Praise for

SIMON
THORN
AND THE
WOLF'S DEN

"Simon Thorn is a hero worthy of a young Harry Potter, and readers are bound to be delighted." —*Booklist*

"Carter unveils a magical world full of amazement and adventure. . . . A thrill from start to finish, the book will have readers eager to return to the magical world of Simon Thorn." —*Kirkus Reviews*

"Readers of fantasy will savor this new series; the theme of good versus evil will satisfy those middle grade readers with an insatiable hunger for superhero kids. . . . The dark, suspenseful plot will keep readers eager for sequels. Highly recommended." —*School Library Connection*

"Unique . . . unpredictable and entertaining. . . . This title is likely to be popular with a whole zoo full of readers." —*School Library Journal*

D0348559

BOOKS BY AIMÉE CARTER

Simon Thorn and the Wolf's Den
Simon Thorn and the Viper's Pit

SIMON THORN

AND THE
WOLF'S DEN

AIMÉE CARTER

BLOOMSBURY
NEW YORK LONDON OXFORD NEW DELHI SYDNEY

First published in the United States of America in February 2016
by Bloomsbury Children's Books
Paperback edition published in February 2017
www.bloomsbury.com

Bloomsbury is a registered trademark of Bloomsbury Publishing Plc

For information about permission to reproduce selections from this book, write to
Permissions, Bloomsbury Children's Books, 1385 Broadway, New York, New York 10018
Bloomsbury books may be purchased for business or promotional use. For information on
bulk purchases please contact Macmillan Corporate and Premium Sales Department at
specialmarkets@macmillan.com

The Library of Congress has cataloged the hardcover edition as follows:
Carter, Aimée.
Simon Thorn and the wolf's den / by Aimée Carter.
pages   cm
Summary: Simon Thorn, twelve, is able to talk with animals, but when his
mother is kidnapped by a herd of New York City rats he learns he, his mother, and
his uncle are all Animalgams—able to change into an animal at will—and that
Simon may be able to save the beleaguered Five Animal kingdoms.
ISBN 978-1-61963-704-7 (hardcover) • ISBN 978-1-61963-705-4 (e-book)
[1. Human-animal communication—Fiction. 2. Shapeshifting—Fiction. 3. Animals—
New York (State)—New York—Fiction. 4. Adventure and adventurers—Fiction.
5. Kidnapping—Fiction. 6. New York (N.Y.)—Fiction.] I. Title.
PZ7.C24255Sim 2015   [Fic]—dc23   2014032526

ISBN: 978-1-61963-706-1 (paperback)

Book design by Donna Mark
Typeset by Westchester Book Composition
Printed and bound in the U.S.A. by Berryville Graphics Inc., Berryville, Virginia
4 6 8 10 9 7 5 3

All papers used by Bloomsbury Publishing, Inc., are natural, recyclable products
made from wood grown in well-managed forests. The manufacturing processes
conform to the environmental regulations of the country of origin.

To Dad

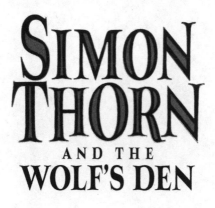

SIMON THORN
AND THE
WOLF'S DEN

PIGEON PANCAKES

Tap tap. Tap tap tap.

Simon Thorn's eyes flew open. He lay in bed, breathing heavily and squinting against the early morning light. He'd been in the middle of a dream, and the harder he tried to remember it, the faster it disappeared. It felt important though, and while he couldn't remember seeing her face, he was sure his mother had been in it.

Tap. Tap tap tap.

He rolled over, his head fuzzy from a lack of sleep. The cramped New York City apartment he shared with his uncle smelled like pancakes, and his stomach churned. Not even chocolate chips could make up for the fact that it was his first day of seventh grade.

Tap. Tap tap. Tap tap tap.

A pigeon perched on his windowsill, rapping its beak against the glass. Simon groaned. "You're too early. Come back later."

The pigeon continued to tap, growing more and more insistent. This wasn't all that unusual. Simon had found that pigeons were, as a general rule, extremely rude and had an inflated sense of self-importance. Never mind the fact that Simon hadn't fallen asleep until nearly midnight, thanks to his racing thoughts and fluttering stomach. The pigeon cared about only one thing, and that was—

"Food!" it cooed as Simon pushed open his window. Another dozen pigeons landed on the fire escape. "Food! Food! Food!"

"I don't have any yet," said Simon.

"Do, too. Smell it," said the first pigeon. It flew into his room and landed on his nightstand. The others crowded together, vying for the empty place on the windowsill. "Food! Food!"

"Leave me *alone.*" Simon tried to shoo them away, but they continued to multiply. Normally he wouldn't have minded. Simon liked animals. They didn't care that he was smaller and scrawnier than the other twelve-year-olds at his school, and they were usually around whenever he needed someone to talk to. This morning, however, it was too much. He had enough to worry about without adding hungry pigeons to the list.

"If you don't leave, my uncle's going to come in, and you know what he does to pigeons," he said.

That brought them up short, and they all glanced at one another nervously. "Us food?" said the first.

"Yeah—my uncle loves pigeon pancakes," said Simon. "Can't you smell the batter?"

The first pigeon ruffled its feathers and eyed the open window. As far as Simon knew, Darryl had never really tried to hurt a living creature (except for the spiders that lurked in the corners of their hallway, though Simon *had* warned them for weeks before Darryl spotted them). But for all of Simon's life, his uncle had had only one rule that never changed:

Stay away from animals.

For years, Simon hadn't had any trouble with this. He liked animals just fine, but he had never wanted a pet, and his uncle was usually diligent about keeping bugs and rats out of the apartment. That had all changed a year ago though when one morning Simon had woken up to the sounds of conversation, making him think his neighbor was blaring the TV. Instead, much to his shock, he had discovered that it wasn't the TV at all—it was the pigeons on the fire escape outside his window. Not only could he understand everything they were saying, but they could understand everything he said in return.

It wasn't just pigeons, either. Simon could talk to the tom-cats that prowled the alleyway, the rats that scavenged in the Dumpsters, and even the mosquitoes he swatted away during the summer. He had thought he was going crazy—he still wasn't sure he hadn't cracked—but ever since then, animals had flocked to Simon, and it had become increasingly difficult to keep his secret from Darryl.

Thankfully his uncle, who was tall with broad shoulders, was a much stronger and more intimidating man than Simon could ever hope to be, and most animals were scared of him without Simon having to resort to empty threats. He didn't fully understand why Darryl hated animals so much, but Simon was fairly sure it had to do with the scars that riddled his uncle's body, including the angry red one that ran down his left cheek. No matter how many times Simon asked, however, his uncle never talked about how he'd gotten them.

"I'll have food for you later," said Simon to the pigeons. "But not—"

Suddenly a strong breeze burst through his window, and several of the pigeons squawked and flew away. Before Simon could feel too relieved, however, a golden eagle landed in the space they had vacated.

Simon froze. He had never seen an eagle in person before. Some of its feathers stuck out at strange angles as if it had been in a skirmish recently, and Simon could see it was missing an eye.

The remaining pigeons shifted nervously, and Simon frowned. "Listen, I don't have anything for you yet. If you come back in thirty minutes—"

"I'm not interested in food," said the eagle in a lofty voice.

"Then what do you want?"

The eagle turned his head so he could see Simon with his good eye. "You're in grave danger, Simon Thorn. If you don't come with me at once—"

"Simon?" said a rough voice outside his door. "Who are you talking to?"

Darryl.

Simon hastily shut the window, cutting off the eagle before he could explain. Unfortunately that left the first pigeon trapped inside his bedroom. Simon darted across the room to shove his foot against the door, preventing Darryl from opening it all the way. He might be able to explain a pigeon in his room, but an eagle on his fire escape was another thing entirely.

"What's going on in here?" said his uncle, raking his long, dark hair out of his eyes and trying to peer around the room. The pigeon on Simon's nightstand edged toward the window.

"Nothing," said Simon, his heart pounding. "I was just getting ready for school."

Outside his window, several pigeons began to coo, and Simon winced. Darryl's jaw tightened, and he flexed the muscles in his massive arms. "Did you feed them again?"

"I accidentally left my window open on Saturday," admitted Simon. "They stole half my sandwich." He couldn't tell Darryl the truth—that he'd given his sandwich to a sick pigeon that didn't have the energy to scavenge.

His uncle grumbled. "How many times do I have to tell you? If you feed them once—"

"They'll come back again and again until their stupid pigeon brains rot," recited Simon. "I know. I'm sorry."

Darryl cast another look around the part of the room he could see from the doorway, and Simon could have sworn he heard him growl. "Just keep your window shut. Breakfast will be on the table in ten. You'll need your protein today."

Simon would need more than protein to make it through today. More like a minor miracle. "I'll be right out."

Once his uncle's footsteps faded, Simon hurried back to the window, but the golden eagle was gone. He bit his lip. What had the eagle meant by saying Simon was in grave danger? And how had he known Simon's name?

He opened his window enough for the remaining pigeon to escape. "If I were you, I'd get as far away from here as I could before my uncle really does serve you for breakfast."

"Far away, far away," said the pigeon, spreading its wings and taking off. Despite the trouble it had caused, Simon was sorry to see it go. Pigeons may be rude, but one was almost always nearby when he wanted company.

"You should tell Darryl about the eagle," piped a small voice nearby.

Simon groaned. "Today's going to be bad enough. If Darryl finds out I lied to him, I'll be grounded for a month."

A brown mouse scampered up the leg of Simon's

pajamas. "Better than being in grave danger, whatever that means."

"And how am I supposed to explain that to my uncle? Tell him a little bird told me?" Simon scooped the mouse into his hand. "I'll be careful, Felix. Don't worry."

Perched on his hind legs, Felix rubbed his paws together. "I should go with you today. Someone needs to watch your back."

"I'm a thousand times your size. If anything, I'll be the one protecting you from becoming that eagle's lunch."

"But—"

"No buts. If something goes wrong, I'll come straight home." Simon set Felix on his pillow. "And don't try to watch TV while I'm gone. One day Darryl's going to come home early and catch you, and you know exactly what he'll do to you then."

Felix huffed, and Simon headed into the bathroom to brush his teeth. He'd found Felix in his closet half-starved to death eight months earlier, and after Simon had nursed him back to health, Felix took up permanent residence in their apartment. They had struck a deal: Simon would continue to feed him so long as Felix never let Darryl know he was there. It had worked out so far, even though Simon worried constantly that his uncle might find the mouse.

Once Simon finished with his teeth, he tried to tame his shaggy brown hair. It was almost time for a haircut, which Simon looked forward to about as much as his pre-algebra homework. His uncle tried to do a good job, but his massive hands made him clumsy with scissors, and the end result was always uneven. While Simon didn't particularly care what his hair looked like, the kids at school did, and their endless taunts never became any easier to bear.

Other than his weird haircuts, Simon thought he looked normal enough, with blue eyes and freckles. He was a little too skinny, and his head was a little too big for his body, but he wasn't a total freak. He didn't understand why his classmates liked to pick on him so much. Last year his best and only friend, Colin Hartwood, told him it was because Simon sometimes talked to animals as though they could understand him. After that, he had stopped, at least in public. No matter what he did, however, the taunts kept growing worse. Even Colin had started to keep his distance—which only made today that much more important.

"Here you go," said Darryl when Simon entered the kitchen. He handed him a plate piled high with bacon and lopsided chocolate-chip pancakes. "I packed you a lunch, too. Peanut butter and jelly isn't suddenly uncool, is it?"

"I wouldn't know," said Simon as he sat at the wooden table that took up most of the kitchen. His stomach protested at the first bite, and he had to fight to keep his breakfast down.

"Nervous?" said Darryl, and Simon shrugged. "Don't be. It'll all be fine."

"If it's anything like last year, it won't be."

The chair groaned in protest as his uncle sat down. "We can't control what other people think of us, but we're the only ones who get to decide who we really are. As long as you act like yourself—"

"I can't lose. I know," muttered Simon, stabbing at his pancakes with his fork. "Colin said he wanted to join the wrestling team this year because he thinks it'll make the popular kids like us."

"Keeping your enemies close isn't a bad strategy."

"Not when it gives them an excuse to beat us up every day." Simon had spent all summer hoping he would be able to spend seventh grade in the background, unnoticed and left alone. But with the way Colin was avoiding him now, his only hope of keeping his friend was to join the wrestling team, too. "Tryouts are next week. You might want to buy some frozen peas just in case."

"After I show you a few moves, they'll be the ones needing frozen peas." Darryl frowned. "This year *will* be better, Simon. Trust me. I know things have been rough lately, especially with your mom, but—"

Simon stood suddenly. He was nauseated enough already without bringing his mother into it. "I have to finish getting ready. Thanks for the pancakes. I'll eat the rest in my room."

"Simon . . ."

"It's fine. Really."

Ignoring Darryl's protests, Simon carried his breakfast back into his bedroom. Closing the door, he set the plate down on the desk and sank into the chair. On the wall in front of him, he'd painstakingly hung the one hundred twenty-four postcards his mother had sent since she'd left him with Darryl. They arrived once a month from cities across the country, boasting colorful pictures of all kinds of animals—wolves, eagles, rattlesnakes, honeybees, bears, dolphins, everything he could think of and more. He had memorized the words on the back of each one, written in a loopy handwriting he knew better than his mother's face. She was a zoologist, so most of the time she wrote about whatever animal was pictured on the postcard. But every now and then she told him how much she missed him, too. Those were his favorite postcards.

Simon and Darryl never talked about his mother. She traveled all the time for her job, so she had dumped Simon with his uncle in the city, and Darryl had become the closest thing Simon had to a parent. Sometimes his mother made it home for Christmas or Simon's birthday, but only for a few hours, and she always seemed distracted. Lately her visits were less and less frequent. The last time Simon had seen her was a year ago, the week after he'd learned he could talk to animals.

More than anything in the world, Simon wanted her to come home. He could put up with all the taunts and bullying if she were there. He would eat lunch alone every day for the rest of his life if he got to eat dinner with her. She would understand his weird ability to communicate with animals.

She wouldn't think he was crazy.

No longer hungry, Simon dropped some bacon and a piece of pancake underneath his desk for Felix and then tossed the rest of his breakfast onto the fire escape, where the waiting pigeons fought over his leftovers as he numbly finished getting ready for school. The eagle hadn't returned.

His uncle was waiting for Simon when he emerged from his bedroom, and Darryl handed him his brown-bag lunch. "I have time before work to walk with you if you'd like."

There was nothing Simon could think of that would be worse than showing up on his first day of seventh grade with his uncle at his side. "I'm supposed to meet up with Colin," he said. Or at least he thought he was. They had always walked to and from school together the year before.

To Simon's relief, Darryl didn't argue. Instead he knelt in front of Simon, the scar on his cheek wrinkling as he peered at him. His uncle was so big that they were nearly eye level. "Nothing lasts forever, no matter how it might feel. Just remember, you'll be my size someday. No one's going to mess with you then."

"Today isn't someday though," muttered Simon.

"No, it's not. But in the meantime, do your best and be yourself. That's all any of us can do." He stood and pressed a scratchy kiss to Simon's forehead. "Do good, kid. Make me proud."

Simon stuffed his lunch into his backpack and left the apartment, trudging down the steps in silence. Their building was across from Central Park, and Simon gazed at the trees lining the street as he waited on the corner where he and Colin had met up the year before. Colin wasn't there yet though, which only made Simon more nervous. He was usually the one who was running late.

Simon checked his watch. Ten minutes. If Colin wasn't here in ten minutes, then he wouldn't be coming at all.

He tried to act casual, leaning against a street sign and pretending his palms weren't sweating. He checked his watch again. Nine minutes and thirty seconds. Colin lived down the block—he had to come this way to get to school.

A loud screech in the street made the hair stand up on the back of Simon's neck, and for a moment he was sure the eagle had returned. He peered over the edge of the curb. Half a dozen rats clawed at what Simon first thought was a balled-up newspaper they'd picked out of the garbage. But when that lump screeched a second time, horror shot through him. The rats were attacking a pigeon.

"Hey—cut that out!" he cried, jumping into the street. "Leave him alone!"

The rats froze. They took one look at Simon and darted into the sewer, leaving the injured pigeon on the pavement. Simon knelt beside it, all too aware that several people waiting to cross the street were staring at him, but he couldn't leave the pigeon there to die.

"Are you okay?" he asked.

The pigeon cooed feebly. "Fly," it said, and with effort, it spread its wings and took off into the sky. Simon straightened, trying to track where the pigeon went, but as soon as it rounded the corner, he lost sight of it.

Over the next eight minutes, Simon witnessed several more fights between pigeons and rats: one in which a bunch of pigeons attacked a single rat, a second where the rats once again had the upper hand, and a third that featured an entire flock of pigeons facing off against a large gang of rats, taking up half the sidewalk and forcing everyone to walk around them. Simon did his best to break up each skirmish, but there was only so much he could do on his own. No one else seemed to notice the animals were acting strangely, and Simon heard the eagle's warning echo in his ear. Maybe he should have stayed home.

At last ten minutes were up, and still there was no sign of Colin. Simon's heart sank. Maybe he had gone to school early, Simon reasoned as he crossed the street. Or maybe Colin would be waiting for him in Central Park.

Darryl hated the park almost as much as he hated animals, and he had expressly forbidden Simon to go inside without him there—which naturally meant Simon sneaked inside as often as he could, especially during the summer while his uncle was at work. A thrill ran through him as he darted up a path that cut a full ten minutes from his walk to school. The rustling trees, the green grass, and the smell of damp dirt made his mood brighten, and, since the trail was nearly abandoned, he even dared to greet a few of the ducks meandering through the park.

"I see you did not heed my warning, Simon Thorn."

Simon whirled around. Perched on a branch over his head was the golden eagle from his fire escape. "What was I supposed to do? It's the first day of school."

"Some things are far more important." The eagle flew down and settled on a bench featuring a bronze plaque. "You must come with me immediately, Simon—for your own safety."

"In case you haven't noticed, I don't have wings," said Simon. "How do you know my name?"

"Because," the eagle said with a long-suffering sigh, "your mother told me."

Out of all the things the eagle could have said, this was the one Simon least expected. "You—you know my mother?"

"Indeed," said the eagle. "If you would come with me—"

A snarl cut through the crisp air. Startled, the eagle took flight, and Simon cursed. "Wait—come back!"

But the eagle had already disappeared. Muttering to himself, Simon glanced into the bushes for the source of the sound. Before he could spot anything, a chorus of snickers started behind him.

"Talking to animals again, Psycho?"

Simon's blood ran cold. Bryan Barker and his gang of eighth graders. They were the biggest, meanest boys in school, and Bryan, with his broad shoulders and towering height that had come out of nowhere two summers ago, was the biggest and meanest of them all. He was practically guaranteed to be named captain of the wrestling team, and getting on his good side was exactly why Colin wanted to join. As far as Simon saw it, Bryan had no good side.

Without looking back, Simon hurried down the path, hoping they would leave him alone. But their footsteps grew louder, and he could sense them surrounding him. No matter how fast he ran, they would be faster, and trying to get away would only give them an excuse to turn him into dog meat.

"Answer me, Psycho." Simon felt something bounce off his backpack—a rock or a stick. "Or did you forget how to speak human?"

Two boys cut in front of him and stopped, leaving Simon no room to escape. He whirled around. "If you don't let me go, we're all going to be late for—"

A pale boy with a round face peeked out from behind Bryan, and Simon wilted. "Colin?"

He was the only boy in seventh grade who was shorter than Simon. He wore thick glasses, and his eyebrows were set high on his forehead, making him look as shocked to see Simon as Simon was to see him. Colin said nothing though, staring at the ground instead.

Simon didn't care that he was surrounded by the four toughest boys in school. All he could focus on was the fact that his supposed best friend couldn't even look him in the eye. "I thought you were going to wait for me at the corner."

"Is it true, Colin? Is Psycho Simon your boyfriend?" said Bryan, and the other boys laughed. Colin turned a deep shade of red.

"He's—he's not even my friend," he stammered. "He's crazy."

Colin might as well have punched Simon in the gut. As much as Simon had been dreading it, hearing Colin confirm his worst fear made the world tilt, and he swallowed a hard lump in his throat.

"Don't cry, Psycho. I'm sure the rats still like you," said Bryan. The older boys' laughs ripped through him as they each shoved him in turn while they passed. Simon didn't fight back. Instead he looked at Colin, who trudged after them, weighed down by five backpacks.

"Colin—" he started, but Bryan Barker made kissing noises, and Colin's face grew redder.

"M'sorry," mumbled Colin, and he walked away.

Not caring whether he was late anymore, Simon stayed glued to the spot on the path until their laughter faded. He wanted to think Colin would change his mind once he saw how terrible Bryan really was, but he already knew. They both knew. And now Simon was alone.

At last he dragged himself the rest of the way through the park, his head buzzing with their taunts. Over and over he tried to convince himself they didn't matter. Bryan didn't matter. Colin didn't matter.

They did matter though, and Simon ducked his head as he walked up the empty concrete stairway leading to the school. By now, half the students probably knew what had happened in the park, and he considered not going inside. But the thought of how upset and disappointed Darryl would be made him climb the last few steps. He couldn't do that to his uncle. Bryan Barker would forget about him eventually, and even if he didn't, at least he couldn't get much worse.

"Simon!"

A hair-raising screech rose above the noise from the street, and Simon spun around. The golden eagle perched on a street sign nearby, staring straight at him.

Simon narrowed his eyes. Everything that had happened in the park was the eagle's fault. If he had just left Simon alone, Bryan Barker wouldn't have overheard their conversation, and maybe Simon would have had a chance at a good year.

He turned his back on the eagle and disappeared into the school. If the eagle wanted something from him, he would come back soon enough. Right now the only thing Simon could think about was exactly how bad today was going to be, and how he was going to survive it.

2

ANIMAL INSTINCTS

By the time Simon left his first class, it seemed like every seventh grader at Kennedy Middle School had heard about what happened in the park. Even a group of sixth graders taunted him as he passed, and one boy stuck out his foot to trip him. Simon staggered forward, barely managing to catch himself before he fell.

"Watch it," said the boy. "These shoes are new."

"Then maybe you shouldn't stick them in front of people," said Simon. Before the boy could retaliate, Simon bolted down the hall.

As the hours wore on he felt smaller and smaller, until he might as well have been nothing at all. By the time the lunch bell rang, Simon couldn't walk down the hallway without kissing sounds following him, and he sat down at the only empty table in the cafeteria, right next to the trash cans. He pulled out his book and unwrapped the sandwich his uncle had packed, and laughter exploded from Bryan Barker's table. Simon glanced up long enough to see Colin sitting there, eagerly hanging on Bryan's every word. Simon bit his lip and looked back down at his book, trying to ignore them.

Without so much as a hello, a girl with long dark hair sat down in the chair beside him. Simon froze. There were plenty of empty seats at other tables—and at his, too—but she was close enough that he could smell her hair over the peanut butter in his sandwich.

He started to edge away. Before he could move too far, however, the girl pulled a book from her backpack. It was exactly the same as the one Simon held. Opening to a marked page, she began to read.

Simon hesitated. Was she new? He was sure he'd never seen her before. Besides, no one in their right mind would sit with him today—it was social suicide. The kind thing to do would have been to move so that Bryan didn't see them together, but after the morning Simon had had, the possibility of talking to someone who didn't think he was a freak was too tempting to pass up. So before he could stop himself, he turned toward her.

"Hi," he said. "I'm Simon."

"And I'm reading," said the girl without looking up.

His cheeks warmed. "Sorry." She must have known about him after all. But while he busied himself with pulling the crust off his sandwich, she spoke again.

"I'm Winter," she said. "But I'm still reading."

She glanced up, and Simon noticed that her eyes were the lightest green he'd ever seen. He wanted to say something else, to show her that he was reading the same book, but he didn't want to scare her away. For now, he stayed quiet.

Opening his own copy, he noticed a piece of paper stuck between the pages. It was a note from Darryl. His uncle never wrote him notes, but there it was, written in his familiar sharp scrawl.

Good luck today. Proud of you. Don't forget to show them your teeth.

Simon reread it twice. It wasn't much, but it was enough to make him smile, and he tucked the scrap of paper back between the pages of his book.

"Whatcha got there, Psycho? A love letter from your boyfriend?"

Bryan Barker snatched the book from his hands. Simon protested and made a grab for it, but Bryan held it out of reach. Flipping through the pages, he found the note and pulled it out.

"Dear Psycho," he read loudly enough for the entire lunchroom to hear. "I love you more than the moon and the stars. Thinking of you. Hugs and kisses. Love, your boo bear."

Bryan's gang roared with laughter. Colin, who stood behind Bryan, turned bright red, but no one was laughing at him. Just Simon.

A knot formed in his chest. It grew hotter and hotter until he almost couldn't bear it, but he didn't move. Anything he said would only make it worse.

"Oh, look, he drew you a bunch of hearts and flowers, too. How sweet." Bryan grinned down at him, and Simon clenched his fists. "Upset, Psycho? Gonna show us your teeth?"

"Would you jerks shut up and go back to whatever hole you crawled out of?" snapped an irritated voice. Winter set down her book and glared at Bryan.

He shoved the note into Simon's book and tossed it to Colin. "What do we have here? Cheating on your boyfriend with another freak, Psycho?"

"Leave her alone," said Simon.

Bryan poked him hard in the ribs. "Or what? You'll go home crying to your mother? Oh, wait. You don't have one."

There it was: Bryan's favorite taunt. Simon refused to react. He concentrated on his breathing instead—in and out, in and out, until the burning knot in his chest started to cool. "Colin, can I have my book back?" he said.

Colin glanced back and forth between him and Bryan. "Sorry, Simon," he mumbled.

Bryan snorted with laughter, and Simon's vision narrowed. Colin didn't matter. Bryan didn't matter. None of this mattered. Someday he would be Darryl's size, and no one would bother him again. Someday he would be far away from here, and—

"Are you going to give it back or not?" said Winter. When Colin didn't move, she stood and snatched the book from him. "Jerk. And you—" She rounded on Bryan. "Is that the best you can do? Coward."

Bryan turned pink. "You want to see what I've got?"

Winter stepped closer. "Go ahead and show me, Ape Face. I dare you."

Bryan's mouth contorted with anger, and to Simon's horror, he shoved her backward. Winter hit the chair hard, and the crack of elbow against metal echoed through the cafeteria.

Simon didn't stop to think. By the time he realized what he was doing, he had already tackled Bryan to the ground and socked him in the soft spot below his ribs. Bryan cried out, and Simon pulled away, dumbfounded. Where had that come from?

The lunchroom went silent. Simon scrambled to his feet. The other boys closed ranks around them, forming a tight circle and chanting *Fight! Fight! Fight!* But Simon didn't want to fight. It had been an accident.

"You—are a dead man," gasped Bryan.

Simon's head buzzed, and he couldn't think of anything

to say. Instead, he stupidly offered Bryan his hand. "I'm sorry."

Bryan grabbed his wrist and yanked him to the ground. Using his knees, he pinned Simon's legs to the cold floor, still panting. "You think—you can hit me—in front of everyone—and get away with it?"

The burning knot in Simon's chest was back, trying to claw its way out of him, but it had nowhere to go. "Maybe you shouldn't attack girls, Ape Face," he blurted.

"Don't worry. You're a much better punching bag, *Psycho.*"

Bryan shoved his arm against Simon's throat. His fist connected with Simon's abdomen, and Simon curled into a ball.

Bryan laughed and pulled back for another punch. On the other side of the room, the vice principal shouted for them to break it up, but Bryan still had time to get in a few more good hits before he reached them. Worse, Simon knew Bryan would never leave him alone after this, and no doubt he would also set his sights on Winter, whose only crime was sticking up for Simon.

Show them your teeth.

That burning knot in his chest exploded, and Simon roared. His hand shot out, his fingers curled into claws, and he swiped his nails against Bryan's face. Bright red lines sprouted across Bryan's cheek, and he faltered, his mouth open in shock.

Simon didn't give him a chance to fight back. He bit down hard on Bryan's wrist, letting go before he tasted blood.

Bryan howled with pain and scrambled off Simon. "He bit me!" he yelled, clutching his arm. "Psycho *bit* me!"

Simon sat up and wiped his mouth. Dread coiled in the pit of his aching belly, and he climbed shakily to his feet. "Are you okay?" he said to Winter. She glared at him.

"Why did you do that?"

"I—" Simon stopped. "Do what?"

"Treat me like I'm some sad little girl who needs protection. I don't need your help."

Before Simon could respond, the vice principal burst into the circle, his paunch heaving as he wheezed, "My office—both of you—now!"

Taking Simon and Bryan by their elbows, he marched them through the parting crowd. While Bryan shouted that he hadn't done anything wrong, that he was injured and had to see the school nurse, Simon remained quiet. Darryl was going to be furious, but that was nothing compared to what Bryan would do to him now. If he were lucky, it would be fast and painless, but if there was one thing Simon had learned today, it was that luck was most definitely not on his side.

The show in the cafeteria earned Simon detention for a week. With Bryan. Which meant he would have to deal with more of his taunts for a whole extra hour for five days straight. Simon tried to explain that he'd only been protecting himself and Winter, but the vice principal didn't seem to have any idea who Winter was.

By the time he was allowed to leave the office, Simon had missed all but his last hour. He stopped in the middle of the hallway. Bryan had gone to see the nurse, and no one else was around to make sure he went the right way. If he didn't go to class, there was a chance his uncle would find out— but Darryl would hear about the fight before the end of the day regardless. Simon couldn't possibly get into more trouble than he was already, and facing the other students would be much, much worse than any punishment his uncle could dream up.

Simon turned and dashed out the front door. Though people passed on the sidewalk below, the concrete steps were clear, except for a few pigeons that lingered on the railing.

"Food?" said the nearest one. Simon cringed.

"I don't have any food, all right? Just leave me alone."

"You talk to *pigeons*?"

He whirled around. Winter stood at the top of the steps, right outside the school entrance. "Of course not. I was just talking to myself," he said. His forgotten backpack sat at her feet. "Where did you get that?"

"Lunchroom. Figured you might need it," she said. "Do they always treat you so horribly?"

Simon climbed back up the steps. "I'm used to it."

"No one should have to get used to that."

"It doesn't matter." Simon dug through his backpack. His

belongings were all there—even his book with the note tucked between the pages. "Besides, anything I do will make it worse."

"You weren't half-bad in that fight, you know. If you wanted to, you could take out those worms without a problem."

Simon stared at the dried blood underneath his fingernails. He could still feel the burning knot in his chest and the rush of dark satisfaction when it had exploded. No matter how angry he became, he had always been able to suppress it before. So why hadn't he listened to his gut this time?

But he *had* listened. That was the problem.

"Why do they call you 'Psycho Simon,' anyway?" she added. "You don't seem psychotic to me. A little weird, maybe, but—"

"I have to get home," he interrupted. Winter stepped in front of him, blocking his path.

"Not until you tell me why they call you that."

Simon tried to go around her, but she moved with him, and his frustration grew until he snapped, "I don't know, all right? Because they hate me. Because they want to make my life miserable. Because they think I can talk to animals. I don't *know.*"

"So you *were* talking to the pigeon."

"Of course not," he said. "That would be crazy."

He tried to move past her again, and this time she let him

go. Simon stormed down the steps, silently seething. He didn't need Winter to make fun of him, too.

"Hey, Simon," she called after he'd joined the crowd on the sidewalk. "You're not the only one."

He stopped. "I'm not the only what?" he called, his view of the stairs momentarily blocked by a group of tourists.

But by the time the group passed, she was gone. Weaving through the crowd, he returned to the base of the steps and looked around. Winter was nowhere to be found.

Simon thought about her words as he cut through the corner of Central Park on the way home. Had she meant he wasn't the only one who was picked on? A small part of him held out hope that she had meant he wasn't the only one who could talk to animals, but of course that wasn't it. That was crazy. *He* was crazy.

When he spotted the bench with the plaque—the same bench where he'd met the eagle that morning—Simon stopped and sat down. Maybe the eagle would return and explain how he knew his mother. It was a long shot, but he couldn't go home yet anyway, not when a neighbor might spot him and tell his uncle, so instead Simon pulled out his book and waited. It was peaceful in the park, and though a few chatty squirrels stopped long enough to ask him if he'd seen any acorns, for the most part the animals left him alone.

Simon didn't mean to lose track of time, but the pages flew by, and over an hour passed with no sign of the eagle. A chorus of laughter echoed through the trees. In the distance, he spotted some of the kids from school, and he quickly gathered his things and stood. If he walked fast enough, he could make it home before anyone caught up to him.

Halfway down the trail, the air seemed to change, and Simon looked up. Perched on a branch above him was the golden eagle. "Hello, Simon Thorn."

"I'm kind of in a hurry right now," he said, walking faster and glancing over his shoulder. He could make out Bryan's head bobbing above the others.

The eagle ruffled its feathers. "I thought you wanted to know more about your mother."

Simon stopped. The eighth-grade boys were getting closer. "Is she okay?"

"For now," said the eagle. "The longer you stay here, the more danger you are in, Simon. It is only a matter of time before the mammals find you, and once they do, we will no longer be able to protect you."

"Protect me from what? Chipmunks?" said Simon. One of the boys shouted his name, and he inched down the path.

"From the most bloodthirsty beasts in the animal kingdom," said the eagle. "They are coming for you, Simon Thorn, and if they find you, they will kill you."

"*Kill* me?" he blurted. "Why?"

"There is no time to explain. They are closing in as we speak. If you would come with me—"

Another snarl cut through the air, exactly the same as

that morning. Startled, the eagle took flight. "Run, Simon, before it is too late!"

Simon cursed. "Wait—come back!"

But the eagle flew away, leaving him alone on the path. With the eagle's warning rattling around his brain, Simon hurried away from the bushes and the creature that had snarled. It definitely hadn't sounded like a chipmunk.

Before he could get very far, Bryan Barker appeared from behind a thicket on the other side of the path, flanked by three eighth graders. "You really are crazy, aren't you, Psycho?"

"Leave me alone," he said, skirting around them. Four pairs of footsteps followed.

"Do the animals talk back? Do they tell you how worthless you are, or are they too stupid to figure it out?" said Bryan, and Simon walked even faster. Short as he was, the gang of four boys caught up to him easily and surrounded him. Bryan pushed Simon backward, and another boy ripped his bag from him. "Answer me, Psycho."

Simon kept his mouth shut. He wouldn't give them the satisfaction. He glanced around, looking for anything he might be able to use against them. Sticks, pebbles, a bench in the distance—

"No girls here to save you this time," said Bryan, shoving him again. One of the eighth graders caught him and pushed him forward. Back and forth he went, until he was so jarred that he could barely keep his balance.

Shoving. He could handle this. Just as long as it didn't get any worse. But within seconds, Bryan made a fist.

"I don't care how crazy you are, Psycho," he said. "If you think you can humiliate me in front of everyone and get away with it—"

Another snarl echoed through the park, louder and more vicious than the first. It sounded like nothing Simon had ever heard before. All four boys started, and Bryan paused, distracted.

A massive dog stepped out from behind a tree, gnashing its teeth. It wasn't like any pet Simon had ever seen. With its gray fur and sharp fangs, it looked almost like a wolf.

No, Simon realized. Not *almost* like a wolf. It *was* a wolf.

Without thinking, Simon made what was possibly the stupidest move in his life: he kneed Bryan in the stomach. Hard. And as Bryan doubled over, Simon pushed him to the ground, grabbed his backpack, and made a run for it.

The eighth graders shouted, but a howl cut them off. Simon tore down the path. His hair whipped around his face, and his backpack hung off the crook of his elbow and banged against his knees, but he didn't stop, not even when he bolted out of Central Park. His lungs burned, and several pedestrians swore as he shoved past them, but he reached his building in record time.

He ran up the stairs, stopping only when he got to his apartment. As he struggled to catch his breath, he listened for any sign of someone following him, but the building was quiet. Exhausted, he dropped his backpack and groped around for the key. What was he going to tell Darryl? Nothing about the eagle or the wolf, that was for sure. Had the vice principal called about Bryan and—

"Simon?"

Suddenly the door opened. Instead of his uncle, however, a woman stood inside, wearing jeans and combat boots and brandishing Darryl's baseball bat. Simon froze, dumbfounded.

"Mom?"

MISCHIEF OF MICE

Simon's mother dropped the baseball bat and caught him in her arms. She was warm and smelled like fallen leaves, and her blond braid pressed against his cheek, but Simon was too dazed to notice much more than that. After everything that had happened today, part of him wondered if Bryan Barker had knocked him out and this was all a dream.

It wasn't a dream though. She was real, and she was finally home. He hugged her fiercely. "Missed you."

She ran her fingers through his shaggy hair. "I missed you, too. Look at you. Look how tall you are."

"I'm not tall. You're just short." The last time he'd seen her, he hadn't even come up to her shoulders. Now he was nearly eye level with her. His insides pinched as he realized how much time they'd lost. "Why are you here?"

"Would you rather I not be?" she asked as she ushered him inside.

"No, I just . . ." He trailed off. His mother glanced up and down the hallway before she closed the door, almost as if she was expecting someone. "You only ever come on holidays or my birthday."

"I don't need a special occasion to see you, Simon," said his mother, but her smile looked more like a grimace. Something was wrong. Simon pulled off his jacket, and she hung it up for him before he could do it himself.

"What's going on?" he said, and she hesitated.

"Your vice principal called. He said you were in a fight."

Simon's heart sank. The only thing he hated more than Darryl's disappointment was his mother's. "You came home because I got in a fight? How did he even find you?" Not even Simon could reach her when he needed her.

"I was already here when he called," she said.

"But—you've been here all day and you didn't come and get me?" She only ever stayed for a few hours at a time. "Where have you been, Mom?"

She frowned. "I'm sorry, sweetheart. Work's been so busy—"

"For a whole year? You didn't take a single day off?"

"I—" his mother began, but the door burst open before she could say anything else.

Darryl, windswept and red-faced, stormed into the apartment and slammed the door shut. "What were you doing in the park?" he said, rounding on Simon. "I went to pick you up after school, but I saw you there instead. You *know* you're not supposed to—"

"Darryl, he knows," said his mother, sliding her arm around Simon's shoulders. "Calm down."

His uncle didn't look the least bit surprised to see his mother there. "Why did you skip school, Simon?"

Simon faltered. "I—I got sent to the vice principal."

"Why? What happened?"

"He got in a fight. Another student," his mother added quickly at the look on Darryl's face.

"I want to hear this from Simon," said Darryl, but when Simon tried to explain, his mother cut him off.

"Kitchen, Darryl. *Now.*"

Darryl glowered at her, but at last he rumbled into the tiny kitchen. Simon shrugged his mother's arm off. Her brow furrowed, and for a split second guilt stabbed through him. He should have been happy to see her, and part of him was— but another part of him, the part that had waited a year to see her again, was fuming. She was the one who had left him, not the other way around.

"I need to talk to your uncle," she said gently. "Alone."

The burning knot in Simon's chest returned, swallowing his reply. Instead he trudged off to his room, lugging his backpack behind him. It wasn't fair. She didn't show up for an entire year, and now that she was here, she would be gone by morning, just like every other time. As Simon headed down the hall, each footstep grew heavier than the last. How long would it be before she didn't bother to visit at all?

Simon closed his bedroom door and dropped his bag. Sitting down on the edge of his bed, he stared up at the wall of postcards and tried to imagine what his life would have been like if his mother had left him with Darryl and never come back. Easier, maybe. He wouldn't constantly feel like he was waiting for something that almost never happened. He loved his mother, but there were times she made him feel lonelier than Bryan Barker ever could.

"I see you survived." Felix slipped out from underneath his desk.

"Barely," said Simon. "I think Bryan Barker is going to murder me tomorrow."

Felix scurried up Simon's jeans and sweater to perch on his shoulder. "He'll have to get through me first. I'm coming with you."

He started to tell the mouse no—mostly because he had already come up with a dozen different excuses to skip school tomorrow—but someone knocked. Felix leaped behind the curtain to hide.

"Simon?" said his mother as she opened the door. "Who were you talking to?"

"No one. I was just—reading to myself." Snatching a book off his nightstand, he held it up for her to see. "Is Darryl going to yell at me?"

"No, no, I talked him down." She sat on the bed beside him. "How are you?"

Simon shrugged. "Fine."

"You don't sound fine. It hasn't been easy lately, has it?"

He shook his head reluctantly. It felt like he was admitting some sort of horrible defect, and he stared at the wall of postcards.

"Do you want to talk about it?"

He shook his head again. Usually Colin would have been there to commiserate, but that wasn't going to happen anymore. He would just have to get used to dealing with things on his own.

His mother hesitated, and after a moment she fished a wrapped parcel out of her pocket and handed it to him. "This is for you."

"What is it?" he said.

"Open it and see."

Simon ripped through the wrapping paper, revealing a plain black box. When he lifted the lid, he found an ornate silver pocket watch inside. It was attached to a long, thin chain, and the back was engraved with a crest. Simon frowned as he examined it. In the center was an oddly shaped star, and surrounding it were five animals: a wolf, an eagle, a spider, a dolphin, and a snake.

"It was your father's," said his mother. "He would've wanted you to have it."

"Really?" Simon's father—Darryl's younger brother—had died before Simon had been born. Darryl never talked about him, and the few times Simon had asked questions, he could tell how much it hurt Darryl to think about him. Eventually Simon had stopped.

"Really," said his mother. "I was going to wait until your sixteenth birthday, but with all you've been going through, I thought it would mean more to you now."

Simon opened the pocket watch. It was stuck at 8:25 and fourteen seconds.

"It's very old," she admitted. "It might never work again. But I want you to promise me you'll take care of it, all right? Keep it on you always, especially when I can't be there with you, and never forget how much I love you."

Simon closed the watch and slid it into his pocket. The weight felt right somehow, and he hooked the chain around his belt loop. "I will, if you take me with you."

His mother wilted. "Oh, sweetheart. You know I would if I could."

"But you can," he said, his voice cracking. "I won't get in the way. You can do your job, and I'll stay in the hotel and study—"

"Sweetheart . . ." She tried to hug him, but Simon slipped out of her embrace. "Simon. Please. Don't make this any harder for me than it already is."

"Harder for *you*?" The words stuck in his throat, and he had to force them out. "I'm the one who gets left behind. All you ever do is send me postcards and visit when you feel like it, which is practically never. I know you love your job more than you love me, but—"

"I love you more than anything in the world. If there was any way I could be here and spend every single day with you, I would. You must know that, sweetheart."

Simon faltered. He did know it, but sometimes it felt like a lie his mother told him so he wouldn't be angry. "If you love me more, then let me go with you."

"Actually," said Darryl as he nudged open the bedroom door, his body taking up the whole frame, "I don't think that's such a bad idea."

Simon looked at him, stunned. "You mean it?" he said, and Darryl nodded.

"Might do you some good to get away from here for a while. Both of you." Darryl gave his mother a look Simon didn't understand.

"You're really going to do this now?" she said.

"And you aren't?"

She stood and gave Simon a quick kiss on the forehead. "I need to talk to your crazy uncle again." When Simon started to object, she cut him off. "Please."

His uncle gave him a slight nod, and Simon sank back onto his mattress, pretending to return to his book. But once they stepped out of the bedroom, Simon counted to ten and opened the door again. Darryl and his mother argued in low voices that filtered in from the kitchen, and Simon crept down the hallway, avoiding the squeaky floorboard.

". . . can't stay here," said Darryl. "Orion already found him—"

"You can't know that for sure," said his mother. "It's been years."

"I wouldn't have called you back if I wasn't positive."

Simon flattened himself against the wall. Who was Orion?

"We can't just uproot him like this," said his mother. "It's dangerous out there."

"It's more dangerous here. We don't have a choice anymore, Isabel. You wanted to wait, so we waited. Now it's been too long. If Orion's found us, then that means they've both found us."

"You're *absolutely* sure?"

His uncle swore. "I already told you—"

"Simon?"

The squeak near his ear startled him, and Simon jumped backward into the bookcase, upsetting a picture frame. Felix sat on the top shelf, rubbing his paws together nervously. Horrified, Simon gestured for him to leave before someone else heard him, but it was too late.

Darryl stepped out of the kitchen. "Simon, what are you—" He spotted Felix, and cold fear washed over Simon.

The mouse scrambled behind several books, but he had nowhere else to go.

"What are you and Mom talking about?" said Simon quickly, stepping between his uncle and the bookcase. Darryl advanced anyway, brandishing a spoon like a sword. "Who's Orion?"

"Get out of my way, Simon," growled Darryl. One good swing, and he could smash the bookcase into splinters. Felix squeaked again, and Simon's mother appeared in the doorway.

"Darryl, what's—oh, for heaven's sake." She sidestepped both of them and, reaching behind the books, expertly snatched Felix by the tail.

"Mom, no!" Simon tried to grab Felix, but his mother dangled him just out of reach.

"Who sent you?" she said, and at first Simon thought she was talking to him. A heartbeat later, he realized she meant Felix.

He felt like Bryan Barker had knocked the air out of him all over again. "You—you can talk to mice?"

She ignored him. "Tell me who sent you, or you won't have this tail much longer. Then it'll be your whiskers. Then your ears. Then your paws, and then—"

"Stop it!" said Simon. "He's my friend. Let him go."

"Your *friend*?" his mother and Darryl said at the same time, but at least she dropped Felix into Simon's waiting hands.

"You know you're supposed to stay in my room," he said, painfully aware of Darryl and his mother watching him.

"But there are rats outside," said Felix, trembling. "Hundreds."

Darryl swore again. "Simon, pack a bag. Looks like we're going with your mother after all."

4

RATTED OUT

Simon stood in the living room, looking back and forth between Darryl and his mother. He'd come to expect this from his uncle whenever animals were concerned, but the panic-stricken look on his mother's face told him that for once, Darryl wasn't being paranoid.

"I'm not leaving," he said. "Not until someone explains what's happening. Who's Orion? Why are a bunch of rats making us leave? And why didn't you ever tell me you could talk to animals, too?"

This last question was directed to his mother. Neither she nor Darryl looked surprised that he could do the same thing. "I'm sorry, sweetheart," she said. "I never meant to lie, but we don't have much time. You need to pack."

"Pack for *what*? Where are we going?"

"As far away from here as we can get."

"But why—"

"Please, Simon," she said. "For me."

She held his stare for several seconds, her blue eyes silently pleading, and at last Simon caved. "Fine. But you have to tell me everything."

"I promise."

As soon as he closed his bedroom door, Simon emptied his backpack and climbed onto his desk, stripping his wall of postcards. Only after he'd tucked them all into a side pocket of his bag did he bother with clothes. They were really leaving. All of them, together, far away from the city and Bryan Barker. Simon briefly considered pinching himself, but if he was dreaming, he didn't want to wake up.

Darryl opened the door two minutes later, as Simon struggled to close the zipper. His uncle grabbed the backpack and yanked it shut for him, nearly ripping the seam. "Let's go," he said.

"Wait." Simon scooped Felix off his pillow. The mouse squeaked and disappeared into the pocket of Simon's sweatshirt, where he curled up into a trembling ball.

Darryl narrowed his eyes. "That rat is not coming with us."

"He's a mouse, not a rat," said Simon. "And either he comes or I stay."

They glared at each other. Simon wasn't going to abandon the only friend he had left.

Seconds ticked by, and at last Simon's mother called from the living room. "Are we leaving or not?"

"I don't know," said Simon, staring at his uncle. "Are we?"

At last Darryl grunted and lumbered unhappily down the hall. Relieved, Simon pulled on his backpack and hurried after him.

"When are we coming back?" said Simon.

"I don't know," said his mother. "It's possible we won't."

An entire lifetime with no more Bryan Barker. Despite how nervous his mother and uncle were, Simon couldn't contain his grin. "Good."

She smiled back. "That's what I thought you'd say."

"Isabel," said Darryl sharply. He stood by the door. Something metal jingled, and the lock began to turn on its own.

Simon frowned. "Who else has a—"

The door burst open. At first Simon thought no one was there, but Darryl snarled, and a thick odor of rotting garbage and filth assaulted Simon's senses. As he began to breathe through his mouth, he saw them.

Rats—hundreds and hundreds—crowded the hallway and poured into the apartment, surrounding the three of them. Their high-pitched squeaks made Simon's ears ring, and he could see their sharp front teeth. Darryl tried to shove him out of the way, but the rats were already there, clambering over one another to get closer. A particularly eager one tried to climb up Simon's leg, its tiny nails scratching his skin, and he kicked hard. The rat flew off and hit the wall, but before Simon could try to back away, two more began to claw their way up his other leg.

Darryl grabbed the pair of rats and threw them into the hallway. "Come on," he said, grabbing Simon and pulling him back through the apartment. The rats screeched in protest, scurrying after them. They moved like waves, the faster ones crawling over the slower ones to get to the front, and if his uncle hadn't been dragging him along, Simon would have stood staring in wonder.

"What do they want?" said Simon. "Why—"

"In here." Darryl ducked into Simon's bedroom and yanked the window open. Behind them, his mother darted inside and slammed the door shut, and Simon barely had time to suck in a great gulp of fresh air before his uncle lifted him up and shoved him onto the fire escape. Simon stumbled and grabbed the railing, his head spinning as he looked down. Hundreds of rats flooded the alleyway below them.

"Darryl," he said as his uncle climbed out the window. "Look."

Darryl cursed. Instead of going back inside, however, he seized Simon's elbow and started down the fire escape. "Whatever you do, don't stand still."

Simon rushed down the stairs. The fire escape shook beneath his uncle's heavy footsteps, and above them he heard his mother following. Simon jumped the last few feet, and when he hit the ground the rats began to climb up his legs again. This time Simon didn't hesitate to knock them off.

"Stop it!" he cried as a bigger one bit the bottom of his jeans. He ripped his leg away. "Why are you doing this?"

"The Alpha wants, the Alpha wants," said a few nearby rats, and more and more joined until it echoed through the entire alleyway.

"What did I say about standing still?" said Darryl, taking Simon's arm. "Sidewalk, now!"

The rats scurried after them as they ran down the alleyway toward the sidewalk. Simon felt dizzy, a million questions buzzing like bees in his brain, but he forced himself to keep going. His mother had promised she would explain everything, and he added the Alpha to his mental list of things to bring up.

When they were only a few feet from the street, an eerie scream echoed high above them, and goose bumps spread over Simon's arms. Apparently an army of rats wasn't enough right now. The one-eyed eagle had returned.

"Is that—?" His mother tripped, and Darryl caught her before she hit the ground.

"Told you," he said grimly. "He's been stalking Simon all day."

"Who?" said Simon. "The eagle? How do you know?"

Both of them ignored him. "If he's here, then she can't be far behind. We need to get somewhere safe," said his mother. "Simon, you stay with Darryl. I'll be right back."

"No," said Simon. "I'm coming with you."

To his surprise, his mother didn't argue. Instead she led them onto the sidewalk, and Simon trotted alongside her as she tugged on the door handles of each parked car they passed.

"What are you doing?" he said.

"A taxi driver would ask too many questions, and the subway system is the rats' territory. This is our last option."

"Wait." Simon gaped at her. "You're stealing a *car*?"

"Yes. Unless you want to get eaten by vermin."

A horde of rats spilled out from the alleyway, and his mother's pace grew frantic. She made her way down the sidewalk, tugging on door after door, Simon keeping close to her side. A woman on the corner screamed at the sight of the rats, and several others began to take pictures of the odd scene.

Another shriek filled the air, and suddenly a flock of pigeons dived toward the sidewalk. As they'd done that morning, the pigeons attacked the rats, beaks and talons fighting fangs and claws. Simon stared, shocked. The birds were trying to protect them.

"Anytime, Isabel," said Darryl in a warning voice.

"I don't see you helping," she said, but three cars later, she finally found an unlocked door. "Simon, get in."

He eyed the open door. There had to be twenty people watching. "But—"

A hissing rat flew up and latched onto the hem of Simon's

sweatshirt. His uncle grabbed it and hurled it into the street.

"This isn't a game, kid," said Darryl. "If you give them a chance, they will kill you."

"They're *rats*," said Simon.

"And there are hundreds of them, and three of us." Another rat flew through the air, and Darryl knocked it away with his forearm. "Car. *Now.*"

Simon ducked into the backseat, and Darryl squeezed in after him. His mother cursed from the driver's seat as she fiddled with wires, and at last the engine roared to life. She hit the accelerator, and the tires squealed as Simon flew against the seat.

"Okay?" she said, glancing in the rearview mirror.

No, he wasn't okay. He wasn't even close to okay. "Why are the rats chasing us? Why didn't you tell me you could talk to animals? You let me think I was crazy—"

"You're not crazy," said his mother firmly. She sped up to make a yellow light. "I didn't realize your communication abilities had manifested already. Most of the time they don't appear until—" She stopped.

"Until when?" said Simon. "*Until when*, Mom?"

"Don't yell at your mother. It's not her fault," said Darryl as he dug around in his duffel bag. "I suspected, but it was too dangerous to talk to you about it, not until I knew for sure. I shouldn't have kept you in the dark as long as I did."

"Then tell me what's going on," said Simon. When neither of them answered, he grabbed the door handle. The rats had to be gone by now. "If you don't, I'm getting out of the car at the next light."

"If you do, Orion will find you," said his mother.

"Great. Then you can start by explaining who he is."

His mother grimaced. Finally, as if admitting something deeply shameful, she said, "He's my father. Your grandfather."

Simon stared at her in the rearview mirror. "I've had a grandfather all this time, and you never told me?"

"Because he's been trying to take you from me since you were a baby. That's why I left—to lead Orion away from you. To give you a chance at a normal life."

Simon's head swam, and his anger bubbled to the surface. He'd never wanted a normal life, not if she wasn't in it. "You should have brought me with you. That's what real mothers do—they don't abandon their kids."

Her face fell, and for a moment, she looked like he'd slapped her. "I had no choice."

"Yeah, you did. You just didn't love me enough to bother."

"Watch it, Simon," said Darryl, but his mother shook her head.

"You have to understand. Orion's spies know what I look like, and they're everywhere. I couldn't risk them finding you, so I had to run. To keep you safe."

"Spies?" said Simon. "What spies?"

"Every bird you've ever seen is under his command," said his mother. "Including your pigeon friends."

It didn't take a genius to put the pieces together. "So on top of everything else, he can talk to animals, too."

"There are a lot more of us out there than you think. And . . . Simon . . ." She glanced at Darryl, and something passed between them. He nodded. "There's more to it than just talking to animals," his mother continued. "Soon, when you're old enough—"

Thunk.

A rat the size of a football hit the windshield, and his mother slammed on the brakes. "What the—"

An odd scratching sound echoed through the car, and suddenly the engine died. "Get it started again, Isabel," said Darryl as several more rats leaped onto the car.

"I'm trying," said his mother, her head ducked near the steering wheel. The engine started, wheezed, and died all over again.

Something hit the window next to Simon's ear, and the glass cracked. A brick. How were rats throwing bricks? "Mom!"

Another hit the window, and another, and another. Simon scrambled to undo his seat belt. It was jammed.

Darryl pulled a knife with an ivory handle and a wicked-looking blade from his bag. "Hold still."

Within seconds Simon was free, and just in time, too. The window shattered. Shards exploded all over him, clinging to his sweatshirt. The rats screamed in excitement

· 50 ·

and began to crawl through the opening. Simon could feel Felix trembling with fear in his pocket.

"Out of the car," said Darryl. "Isabel, try to hold them off. Simon, here."

He handed Simon the knife. Simon blinked. "You expect me to use this?"

"I expect you to do whatever you have to do," he said, and he shoved open the door. "Stay close."

Darryl landed hard on the asphalt and began to kick the swarm of rats out of the way. Simon scrambled after him. Rats immediately began to climb up his legs again, and though he brandished the blade threateningly, he couldn't bring himself to kill them. It wouldn't have mattered anyway. Even as another flock of pigeons dived from above to fight the rats, Simon could see that there had to be hundreds, if not thousands by now, coming relentlessly for them. They were trapped.

"Run!" shouted Simon's mother. Darryl grabbed his arm, and together they ran as fast as they could through the sea of vermin. Simon stumbled, and a bright circle of light appeared on the ground—his uncle was shining a high-powered flashlight at the rats. They recoiled, forming a path wide enough for Simon to follow.

They ran half a block before he realized his mother wasn't with them. Simon dug his heels in until his uncle was forced to stop. Several yards behind them, his mother struggled to bat away the rats that clung to her sweater and jeans, and some even swung from her braid. Several pigeons flew around her, screeching and lashing out at the rats with their talons, but nothing seemed to help.

"Mom!" Simon tried to wrench his arm from his uncle's grip, but Darryl held on tighter. "Let me *go*."

"She can't fight them if she's worried about you. Come on."

"Mom!" he called as they reached the end of the block. Rats clung to her, and as soon as she threw one off, two more joined.

"Go, Simon—I'll find you. I love you!"

The fiery knot returned to Simon's chest, and the need to do something, *anything*, built up inside him until he couldn't breathe. But he couldn't shake his uncle's grip no matter how hard he tried, and Darryl didn't give him any choice. They rounded a corner, and his mother disappeared from sight.

"Stop—let me go!" yelled Simon. Darryl dragged him forward, nearly lifting him off the ground.

"I can't do that," said his uncle. "I'm sorry. She'll be all right. Soon as they realize you're not with her, they'll come after you again."

"Good. Let them come." Simon clutched the knife. This time he would use it.

"Your mother wants you safe," said Darryl. "That's all that matters to her, do you understand me? Your safety. Not hers, not mine—*yours*. If you want to help her, then stop struggling and let me protect you."

They neared the end of the block. The rats began to thin,

and Simon could see clear pavement ahead. He may have been angry that his mother and Darryl had kept so many secrets from him, but that didn't mean he wanted the rats to kill her, and if they got any farther away, Simon would have no chance of helping her. So at last he said, "Okay. Fine. Just let go of me—you're hurting my arm."

Darryl reluctantly let go. "The rats can't follow us over water. If we can make it to the Midtown ferries . . ."

Simon wasn't listening. Instead, he counted down in his head. *Five, four, three, two . . .*

As soon as he hit *one*, he bolted in the opposite direction. The rats moved aside for him, apparently sensing that he was heading back into their trap, and he ran as fast as he could down the sidewalk. Behind him, Darryl shouted, but Simon didn't slow down. He'd already lived his whole life without his mother. He wasn't going to lose her again.

But when he turned the corner, he skidded to a stop. She was gone, along with the pigeons. And a thousand rats were waiting for him.

They descended on him with impossible speed, climbing up his clothes, flinging themselves at him, biting him everywhere they could reach. He tried to shake them off, but they were bigger than any rats he'd ever seen before. One of them crawled up the knife, and though the blade cut its belly, the rat either didn't notice or didn't care.

"Simon!" yelled Darryl. "Hold on!"

Simon's knees buckled. The weight of the rats was too

much. He couldn't move. Within moments, he wouldn't be able to stand, and there would be nothing stopping the rats from killing him.

A ferocious howl ripped through the air, and Simon looked up in time to see his uncle flying toward him, his enormous form unstoppable. But he didn't barrel into him like Simon expected. Instead, Darryl seemed to shimmer midleap, and to Simon's shock, his body began to change.

Darryl's fingers shifted into claws, his hands into paws, and his nose into a snout. Gray fur sprouted all over his body, engulfing his clothing, and as his torso thinned and lengthened, a tail appeared at the base of his spine. In the time it took Simon to blink, his very human uncle had changed into a real, live, snarling wolf. No, not just any wolf—the wolf from the park.

Simon froze. It wasn't possible. Humans didn't turn into animals.

Humans weren't supposed to be able to talk to animals, either, but Simon could. Maybe he was hallucinating. Maybe he was going crazy. Or maybe his uncle had been keeping a huge howling secret the whole time. Whatever it was, as far as he could tell, a very real wolf stood on the sidewalk in front of him, and no amount of frantic blinking made it disappear.

His uncle—the wolf—*Darryl* tore through the sea of rats and snatched two that clung to Simon's sweatshirt. Within seconds, the others either let go or were yanked away by the wolf's sharp teeth, and at last Simon was free of them. Breath-ing heavily, he watched as they scampered several feet away. At first Simon thought they were retreating, but then they grouped together once more and advanced on them. He held out his knife with a trembling hand.

"Go, Simon," snarled the wolf in Darryl's voice. He snapped as a rat got too close. "I'll hold them off."

"I'm not leaving you," said Simon.

"Yes, you are," said Darryl. "Take a bus to the Midtown ferry terminal and wait for me there. I'll be right behind you."

"I'm not leaving," repeated Simon. He had no idea where his mother was, and if the worst had happened . . . Darryl was all he had left.

The wolf growled and nipped at Simon's knees. "Go. Before you get us both killed."

He stumbled backward. The wolf glared at him, his black eyes exactly like Darryl's, and Simon swallowed the pain-ful lump in his throat. "If you're not there by the time I get there, I'm coming back," he finally said.

A rodent the size of a cat threw itself at the wolf, land-ing on his shoulder. Darryl howled and bucked the rat off him, whipping it back into the horde. "I'll be there."

Simon took one last look at the hulking wolf facing off against the army of vermin, and then he began to run. His uncle could take care of himself. He always could. Every-thing would be fine.

Simon sprinted down the street, dodging pedestrians as

he searched for a bus route heading west to the water. For blocks he ran, until he was breathless and sweaty, trying to remember where the closest stop was. As he turned a corner, he spotted a subway station with a thin stream of rats heading down the steps, and he stumbled to a halt. His mother had said the subway was the rats' territory—that was where they must have taken her. He glanced back over his shoulder. His uncle would kill him, but if there was even the slightest possibility she was down there, maybe he could take a quick look and—

"Simon!"

A hand reached out and grabbed his sleeve, yanking him into an alleyway dark with shadows. He squinted. "Mom?"

"Do I look like your mother?" said an all too familiar voice. Simon's eyes quickly adjusted, and his heart sank. The girl from lunch—the one who had returned his backpack—stood in front of him.

"Winter? What are you doing here?"

She pulled him deeper into the alleyway. "Saving your hide, that's what."

"I don't need you to save me," he said, and she gave him an exasperated look.

"You're about to follow the rats into their own territory. You really think they'll let you see the surface again?"

Simon yanked his arm away. Her grip broke easily, unlike Darryl's, and he started back toward the sidewalk. "They have my mother."

"Not down there, they don't."

"And I'm sure you know exactly where she is," he said sarcastically. He didn't have time for this.

"I don't. But I know someone who does."

He stopped.

Winter smiled. "Got your attention, didn't I?" she said, tossing her hair over her shoulder. "Orion saw the whole thing happen."

Orion. His grandfather. The very man his mother had been trying to evade. Simon's throat tightened. "I'm supposed to be running away from Orion, not toward him."

"He's *trying* to protect you, despite your best efforts," said Winter, and her voice softened. "We don't have much time. We've been trying to hold off the rats all day, but there are too many of them. If you don't come with me, the mammals are going to find you, and they're going to kill you."

"So—you can talk to animals, too," he said faintly.

"Told you you're not the only one."

Simon eyed the bustling street. Something was happening. Something big. If he went back out there and met his uncle at the ferry, part of him—a very large part—was sure he would never find out what it was. And worse, he feared he would never see his mother again.

But if he went with Winter to meet Orion, he would be doing exactly what his mother and uncle didn't want him to do. He wanted to trust Winter though. She'd stood up for him in school, and she'd tried to reassure him that he wasn't crazy, talking to animals like he did. Darryl had no plan to rescue his mother—just a way out of the city. But Orion . . . if he'd really sent the pigeons to help them—if he really knew where his mother was . . .

Darryl was going to kill him.

"Where is he?" said Simon. "Where's Orion?"

"Your mom tried to fly away from the rats, but she was too injured, so Orion's following them," said Winter. "He wanted to be here, but if they drag her underground before he can track them . . ."

Fly away. His mother had tried to fly away. Simon shook his head. His mother didn't have wings. Then again, up until ten minutes ago, Darryl hadn't had a tail, either.

"I'm supposed to meet my uncle," said Simon, feeling light-headed. "I have to make sure he knows I'm okay. If I'm not there when he—"

The squeal of tires echoed between the buildings, and a black sedan appeared at the end of the alleyway. Simon backed away, but Winter didn't seem the least bit surprised, even when two large men exited the car.

"Who are they?" said Simon.

"Our ride," said Winter. When Simon didn't move, she let out a frustrated hiss and lowered her voice. "The rats are almost here, and if they catch us, we're both going to become human chew toys. And if you don't come with me and something happens to you, Orion will never forgive me, and—please." For the first time since Simon had met her, she sounded desperate "He loves you. He's your family, and not everyone's lucky enough to have that, all right? He wants to protect you and your mother, and this is the only way. *Please.*"

Simon's heart raced. Darryl would be furious, but if he didn't go with Winter, he would probably never see his mother again, and Simon couldn't live with that. He'd lost her before, more times than he could count. He couldn't lose her forever.

At last he moved toward the sedan. "If anything happens to my mother—"

"It won't," she said. "Feathers are family, and we protect our own."

As Simon ducked into the car, all he could do was hope Winter was right.

5

THE BIRD LORD

Simon stared out the window as the black sedan navigated through rush hour traffic, his hand in his sweatshirt pocket as he stroked Felix's soft fur. What would Darryl think when he reached the ferry and found Simon missing? Would he assume he'd been kidnapped? Simon couldn't work up much guilt. Darryl had lied to him his entire life. Not only had he secretly been a wolf, but he had also known about Simon's ability to talk to animals. Instead of telling him the truth, he'd let Simon think he was weird and alone. And unlike his mother, he hadn't had a good excuse.

"How did you get away from the rats?" said Winter as they drove toward the Upper East Side. "Have you shifted already?"

"Shifted?" said Simon, but he had an uneasy feeling he already knew exactly what she was talking about.

"Into your Animalgam form, of course," she said.

"Ani-what?" said Simon.

"Ani-*mal*-gam," said Winter, looking at him strangely. "Do you even know what the five kingdoms are?"

Simon stared at her blankly, and Winter sighed. "This is going to be fun."

The sedan stopped outside a glitzy tower on Park Avenue a few minutes later. Winter hopped out of the car, and Simon followed, frowning. The tower had to be at least forty stories tall, and when he craned his neck, he could see a strange glass observatory on the very top level. "I need to let my uncle know where I am."

"Orion will send a messenger," said Winter as she bounded past the doorman and into the building. After taking one last look at the bustling street, Simon followed her inside. His uncle wouldn't leave the city without him, but he would undoubtedly assume Simon had been taken by the rats, too.

"What is this place?" he said once they were inside the lobby. The foyer was lined with trees that seemed to grow straight out of the marble floor, and the ceiling swirled with animated clouds.

"Sky Tower," said Winter. "You've seriously never heard of it?"

Simon had a feeling there was a lot he hadn't heard of.

A security guard in the elevator welcomed them with a nod. Though there were forty floors to choose from, he swiped a card and pressed the top button—a big *P*.

"I take it Orion lives in the penthouse," said Simon as the elevator rose. "Do you live there, too?"

Winter nodded. "My father was the head of his security team."

"Was?" said Simon.

Her expression darkened. "He's dead."

"Oh." His stomach twisted into knots. "I'm sorry. My dad's dead, too."

"I know." She didn't look at him, but her voice softened a little. Simon took that as a good sign.

"Do you really think Orion can save my mom?" he said, and Winter nodded.

"Orion wouldn't let her die. She's his family."

It wasn't much reassurance, but it was all Simon had for now, and he hoped against hope she was right. They spent the rest of the elevator ride in silence, until at last the doors opened, revealing the penthouse.

Simon blinked. Hard. The penthouse was enormous, but instead of marble and chandeliers, he might as well have stepped into the middle of a forest. Dozens of trees grew from a carpet of grass and dirt, stretching up toward a ceiling five stories above them. One oak tree towered above the rest, with gnarled branches that bowed under their own weight. The walls on all four sides were made of glass, and at least a dozen birds flew from tree to tree, chattering in voices that sounded strangely human.

"This is where you *live?*" he said, his mouth hanging open.

"The floor below this is where we sleep, but we spend almost all our time in the tree house," she said, pausing to wave at a robin.

They reached a spiral staircase. Simon tried to peer down into the level below, but Winter began the dizzying climb up instead, and he scrambled to follow.

When they reached the top, Simon stopped and stared. It wasn't a tree house at all, but a circular walkway that extended all the way around the penthouse. Armchairs were scattered around the roomy level, all facing the windows that provided a view of the entire city. There was even a large desk looking over Central Park, and low bookshelves created an inner wall. But the most amazing part was the huge old oak tree that grew from below, its branches so high that the glass ceiling had been specially built to form a dome around them.

"Like it?" said Winter with a smirk.

"Of course he does, my dear," said a voice Simon immediately recognized. Halfway up the massive tree, the trunk twisted into a seat, and perched in the center was the one-eyed eagle.

"What are you doing here?" said Simon.

"This is my home," said the eagle. "I am so very glad to see you safe at last."

"Winter said Orion knew where the rats took my mother," said Simon. "I want to talk to him."

"Of course, of course," said the eagle. "If you'll indulge me for a moment."

"What—" started Simon, but the eagle took flight, landing gracefully at Simon's feet. The air shimmered, and the eagle began to change shape just as Darryl had. His body elongated; his massive wings turned into arms, and his brown feathers melded together to form clothes. The eagle's one beady eye stayed the same, but the beak retracted, morphing into a human nose and mouth. White feathers formed a trim silver beard and a head full of hair, revealing tanned skin where they disappeared.

Within seconds, the transformation was complete. Instead of an eagle, a man stood in front of Simon, tall and regal, with a thin nose half a size too big for his long face. He wore a plain white shirt and brown pants, and what had once been talons were now bare feet, gnarled with age. One eye was scarred over, and he fixed the good one on Simon and smiled.

"My boy," he said warmly. "I have waited for this day for a very long time."

"You're Orion," said Simon. His mouth went dry. This was who his mother and Darryl had been so afraid of—the same eagle that had been stalking him all day. "Where's my mother?"

Orion's bushy eyebrows knit together. "I followed them for as long as I could, but despite my efforts, the mammals took her hostage. I am certain they will not kill her, not when she is so valuable to both of us, but how long that mercy will last, I cannot say."

Cold fear washed over Simon, and he gulped. "So get her back."

"I'm afraid it isn't that simple," said Orion. "My kingdom has been at war with the mammals for years. I have no more control over the rats than you do."

"Then who—"

"The Alpha, of course."

The Alpha. The same name the rats had murmured. "How do we find them?" said Simon, clutching the hilt of Darryl's knife where it hung from his belt.

"Not *them. Her.* The Alpha is well protected by her subjects, and even without their support, she is a formidable foe," said Orion. "By now, I do not doubt your mother has been taken deep into mammal territory. To try to save her would be suicide."

"But the pigeons—they can help us." There had to be a million in the city.

Orion regarded him with his one good eye. "How much did your mother tell you about me?"

Simon fidgeted. Talking to Orion felt like he was betraying her, but he *had* tried to save them from the rats. "She told me you're my grandfather, and that you've been hunting us since I was a baby," said Simon. "That she had to abandon me just so you wouldn't find us."

Orion sank wearily into the nearest chair. Despite his

apparent frailty, he gripped the arms of the chair hard enough to turn his knuckles white. "Your mother abandoned you to stop the Alpha from finding you. *I* have only ever wanted to keep you and your mother safe, but I am growing older and weaker. After the Alpha's soldiers killed your father while he was supposed to be under my protection, your mother feared I would fail to protect you, too."

Suddenly the room tilted and Simon's knees buckled. "The Alpha murdered my father? But—my mother never said—"

"No, I suspect she did not." Orion leaned toward the window, his brow furrowing. "Perrin!"

Half a dozen birds flew up into the tree house, and a hawk rose above the rest, perching on the back of the chair beside Orion's. "Sir," he said in a man's voice.

"I see movement," said Orion, nodding toward Central Park. "Double the park guard, and keep me apprised of the pack's whereabouts. The Alpha no doubt knows of our involvement by now, and we must remain one step ahead of her if we are to succeed."

"As you wish, Your Majesty," said the hawk, and he spread his wings, taking off toward the highest branches of the tall oak. One of the glass panels must have been open, because he turned sharply and glided out into the open air above the city.

Simon's head was spinning. The Alpha had murdered his father, and now she was after his mother, too. "I have to find her," he said, his voice breaking. "Please—you have to help me."

Orion refocused on Simon and patted the seat beside him. Simon didn't budge. "I will do everything I can, my boy, I promise. But the might of the mammal kingdom surpasses even my own, at least within the city."

"You mean rats and dogs and . . ." *And wolves,* but Simon couldn't say it.

"He doesn't know anything about us," said Winter from her armchair. She had pulled her book out and was steadily turning pages. "He doesn't even know about the five kingdoms."

"I don't care about any of that," said Simon, his voice shaking. "I just want to find my mother."

"Then despite what you may think, you do care, for it is an integral part of why this happened to her. To both of you." Orion stood and limped to the edge of the glass, flinching with each step. Winter dropped her book and hurried over with a cane, and he took it with a grateful smile. "I hear you have been able to talk to animals for quite some time."

"They come to me for things. For food, and when they're sick and stuff."

"Birds in particular?" said Orion. Simon nodded. "That is because you are my grandson."

"What does that have to do with anything?"

Orion set his hand against the glass and gazed out toward Central Park. "I am the King of the Skies, and I rule over every animal with the ability to fly. Except for insects, of course, but I consider that quite a bit of luck."

Several of the birds in the oak's branches tweeted with laughter. Simon didn't see what was so funny. "You're a—king," he said.

"Indeed," he said. "Animalgams—people born with the ability to turn into animals, like us—are split into five kingdoms: birds, land mammals, insects, reptiles, and the underwater kingdom. We all have the ability to shift into animals. For instance, as you have seen, I am a golden eagle, and the leader of the bird kingdom. Your mother, as my heir, is also an eagle, and your guardian is a wolf and a member of the mammal kingdom."

"But I can't shift into an eagle," said Simon. "I can't shift into anything."

"Not yet, but you will. Rather soon, I'd say. The first transformation usually comes around twelve or thirteen. Winter has not yet shifted, either, but when she does, she will be a hawk like her father," he added. "I guarantee you are one of us, Simon. Your ability to talk to animals has already proven that. Most don't develop that gift until they have shifted, but you—you are special."

Simon wasn't sure he believed it. He'd never been extraordinary or talented at anything, except for accidentally egging on bullies. "Is that how the Alpha found us? Because of me?"

Orion grimaced. "No, no, my boy. You did nothing

wrong. I have been searching for you for a very long time, but it wasn't until I heard rumors of a boy who could speak to pigeons—who helped and befriended them even when so many believe them to be nothing but nuisances—that I learned where you were. And I fear in the process of finding you, I am regrettably the one who led the Alpha directly to your doorstep."

A lump formed in Simon's throat. So the fault lay with both of them. "I don't understand why she wants to kill us."

"The Alpha wants to enslave all five kingdoms and seize ultimate power for herself," said Orion. "She has already threatened and blackmailed the other three kingdoms into bowing down to her and giving her the means to control them. I am all that stands in her way now, and because I refuse to yield, the Alpha has made it her mission to destroy my line, allowing her to take control. That is why she sent the rats to attack you and your mother. Without an heir, my kingdom will fall, and with it the final resistance to the Alpha's tyranny. Should I surrender, she will strip the kingdoms of their rights and slaughter anyone who opposes her. Mammals will run wild and unchecked, and there will be chaos. But you and I will not be around to see it," he added. "Nor will your mother, because we will all be dead. That is what I am fighting for, Simon—our family, our kingdom, and the freedom of every Animalgam. If we do not fight, no one else will."

Simon swallowed hard. He didn't know whether Orion

was telling the truth, but he had witnessed the fights between rats and pigeons in the streets with his own eyes. He had seen the rats band together by the thousands. If that was what the Alpha was willing to do in order to get to him and his mother . . .

"I need to tell my uncle where I am," he said.

"Darryl Thorn is a wolf," said Orion, his lips twisting with disdain. "While I . . . *admire* the lengths he has gone to in order to secure your safety, against the very foundation of his breed, it is far too dangerous for you to see him."

"But he protected me from the rats," said Simon, his hands balling into fists. "He would never hurt me. He *raised* me. He's my family."

Orion hesitated. "Perhaps one day, once the Alpha is defeated, it will be possible. But for now, you must stay here, where it is safe." He turned to the window, wincing and touching his back. "There are millions of mammals in the city, and every single one of them will be searching for you. The moment you step out of Sky Tower, I can no longer protect you."

Simon sputtered. "But—"

"I am sorry, my boy. Truly. I know what it is to be caged, and I would not wish that on anyone. But your life, and the fate of the five kingdoms, is in jeopardy. I do not know if I will be able to save Isabel, but I *can* protect you."

So that was it. He might never see his uncle again—not if Orion had anything to say about it—and if they didn't find his mother before the rats handed her over to the Alpha . . . "You can't make me stay here."

"I do not wish to do so, but I must keep you safe. It is my highest priority."

"Your highest priority should be finding my mother."

"I am doing everything I can—"

"That isn't good enough." The urge to lash out at Orion overwhelmed him, and he backed away toward the spiral staircase, the glass windows spinning around him. "If you don't find her, I'll—I'll—"

"You will what?" said Orion gently. "Put your life at risk by leaving? Destroy everything your mother has worked for by letting the Alpha kill you?"

Simon said nothing. Instead he stormed to the staircase and down the winding steps, nearly tripping over his own feet. He didn't care about what the Alpha would do to him. He didn't care about the five kingdoms or their wars or whether Orion kept control over the bird kingdom. Somehow, some way, he would escape. He would track down the rats. And as soon as he got them to tell him where his mother was, he would save her. It didn't matter if it put his life in danger. If he didn't do something, she would die, and he would never see Darryl again. No matter what it took, no matter what it cost him, Simon refused to let that happen.

BIRDS OF PREY

The spiral staircase let out into a corridor that, like the floor above, nature seemed to have overrun. Even though Simon was short for his age, he had to duck to avoid several low-hanging branches that grew out of the leafy walls, and the ceiling swirled with animated clouds just as the lobby of Sky Tower had. Compared to the openness of the level above, however, Simon found himself feeling claustrophobic in the maze of hallways.

It didn't matter. He wasn't staying. Reaching into his pocket, he scooped Felix out. "We have to get out of here."

"And do what?" said Felix, cleaning his whiskers. "You have no idea where your mother is."

"But the rats do," he said, and Felix let out an annoyed squeak.

"I thought the idea was to survive this," he said. "They'll kill you."

Simon ducked around the corner, narrowly missing another branch. "You heard Orion—he's practically given up on finding her. I have to do *something*. So if you have any brilliant ideas, now's the time to speak up." They turned another corner, and at last he spotted the elevator.

"Simon?"

Orion's voice echoed down the hallway, and Simon froze. He sounded close, and as Simon listened, he could hear the flap of wings. He hastily tucked Felix back into his pocket, muffling his squeaky objections, and pressed the down button.

Nothing happened.

He pressed it again. Still nothing. Was the elevator out of service? He examined the wall beside the door. There was a slot next to the buttons for a keycard like the one the elevator attendant had used.

Terrific. He was trapped. The rustle of leaves grew closer, and Simon swore he could feel a breeze on his face.

There had to be another way out of here. He searched the hallway, opening various doors one by one, his heart pounding as Orion called his name, his voice growing closer with each passing moment. He couldn't stay here. He couldn't let Orion keep him imprisoned while the Alpha killed his mother. There *had* to be a way.

Two large closets and a bathroom later, Simon at last opened a door to find a dingy stairwell. Fluorescent lights flickered above the concrete steps, and he swung his backpack over his shoulder as he closed the door behind him and then bolted down the stairway. Twice he tripped, but he caught himself before he barreled headfirst down to the landing below. After that he took the steps more cautiously, straining his ears for any sign that Orion was following him. But as far as Simon could tell, he was alone. It was almost too easy, but he couldn't afford to think about that right now. He had to get out of there and find his mother—that was all that mattered.

Forty floors later, he reached the ground level and peeked through the doorway. The elevators were only a few feet away, and beyond them, a security guard sat at the front desk. Simon looked around, but he didn't see any other way out. Sneaking past the desk wouldn't work; the guard would see him in the open lobby. That left him with only one choice.

Gathering his courage, Simon walked toward the exit with as much confidence as he could muster. He was Orion's grandson. That had to count for something, and if the guard asked—

"Fifteen minutes. I expected better from you, Simon Thorn. You're a disgrace to seasoned runaways everywhere."

Simon stopped. Lounging in a plush armchair near the door was Winter, book in hand. She didn't bother looking up.

"You can't stop me," he said. "I'm leaving."

"You see that guard?" she said, nodding to the tall man behind the desk, who watched them out of the corner of his eye. "And the doorman who looks like he wrestles bears for fun? They're not going to let you set foot outside Sky Tower. Even if you did manage to make it past them, there are a hundred rats swarming the sidewalk outside. You won't get to the end of the block."

Simon glanced through the floor-to-ceiling windows looking out onto the street. Just as Winter had said, the rats were back, and so were the pigeons. They weren't fighting alone this time though—a swarm of robins and sparrows had joined them, doubling the bird kingdom's numbers in their attempt to defend their territory. His throat went dry. There was no way he would be able to get past all of them.

"There has to be another way out of here, one the rats don't know about," he said, his voice cracking with desperation.

Winter shrugged and climbed to her feet. "Wait until you grow wings, and then fly away. The rats won't be able to touch you."

"That could take years," said Simon. "Please, Winter. If it was your mother, wouldn't you—"

"My mother's dead, too."

Simon's heart sank. "I'm sorry."

"Don't be sorry. Be smart. You're not going to get around the Alpha's guards, and she's been trying to end Orion's line for ages. Even if Orion's right and your mother's still alive, the Alpha won't give her back just because you asked nicely."

"I have to try. I can't let my mother die if there's anything I can do about it."

"And what if there isn't?"

Simon opened and shut his mouth. What then? "I don't know, and I don't want to know. I have to try, Winter. She's my family. Would you sit here locked in a tower if she had taken Orion instead?"

Now it was her turn to hesitate, and she looked out the window again. "There are only so many places in the city where the Alpha would keep her, and Orion's already scouting them out. If he can't save her—"

"The Alpha has to know he's going after her," said Simon, his mind racing. "But she won't expect me to try, too. She'll be ready for him, but she won't know I'm coming. It's a long shot, but it's something." He took a deep, shuddering breath. "Please, Winter. I need your help getting out of here."

Several seconds passed in silence, and Simon exhaled sharply. Before he could say anything else, however, Winter whipped back around to face him.

"Fine, but you have to listen to everything I say. No arguing, got it?"

He nodded, relieved. "We do this your way."

"The rats outside are soldiers—they just do what they're told, and they won't know where your mother is," she said, her green eyes steely. "But I know someone who will."

"Who?" he said, gripping the strap of his backpack.

"The Rat King." At the confused look that must have been on his face, she rolled her eyes and added, "He's not a *real* king—not like Orion or the other rulers of the kingdoms. It's just what you call it when . . ." She shook her head. "Anyway. He's a joke, and he smells terrible, but he knows everything that goes on in the city. If your mother's still in Manhattan, he'll be able to tell us where."

Simon could put up with a stench if it meant finding his mother. "Where is he?"

"Rat Rock Boulder in Central Park. It's sort of hard for him to get around, so he doesn't go too far." She eyed him. "How fast can you run?"

"Pretty fast. Why?"

"Because I'm going to kick the guard in the knee, and you're going to make a break for it."

"You're what?" said Simon, but she was already halfway to the desk. "Winter—Winter!"

"You get only one chance, Simon," she said, and before he could react, she did exactly as she'd said she would and kicked the unsuspecting guard. Hard.

His cry of pain echoed through the lobby, and Simon darted forward. He could do this.

He rushed the glass door and threw his whole body

weight against it. Part of him expected resistance and pain, but the door flew open, and Simon spilled out onto the pavement.

"Hey!" yelled the doorman, but Simon was already running. The rats had nearly taken over the sidewalk, but seemingly oblivious pedestrians had formed a path through the battle, and Simon jumped from one clear spot to the next, narrowly missing several tails.

He managed to get halfway down the block before a rat cried out, "Simon Thorn!" His name rose from the horde in waves, and before he knew it, the rats began to converge on him. Several people made sounds of disgust, and a nearby tourist screamed, but the rats ignored them.

Simon's heart hammered. The rats were coming from every direction—even the street—and now that he was there, they seemed to be multiplying. The birds screeched as they flashed their talons and ripped at the rats' fur, but in seconds, they were vastly outnumbered.

"Simon!" cried another voice—Winter. She waded through the rats, kicking several aside. "Ew, ew, *ew*! This is disgusting."

"Get back inside!" he called as he stumbled forward, the rats' sharp claws scratching his legs as they tried to climb up his jeans again. Simon grew heavier and heavier as more rats joined them, and he became dizzy with panic. This had been a terrible idea. He should've listened to Winter and stayed in Sky Tower, or at least waited until the rats vanished. This time, his uncle wasn't here to save him, and if any more rats appeared—

A shriek filled the air, and Simon looked up in time to see a flock of hawks and falcons diving toward them from the top of Sky Tower. Leading them was the one-eyed golden eagle—Orion.

Before Simon could move, talons ripped the rats off his clothing, and more vicious screams echoed in his ears as the birds and rats clashed. The rodents were no match for the larger raptors, and within seconds, they began to scatter.

"Come on, before they force us back inside!" Winter grabbed his elbow and tugged him forward, away from the tower and toward Central Park.

"But—you really don't have to come with me," he said as they raced down the sidewalk.

"Someone needs to make sure you don't get eaten by a pack of hungry wolves. Now come on, before they catch us."

Simon didn't need any more prompting. He ran as hard and as fast as he could, and to his surprise, she matched him. Together they raced through the city streets, past vendors selling hot dogs and ice cream, past groups of tourists staring upward, past countless men and women who protested sharply as they went hurtling by. They zigzagged around corners and through crosswalks, always heading west. By the time they reached the edge of Central Park, Simon's lungs burned, and his legs shook beneath him.

"Not bad," said Winter, who despite looking as if she had

never run anywhere in her life, had barely broken a sweat. They slowed to a fast walk as she led him down the sidewalk along a street that cut through the park. "Rat Rock isn't far, and the flock won't expect us to go there, not now. We should be able to get in and out."

"Unless the rat army is waiting for us," said Simon breathlessly, his skin crawling with the memory of vermin climbing all over him.

"If that happens, then I hope you figure out how to shift before they eat you," she said, turning onto a path that led south.

That was comforting. It took Simon a minute to catch his breath, but once he did, he peered at her curiously. "Have you shifted?"

She stared straight ahead, but Simon could see her brow furrowing. "You heard Orion."

"And I also saw the look on your face when he said it."

"I should have by now, but I haven't, all right?" she said sharply. "It's a sore subject."

Simon wasn't so sure he believed her, but he let it drop for now. "Do you know what my father shifted into?"

Winter shrugged. "A wolf, I guess, like the rest of his family. The mammals don't like Hybreds."

"Don't like what?"

"Hybreds. The five kingdoms don't exactly encourage mingling, but sometimes it happens, and that's the result. A Hybred."

She said "Hybred" as though it were a particularly bad curse word, and Simon blinked, still not understanding. She must have sensed his confusion, because she stopped suddenly and faced him, her expression pinched in annoyance.

"Most of the time, Animalgams know which kingdom they belong to before they shift. If you have two birds for parents, that's what you're going to be. Two mammals, there you go. Two fish, two insects, two reptiles—you get the picture. But you, for instance—your mother is an eagle. Your father was a wolf. No one really knows which one you're going to be. You're the product of two kingdoms, and that makes you a Hybred."

"I don't see how that's a bad thing," said Simon.

"Do you like knowing where you don't belong?" she said, and he shrugged.

"Haven't really thought about it much yet."

"Well, believe me, everyone else won't like it. Especially when, out of all five kingdoms, you're half bird, half mammal. It's dangerous, and no matter what you are, someone will always remember that your mother's a bird and your father's a wolf."

As far as Simon saw it, it wouldn't matter what his parents were. He didn't plan on sticking around long enough for anyone to care. But before he could say anything, Felix nudged his way out of his pocket, his whiskers twitching. "That was a rather bumpy ride, wasn't it?"

Simon frowned. "Sorry. At least the rats are gone now. Here—it'll be safer for you in my backpack."

He set the little mouse on his shoulder, but before Felix could reply, Winter shrieked and scrambled backward, straight into a bench. "You brought a *rat?*"

"Excuse me?" said Felix, his whiskers twitching. "I am not a *rat*—"

"He's a mouse, and he won't hurt anyone," said Simon, glaring at her.

"Didn't you listen to anything Orion told you?" she said. "Mammals are ruthless. They're all working for the Alpha, and they all want to kill you."

"Felix is my friend," said Simon. "He doesn't even know who the Alpha is."

"You have to dump him," said Winter, her eyes wide and wild. "Now."

"I'm not going to dump him! He'd die," said Simon.

"If you want a pet, get a canary or something. Not a rodent."

"I already told you, he's not a pet. He's my fr—"

"Either he goes or I go," said Winter. "Which is it?"

Simon crossed his arms over his chest. "Then I'll just go to Rat Rock on my own, and you can explain to Orion why you helped me escape in the first place."

Her mouth dropped open. "You're seriously as brainless as a sea monkey. You're going to get us *killed*."

"Maybe. Maybe not. But if we die, it won't be Felix's fault."

With a huff, Winter stormed off down the path, and Simon paused long enough to unzip his backpack for Felix.

"You can stay in here," he said, setting Felix on top of his socks. "The Rat King will never know you're there."

Felix's nose twitched indignantly. "I don't trust her."

"Well, I do. Make sure to find a soft spot so you don't get squished."

Simon zipped up his backpack and scrambled after Winter. "I'm sorry," he said. "Felix won't get us into trouble, I promise."

"You better be right." She veered off the path and ducked through a thin line of trees. "When we get there, let me do the talking. And whatever you do, don't stare."

"I've seen rats before," said Simon, following her across a patch of wood chips.

"Not like this, you—"

"*Who goes there?*"

An angry hiss filled the air, and Winter jumped. Simon automatically stepped in front of her and looked around. Rocks at least twelve feet high loomed around them, casting shadows across an open space that smelled faintly like sewage.

From the depths of the boulders came a strange dark shape that looked like nothing Simon had ever seen before. It lurched across the ground in a zigzag pattern that seemingly had no direction at all, as if something were holding it back. The closer it got, the tighter Simon gripped the knife hanging from his belt, until at last it stepped into the afternoon sunlight.

A dozen rats the size of small dogs inched toward them, their razor-sharp teeth bared and their fur matted and dirty. Finally Simon understood why they moved so slowly: their tails were tied together, making it impossible for them to separate.

"Is that—?" said Simon.

"Yeah," said Winter with a gulp. "That's the Rat King."

THE RAT KING

Simon knew it was rude to stare, but he couldn't help it as the tangle of rats stopped a few feet away. He had never seen anything like it. "Which one's the Rat King?" he whispered to Winter.

"None of them. It's how rats punish one another—by tying their tails together and mocking them," she whispered back. "I told you, they're a joke, even to their own kingdom."

They didn't seem like a joke to Simon. Even if they couldn't move well, they were still what nightmares were made of.

"Answer us," one of the rats demanded. It was the biggest of them all, with an abnormally thin face and greasy, matted gray fur. "Who are you?"

"I—I'm Simon," he said. "This is Winter."

"Simon," murmured the rats surrounding them. "Winter."

"Trespassers," said the leader, and the murmuring grew. "We do not allow trespassers."

"We don't exactly want to be here, either," said Winter, and Simon elbowed her in the side. She glared at him.

"I'm looking for my mother," said Simon, sounding much braver than he felt, with his insides quivering. "A bunch of rats kidnapped her earlier, and I need to know where she is. Her name's Isabel Thorn."

"Isabel Thorn, Isabel Thorn, Isabel Thorn," murmured the rats in unison. "We know everything, for a price."

"I'll give you anything you want."

"What could you possibly offer us that we do not have already?" said the Rat King.

Simon glanced around, searching for anything they might be interested in. He had only clothes, books, and his mother's postcards in his backpack, and all he had of any value was the pocket watch his mother had given him. He would rather cut off his right hand than let them have that.

"My knife," he said suddenly, pulling out the dagger Darryl had given him. "I'll give you my knife."

The leader scoffed. "What need have we of a human weapon?"

His desperation grew. There had to be *something*. His gaze fell on the Rat King once more, and an idea formed in his mind. "I'll untie you."

The hissing stopped. "What did you say?" said the leader.

Simon tucked his knife back into his belt. "It can't be easy to find food or run around. I bet you haven't been down in the subway stations in forever." He couldn't imagine all of them managing the steps at once. "Tell me where my mother is, and I'll untie you."

The rats glanced at each other. Simon heard a few whispered words, and at last the leader rose on his hind legs. "Untie us, and we will consider your offer."

"How do we know you won't just run away?" said Winter.

The leader rubbed his paws together. "You trust us."

She snorted. "Please. I'd trust a pigeon before trusting a rat."

Immediately the Rat King shivered, and several of them eyed the blue sky. Simon had an idea.

"I'll untie you. But if you run away—if any of you run away before you tell us where my mother is, then I'll tell all the pigeons in New York to hunt you down. They're my friends," he added. "And if you want to ever see your subway tunnels again, you'll keep your word. Got it?"

The rats whispered to one another, and several squeaked nervously. "Fine," said the leader at last. "Untie us, and we will tell you."

Simon knelt on the ground beside them. "Hold still," he said as he pushed aside their matted fur as best he could. The tangle of tails was much worse than he expected, forming a hard lump the size of a baseball. He made a face and began to search for a starting point. He'd never been very good at knots, but at last he found the pitiful end of a tail.

"Just hold on and stop squirming," he said, and he slowly began to undo the twisted mass. Minutes passed, and a bead of sweat trickled down his cheek. The stench coming from the Rat King was so bad that Simon had to breathe through his mouth, but even then he could taste the rot.

"What's taking so long?" said Winter, glancing at the late afternoon sky. "If the flock finds us, we're sitting ducks out here."

"Do you want to do this instead?" said Simon. He had half a tail free and thought he'd spotted the end of another, but his fingers were already coated with grime and other stuff he didn't want to think about.

Winter knelt beside him and made a face. "That's *disgusting.*"

The rats' mutterings grew louder, and Simon glared at her. "They can hear you," he said. She huffed and elbowed him in the side.

"I don't care. Move over."

"Be my guest," said Simon, and he wiped his hands on a patch of grass. "It's not as easy as it looks."

"Maybe not for *you.*" Winter took a deep breath and dived in, her nimble fingers somehow unknotting the tails with ease. Simon stared, stunned. By the time he opened his mouth to speak, she'd already freed three rats.

"How are you   "

"I'm not a clumsy baboon, that's how." Another two tails slipped out of the knot. "Most of it is just fur and rat droppings. They're all clumped together, and the tails aren't as tangled as you think they are."

Simon watched as, one by one, Winter freed the members of the Rat King. Most of the tails were bent at odd angles, but the rats didn't seem to mind; like Felix so often did, they clutched their tails lovingly. Simon couldn't blame them.

"How long have you all been knotted up like this?" he said to the leader.

"Many moons, many moons," he said, his eyes shining as Winter finally freed him. He gingerly took his crinkled tail and ran his paws over the angles. "How I've missed you."

Winter wiped her hands on the ground and stood without touching her outfit. "There. Disgusting, but done. Where did you take Simon's mother?"

"It wasn't us," said the leader. "It was the rat army. We were not allowed without our tails."

"So where did they take her?" said Simon, his frustration growing.

"To the safest place in the mammal kingdom," said the rat. "Where only the strongest may go."

Beside him, Winter muttered a curse under her breath. "You mean—?"

"Yes," said the rat. "The zoo."

Winter let out a screech so loud that half the rats

surrounding them bolted. "Of course. Of *course*. Out of all the places the Alpha could've taken her—that's just perfect, isn't it?"

"At least we know where she is now," said Simon, standing. He didn't see what was so dangerous about a zoo, but before Winter could elaborate, the former leader of the Rat King limped toward them.

"If you follow, you will surely perish," he said, his beady eyes flashing. "Beware the Beast King, Simon Thorn."

"Is that the leader of one of the other kingdoms?" said Simon. The last thing they needed was someone else hunting them, too, but the rat disappeared into the scraggly brush without an answer. Simon frowned, turning back to Winter. "Please tell me you know what he was talking about."

Winter laughed humorlessly. "The Alpha took your mother to the Central Park Zoo."

"That's not what I—" He stopped. It didn't matter. "So let's go get her."

"Have you ever even *been* to the Central Park Zoo?" she said, and Simon shrugged.

"I've seen parts of it from the street. But—"

"But your uncle never took you inside. Orion doesn't let me go near the zoo, either," she added. "You want to know why?"

"The lions aren't very friendly?"

Winter gave him a withering look. "The Central Park Zoo is really a cover for the L.A.I.R.—the Leading

Animalgam Institute for the Remarkable. It's the academy where the Alpha trains her army. She handpicks the smartest and deadliest Animalgam kids from the mammal, insect, reptile, and underwater kingdoms, and because they're all under her control, they can't say no. The Alpha brainwashes them and turns them into killing machines. After five years, the students are sent back to their kingdoms, completely loyal to her. Anyone who's anyone in the five kingdoms trained there. Except for us," she said sourly. "She stopped letting birds attend when she took over."

"I still don't understand why she would take my mother to a school," he said.

"There are other places she could have taken her—the Alpha owns property all over the city, even a few islands north of here. I thought . . ." Winter trailed off and shook her head. "But of course the Alpha took her to the L.A.I.R. instead. It's the safest place in all five kingdoms. If anyone tries to break in, the wolf packs will rip them to pieces before they can get anywhere near the students. Not even Orion's flock can get very far."

"But tons of people go to the Central Park Zoo every day," he said. "You can't tell me it's impossible to sneak in when all we have to do is buy a ticket."

"That's because the L.A.I.R. is hidden. It's—"

A soft trill echoed through the air, and Winter whipped around, her eyes searching the sky. The branches above them rustled, and her face drained of all color. "Orion's coming."

Simon didn't stop to think. He took off eastward down the path, toward the Central Park Zoo. If Orion already knew they were here, then it wouldn't be long before he and every bird in the city came after them.

"Simon—no!" yelled Winter, chasing after him. "We *can't.*"

He didn't reply. Maybe *she* couldn't go to the zoo, but if there was a chance his mother was there, he had to take it. Even if it meant a pack of wolves would probably tear him apart.

"You don't understand—Orion will kill me if I let something happen to you." Winter ran up beside him.

"Then go back to Sky Tower and tell him you tried to make me come back, but I refused," he said. "I'm going to the zoo."

Winter let out another strange sound, this one more a cross between a huff and a strangled curse. "If you go, I go, too."

"Then stop complaining and keep up."

He could practically feel her stare burning holes in the back of his head. "You're going to get us both killed."

"The only person I'm going to get killed is me," he said. "If you want to come, that's on you."

"I can't just let you go off on your own, now, can I?" she said. "You wouldn't know the Academy from a hole in the ground."

Simon said nothing. She could pretend all she wanted that

she was coming along for his safety, but he had seen how much Winter loved Orion, and he knew the truth: she would rather have faced a pack of wolves than return to Sky Tower without Simon.

He ran through the park as fast as he could, and Winter darted along beside him. By now three hawks circled above them, no doubt signaling to Orion exactly where they were. "This way," he said, climbing up a rock face that separated the zoo from the rest of the park.

Winter stopped beside him, her long hair tangled around her face. "What are you doing?"

"What does it look like I'm doing? Sneaking in the back." Simon peered over the edge. A brick wall surrounded the empty zoo; it must have been after closing time. He looked around. Directly below them was a pond that sparkled in the waning sunlight. If he jumped, the splash might make enough noise to alert someone, but there was no other way to get in. And—he glanced at the hawks circling them— no time to try to find one.

"You're crazy," said Winter. "There could be piranhas in there."

"In a pond in the middle of New York? I don't think so." But as Simon pulled off his backpack and eased over the edge, his legs dangling over the water, his heart pounded. What if Winter was right? What if there was something in there that would be more interested in eating him than helping him? Or what if he broke his leg in the fall?

An eagle's cry pierced the air. Orion had found them. No time to think—taking a deep breath, Simon let go of the wall and fell into the pond. The water was deeper than he expected, and for a moment his whole body was submerged, his feet touching the bottom. Something thin and slimy brushed his leg, and he immediately pushed back up.

"It's all right!" he called when he surfaced. Above him, the hawks continued to circle, now joined by the one-eyed eagle. As he climbed out of the pond and onto a wooden bridge, he expected them to soar down, but none of them made a move. He held out his arms. "Throw my backpack down!"

Winter tossed it to him, muttering inaudibly and eyeing the birds. He caught his bag and immediately checked the nest of socks he'd made for Felix. "Are you all right?"

Felix was trembling, and his whiskers twitched nervously, but he was in one piece. "I cannot *believe* you went into the zoo. Your uncle would be furious."

"He isn't here right now," said Simon. "Besides, we aren't staying long."

Winter fell into the pond with a splash. Within seconds she surfaced, sputtering. "Are—you—*kidding* me?" she screeched. "There are *eels* in here!"

"Eels aren't going to kill you. And the flock isn't following us in," noted Simon, offering her a hand. The birds still circled overhead, but they made no move to land.

"Nothing they can do now. We're stuck." She ignored

Simon and climbed out on her own, dripping wet. He had to bite his tongue to keep from laughing. With her oversize cardigan and long hair soaked, she looked more like a half-drowned cat than a human being. "Orion isn't the one we have to worry about, anyway. If your rat—"

"Mouse."

"—*bloodthirsty mammal* squeals on us, I'm turning him into a rat-kebob."

Felix snorted. Figuring it was best to keep them separated, Simon zipped his backpack shut. "You don't need to be so mean to him, you know. He's my friend. He's not going to give us away."

"Please," said Winter. "Rodents are about as dumb as they are smelly."

"How many rodents have you ever talked to? Because I've talked to plenty, and they might not be geniuses, but they're smarter than pigeons."

"*Everything's* smarter than pigeons. They're an embarrassment to the kingdom. Birds are supposed to be noble, loyal, intelligent—"

"Stuck-up . . ."

Winter sniffed. "We fly high. It isn't our fault everyone else is grounded."

Simon pulled off his sweatshirt and wrung it out. "Come on. Show me where the L.A.I.R. is so I can find my mother and we can get out of here."

"We're going to die," she grumbled as she started down

the stone walkway. Simon took one last look at the circling birds before he followed her.

As they walked, he kept an eye out for anything that seemed out of the ordinary. The only other time Simon had ever been to a zoo was on a class field trip last year, and that had been the Bronx Zoo, where he'd spent the day trying not to laugh as the monkeys and elephants and giraffes made fun of the guests. The Central Park Zoo was tiny in comparison, and with its hills and hidden pathways, it looked more like a normal section of the park than a place full of exotic animals. He wasn't even sure how there was enough room to fit them all, let alone an entire academy.

He spotted a looming brick building on the other side of the zoo, close to Fifth Avenue and Sky Tower. "Is that it?" he said, pointing.

"No, that's the Arsenal," said Winter. "It's where—"

A vicious snarl cut through the evening air, and Simon clutched the strap of his backpack. "Who's there?" he called.

With a low chorus of growls, half a dozen wolves emerged from the trees on either side of them. Simon grabbed Winter's hand, but before he could drag her down the path, a massive gray wolf blocked their way, and the others closed ranks around them.

They were surrounded.

8

THE L.A.I.R.

Simon stumbled backward, his heart racing. Behind him, Winter stood frozen, her face drained of color. The leader, the big gray wolf, slinked toward them. "What do you think you're doing out here?" he growled. A string of saliva dangled from his sharp fangs.

"We—we were just—walking around," said Simon lamely.

The wolf moved closer until he was only a few inches away, and Simon felt his hot breath on his face. "How many times have I told you not to wander into the zoo?" said the wolf in a deep, dangerous voice that sounded more human than animal.

Simon blinked. The only wolf he'd ever seen was

Darryl, but this one was smaller, with blue eyes that didn't match his uncle's. "I don't—"

The wolf snarled. "*Enough.*" Behind Simon, Winter let out a squeak that sounded remarkably like one of Felix's. "The flock is everywhere. Unless you want me to inform the Alpha of your little adventure, you and your friend will follow me without another word."

"Y-Yes, sir," managed Simon. But instead of calming down, the wolf bristled, bearing his teeth once more.

"What are you playing at, pup?" He moved closer a second time, sniffing Simon's damp sweatshirt.

"His scent, Malcolm," said a female wolf behind them. "It isn't right. Neither is the girl's. They reek of rats."

"*Excuse* me?" said Winter, but the massive wolf in charge—Malcolm—snarled again, and she shut her mouth.

He continued to sniff Simon, moving from his clothes to his hands to his backpack. Simon stood as still as he could, barely daring to breathe. Who did the wolves think he was?

"Impossible," said Malcolm at last, and he gnashed his teeth half an inch from Simon's nose. "Who are you? What are you doing here?"

A dozen thoughts ran through Simon's head. What lie could he tell to get them out of this without becoming an evening doggie treat?

"Your Beta asked you a question, pup," growled the female wolf behind them, and she snapped at his heels.

Winter shrieked, but another snarl ripped through the air, making the hair on the back of Simon's neck stand up.

"You will not touch him," said Malcolm. "Not until he answers me. Who are you, boy? What game are you playing at?"

Simon hesitated. If the pack knew his uncle, there was a possibility they would let them go. "My name's Simon Thorn," he said. "I'm here because—"

"Thorn?" Malcolm's ears stood straight in the air. "Of what pack?"

"I don't have a pack. I live on the Upper West Side with my uncle Darryl."

This name seemed to send a shock wave through the pack, with several growling and backing away. Malcolm's ears flattened against his head.

"I will warn you only once, boy. I do not show mercy. You will tell me the truth, or I will rip out your throat."

Simon swallowed hard. "I'm telling you the truth. I've lived there my whole life. My uncle raised me."

"*Impossible.*"

"Why?" demanded Simon.

"Because Darryl Thorn is dead."

Simon's insides clenched, and his eyes darted from one wolf to the next. "Are you sure about that? Because I know for a fact he's still alive," he said as boldly as he dared. The wolves were silent. "Go ahead and kill me. I'd hate to be you when he comes looking for me."

Malcolm stared at Simon for a long moment, and the others shifted around them. One word from their leader, and they would turn Simon and Winter into oversize chew toys in no time. Winter clutched Simon's hand, and he squeezed back.

"Malcolm," said the female wolf. "Look. The knife."

The wolf's narrowed eyes focused on the ivory-handled knife hanging from Simon's belt. Simon's heart skipped a beat. "My uncle gave it to me," he said.

"Quiet," snarled Malcolm, and Simon shut his mouth.

Heavy silence hung in the air. Simon expected the wolf to lunge at him at any moment. Instead Malcolm examined the knife, his snout a fraction of an inch from Simon's hand. Beside him, Winter shook so hard that he was surprised she could still stand.

At last Malcolm tilted his head back and howled. It was a lonely sound that made Simon ache. In the distance, he heard several dogs join in, but none of them were as haunting as Malcolm.

Finally the howl ended, and the wolf lowered his head. "Both of you, come with us. Run, and you may not live to see sunset."

He trotted ahead, and the others formed a wall behind Simon and Winter, trying to force them down the stone path. Winter refused to move.

"Trust me," said Simon. "It'll be all right."

"If you want to be their dinner, then fine," she said, "but I'd rather not be eaten alive by a bunch of mangy mutts—"

One of the wolves snapped at her ankles, and she yelped. "I don't think they like being insulted," said Simon. Winter grumbled, and at last trudged forward.

As they made their way to the center of the zoo, Simon's skin prickled. He had the strangest feeling they were being watched. When he looked around, however, all he saw was the empty path, surrounded by trees and the New York City skyline. There was something undeniably strange about the zoo. It was quiet—too quiet, especially for the city, and it took him several seconds to figure out why. Though the flock still circled high overhead as the pack watched warily, Simon didn't hear any birds nearby. Not even pigeons.

As Malcolm led them through the exit, Winter let out a muffled sob, and Simon glanced over his shoulder. For all her bravado, her eyes were red and her cheeks flushed, and she looked as though she was on the verge of a panic attack.

"We'll do anything you want," she said in a choked voice. "Just please don't eat us."

"Eat you?" said the female. "Look at you—runt of the litter. Runts don't amount to much here, do they?"

"I see plenty of potential," said another, wearing a sadistic grin. "Fatten her up, and there might even be enough for leftovers."

Several of the wolves laughed, and Simon clenched his fists. "Stop it," he said. "I don't care what you do with me, but you *will* let Winter go."

To his surprise, the wolves grew quiet and glanced

uneasily at one another. Finally they all seemed to focus on their leader.

"What's your name?" said Malcolm.

"Winter Rivera," she said, her voice shaking. The wolf cocked his head.

"Rivera? As in Councilman Robert Rivera?"

"He's my grandfather," she said with a hint of defiance, as if daring him to comment. Simon looked back and forth between them, trying to figure out whether Winter was telling the truth.

"I see." The wolf considered her for a long moment. "The flock has the zoo surrounded. For your own safety, we cannot let you go. However, if you follow my orders, both of you will be safe here."

"How are we supposed to trust you when we don't even know who you are?" said Simon.

"I am not asking you to trust me. I am demanding your cooperation. Now, if you will."

They stopped in front of the large, old-fashioned brick building that Winter had called the Arsenal. A stairway led up to a pair of wooden doors that looked firmly closed, and above them, a metal casting of an eagle spread its wings.

"Is this the Acad—" Simon began, but suddenly the air around the pack leader shimmered, and Malcolm began to shift. His snout turned into a human face, and his thick fur wove together to form a crisp black uniform. Soon enough, a hulking man stood in front of them, and Simon tried not to stare. His hair was curlier and his face unscarred, but with his bulging muscles, chiseled jaw, and broad shoulders, he looked startlingly similar to Darryl.

"No, it's not. Give me the knife," said Malcolm, holding out his hand.

Simon bit the inside of his cheek and handed it over. Malcolm inspected the wicked blade and polished handle, and after several seconds he slipped the knife into his belt.

"You will come with me, and you will not say a word unless spoken to."

"I'm not going anywhere until you tell me who you are," said Simon.

The man narrowed his eyes. "I am Malcolm Thorn, Beta of the mammal kingdom, leader of the Brotherhood of Wolves, and head of security at the L.A.I.R."

"Malcolm Thorn?" said Simon. "Are you and my uncle—"

"Darryl Thorn was my eldest brother," said Malcolm, and a muscle in his jaw twitched. "If he is still alive, then he has done an excellent job faking his own death. Even our mother believes him to be dead."

"Your mother?" said Simon faintly. Darryl had family in the city, and he'd never mentioned them?

"Yes, our mother. The Alpha. I expect she'll want to meet with you as soon as she returns."

Simon's mouth dropped open. The Alpha was Darryl's *mother*? Which made the Alpha his grandmother, he realized. But why—

"Meet with us?" said Winter, who had apparently regained some of her confidence now that they were facing down a human instead of a wolf. "No way. I'm not going anywhere near that—"

"I would choose your next words very carefully if I were you," said Malcolm. "Nothing inside is going to bite you. Yet. But I can't guarantee my pack won't get hungry."

Turning away, he climbed up the stairs, and Simon followed. If Darryl was the Alpha's son, then why had he faked his death? To protect Simon from his own family? Malcolm might have been afraid of what the birds would do to them, but Simon knew the real danger wasn't the flock. It was whatever lay inside the Arsenal.

He couldn't turn back now though, and he wouldn't have even if he could. His mother was inside, and no matter what it took, he was going to find her.

Malcolm led them into the entrance hall, and the wooden floor squeaked beneath their feet. Weak light filtered through the window above the door, and Simon examined a mural as they passed—falcons and wolves and rattlesnakes and bears and even a swarm of wasps, all united against an enemy Simon couldn't see. Instead of leading them up the nearby winding staircase as Simon expected, Malcolm turned right and ducked through a door in the corner of the hall, guiding them down a narrow stairway that led deep below the Arsenal.

As they descended the steps, Winter found Simon's hand

again and clutched it. His fingers started to ache, but he didn't pull away. The other wolves must have stayed outside, because when the three of them reached the bottom, Simon noticed they were on their own. And standing at a dead end.

"Where—" Winter began, but Malcolm shushed her and flipped open a wooden panel in the wall, revealing a keypad. He punched in a code, and for a moment, nothing happened. Grumbling under his breath, Malcolm kicked the wall, and suddenly a grinding sound filled the air. A sliver of light appeared, slowly growing larger.

Simon stared, his mouth agape. The hidden door slid open, revealing a cavern that housed a brick structure even larger than the Arsenal—so large, in fact, that Simon was pretty sure it took up all the space beneath the entire zoo. It looked a lot like any normal building in the middle of the city, other than the fact that it was deep underground, had no windows, and happened to be surrounded by a moat. A narrow bridge swayed over the dark water, leading to a set of double doors on the other side. Malcolm started across, and Simon followed nervously. What was this place?

Before he could ask, he spotted a silhouette in the murky water, one that looked disturbingly familiar. "Uh, there's a shark in your moat," he said.

"Security is our first priority," said Malcolm. He nodded to the shark. "Captain."

The captain rose to the surface. "Malcolm," he said in a

gravelly voice, and Simon had to tighten his grip on Winter's hand to keep her from darting back into the Arsenal.

"I thought sharks needed salt water," said Simon, sneaking Winter a reassuring look. She didn't look terribly convinced.

"As most of our students from the underwater kingdom come from the ocean, the Aquarium is specifically designed to house saltwater creatures," said Malcolm.

Simon kept his eyes glued to the water as they crossed the bridge. As soon as the shark sank back into the depths, a smaller silhouette appeared.

"There's another one?" moaned Winter, but as the shadow grew larger, Simon realized it wasn't a shark at all. Instead, a dolphin surfaced.

"Hello!" said the dolphin, waving a fin. "You must be new! I'm Jam."

"I'm Simon," he said warily. Were dolphins always this friendly, or was Jam really an Animalgam?

Instead of replying, Jam cocked his head toward him, looking confused. It was then that Simon realized the dolphin hadn't been talking to him—he'd been talking to Winter. "But—" Jam began.

"Fluke," said Malcolm sharply. "Back to your lessons."

"Yes, sir," said Jam. Though he still looked as uncertain as any dolphin could, he bobbed his head. "See you, Simon!"

"See you," said Simon faintly.

The dolphin disappeared back into the water as they

reached the other side of the underground bridge. Apparently not very pleased that Jam had seen them, Malcolm muttered a curse under his breath and pushed open the heavy door, revealing a dark hallway that looked more like the entrance to an old castle than a school. The walls were made of stone, and a wrought iron chandelier hung above them. The low light gave the building an eerie feeling, and a chill crept down Simon's spine. Worse, while framed paintings of all kinds of animals, from mountain lions to vipers to a dolphin that looked like an older version of Jam, lined the hallway, there weren't any portraits of birds. Simon shoved his hands into his pockets.

"I'm guessing this isn't an official part of the Central Park Zoo," he said.

"No, it's not." Malcolm paused in front of a painting of a wicked-looking spider with a red hourglass on its abdomen. "This is the Den—the temporary home of the L.A.I.R., which is the most prestigious academy for our kind in North America, catering exclusively to the future rulers of our world. The L.A.I.R. is the only school of its type that is interspecies—meaning we teach students from all kingdoms."

"Except birds," said Simon, and Malcolm's expression darkened.

"The bird kingdom lost the right to attend when their leader ordered an attack on the original L.A.I.R. and destroyed half the school."

Simon fought to keep his expression neutral as he glanced at Winter. She didn't react, seemingly too busy examining a portrait of a wolf that looked strikingly similar to Malcolm. "Why would they do something like that?"

"Up until a decade or so ago, the Bird Lord was the head of the L.A.I.R. When the kingdoms voted the Alpha as his replacement, he didn't go quietly," said Malcolm, gripping the handle of Darryl's knife. "Afterward, it was too dangerous for us to stay beneath the open sky, so we had to hide underground like a pack of moles. The middle of the city is far from an ideal location to host a school of Animalgams, but the flock can't attack us down here. Not easily, at least."

Malcolm pushed open another door at the end of the short corridor and ushered them through. As soon as Simon saw what was on the other side, he nearly tripped over his own feet in shock. It seemed like they'd stepped into a glass tunnel in the middle of the ocean. Surrounding them on all sides was the kind of marine life Simon had only ever dreamed of seeing. Colorful schools of fish swam in tight formations among the coral and seaweed, as if doing military exercises. Sharks weaved among them, showing off rows of sharp teeth. Spotting Jam the dolphin, Simon gave him a weak wave.

"This is the Aquarium," said Malcolm. "The underwater kingdom's section."

Simon wasn't in the mood for a guided tour, but the more he knew about this place, the easier it would be to find his mother. "So each kingdom has a section, then."

"Yes," said Malcolm, his voice tinged with annoyance. "The Den is shaped like a pentagon—five sides, five sections. This hallway goes all the way around. The outer ring consists of the dormitories, where the students sleep. That's where that trapdoor leads—to the underwater barracks," he said, gesturing to a door beneath their feet. "The inner ring of the Den contains the classrooms, and the pit is in the center of it all."

"If birds aren't allowed here, then what's in the fifth section?" said Simon as he pictured the layout in his mind. If he were the Alpha, where would he keep his mother? No place the students could accidentally find her, which ruled out the dormitories.

"The fifth is for members of the Alpha family," said Malcolm flatly. "It's where you'll be staying."

He opened a door on their left, and Simon blinked, taken aback. This hallway looked to be straight out of an ancient forest. Fully grown trees with leaves as green as the ones in Central Park grew around a dirt path, and the lights were dimmed to make it look like twilight.

"The mammals' section," said Malcolm. "Why aren't you in the pit, Tomas?"

A massive grizzly bear peeked out from his poorly chosen hiding spot behind a pair of trees. He shrugged sheepishly. "Don't want to die."

"You're not going to die." Malcolm opened a wooden door that blended in so well with the rest of the forest that

Simon would have never noticed it on his own. "Pit—now. And don't forget, you're bigger than her."

The grizzly bear—Tomas—shuddered and ambled through the door. Simon craned his neck to see past Malcolm, and he spotted a long hallway that led to the center of the Den. Before he could see what was at the other end, Malcolm closed the door and grunted, gesturing for Simon and Winter to follow him through the rest of the mammals' section. At the end of the hallway, he pushed through a curtain of ivy. They must have been near the very back of the Den now, as far from the entrance hall as possible.

"The Alpha quarters," said Malcolm, and Simon frowned. The walls were painted sky blue, and branches grew out of the walls, low enough that he had to duck to avoid walking into them. If he hadn't known better, he would have guessed they were back in Orion's penthouse.

Even more confusing, Malcolm turned halfway down the corridor and led them into an atrium decorated exactly like the top level of Sky Tower, with lush grass, trees rising several stories high, and a glass spiral staircase in the back leading upward to three other levels. The Den must have been built before the bird kingdom had been banished, Simon realized. This was supposed to be their section.

"You'll wait in here," said Malcolm as he herded them into an office. Simon stumbled after Winter, and Malcolm closed the door, locking them inside. With red walls and leather furniture, the room felt comfortable and warm, almost like his and Darryl's apartment. A huge mahogany desk took up most of the space in the back of the room, and near the door stood a bookcase overflowing with worn books about every species of animal he could think of. The higher shelves were crammed with titles like *The Great Bird War of the Seventeenth Century*, *The Ancient Order of Animalgams*, and *A Brief History of the Insect Migration*—titles that, if Simon weren't staring right at them, he would never have believed. His fingers itched to flip through the pages, but he stopped when he spotted another title: *The Rise and Fall of the Beast King*.

The rat's warning echoed through his head, and Simon reached for the book. If nothing else, maybe he could find out what the rat had been talking about.

"So that's what she looks like," said Winter, her voice cutting through the silence. Startled, Simon dropped his hand. Winter was examining a portrait of a woman with straight dark hair, icy blue eyes, and a narrow nose. Another one of a young man with sandy hair and a playful smirk watched them from behind the desk.

"If that's the Alpha, then who—" Simon began, turning around, but he stopped short. A third portrait hung on the wall beside the door, and this time he knew exactly who the young man with dark hair and even darker eyes was.

Darryl.

"That's my uncle," he said. "He really *is* Malcolm's brother."

"What, did you expect the slobbering mutt to lie to you?"

said Winter, collapsing on a leather couch. Her eyes were still red and puffy from crying. "We have bigger problems to deal with right now. If Malcolm really thinks the flock was trying to attack us, then he must not know the Alpha ordered the rats to go after you, or that Orion protected you. But once he catches on . . ."

"We'll leave as soon as we find my mother," said Simon, wandering around the office, searching for any clues that might indicate where she was being kept. But he saw nothing out of the ordinary—nothing that screamed "kidnapping," at least.

"The Alpha could have moved her by now," said Winter.

"She's here. You heard the rats."

"But how do you know for sure? We could be risking our lives for *nothing*—"

"This is the only lead we have," said Simon. The hot knot settled back in his chest and burned. "She has to be here, all right? If she's not, then—then she's gone, and I can't think like that. Not right now." His mother was counting on him.

Silence filled the office, and somewhere nearby, a clock ticked. "You're right. We'll find her," said Winter quietly. "I'm sorry."

Simon leaned against the desk, not trusting himself to say anything yet. An awkward minute passed, and his eyes landed once more on the portrait of the Alpha. "I don't understand why Darryl faked his death. If his family was trying to kill me, then why—"

"We were not trying to kill you, Simon," said Malcolm from the doorway behind him, and Simon flinched, grateful Malcolm couldn't see his face. "Up until twenty minutes ago, none of us had any idea you even existed."

"Simon . . ." Winter stared at Malcolm as though he had turned into a kangaroo. Simon dug his nails into his palms.

"Then why did my uncle hide me?" he said as he whirled around. "Why—"

He stopped cold. Malcolm wasn't alone.

Beside him stood a scowling boy wearing a black uniform with a matching armband that bore a silver crown insignia. His brown hair was neat and trimmed, and he stood up straight, making him look taller, but that was where the differences ended. From their matching blue eyes to the way their ears stuck out, all the way down to the slant of their eyebrows, he and Simon were identical.

"Simon, you have the honor of meeting the heir to the mammal kingdom, the Alpha Prince Nolan Thorn," said Malcolm. "My nephew, and your brother."

THE ALPHA PRINCE

The room began to spin. Brother? Simon had a brother? He stared at Nolan. Even if Malcolm hadn't told him, it would have been obvious. There was no mistaking them for anything other than twins.

He had a brother. He had a whole family, and his uncle—his *mother* had never told him.

While at first Nolan wore what was likely an identical look of shock, he seemed to brush off the surprise quickly, his expression smoothing into a mask of boredom. "I don't have a brother."

"Hard to say so now, isn't it?" said Malcolm. "After a haircut, we won't be able to tell you two apart."

"If I had a brother, Mother would have told me,"

said Nolan with a sniff, "It's a trick or a disguise, that's all."

"You—you know our mother?" said Simon.

"*My* mother," said Nolan nastily. "I don't know *yours*."

Simon's chest tightened as if a boa constrictor had wrapped around him. His mother had lied to him. Not just about what she did or who he was, but about everything. He had a brother. A *twin*.

"When—when's the last time you saw her?" he managed, feeling like Bryan Barker had socked him in the gut all over again. "Do you know where she is? Have you—"

"I have no idea what you're talking about," said Nolan, and to Malcolm he added, "you dragged me out of training for this?"

"Don't act so annoyed when we both know you jump at the chance to miss training whenever you can," said Malcolm. "You will be polite to your brother, or I'll—"

"Or you'll what? Ground me?" The prince rolled his eyes. "I'm shaking in my boots."

"I'll inform the Alpha of your blatant disrespect for your family," said Malcolm in a warning voice.

Nolan hesitated, but before he could reply, Winter, who had been silent since Nolan had arrived, finally burst. "I've heard all kinds of rumors about how much of a spoiled jerk the Alpha Prince was, but I never actually believed them until now. You really are worse than I am."

"Excuse me?" said Nolan.

Winter stood, her arms crossed over her chest. "You heard me. You're a selfish, spoiled, egotistical jerk who can't even talk to his own brother without making piranhas look polite."

He took a menacing step forward. "How dare you speak to me like that. I am the *Alpha Prince*—"

"Are you?" said Winter. "Because the last time I checked, you were just a bully with a crown."

"I'm sorry," said Simon quickly, stepping between them before Winter could make things worse. The last thing they needed was to make an enemy of the only other person who might care enough about his mother to help them. "She didn't mean that."

"Yes I did," said Winter hotly.

Nolan fumed. "I want you gone. Both of you."

"That's not your decision to make," said Malcolm. "Simon is your brother, Winter is the granddaughter of one of our greatest allies, and Orion is hunting them both. Had they not arrived when they did, no doubt he would have taken them hostage or worse. They will remain here, under the pack's protection, until the Alpha returns and decides what to do."

"But—" said Nolan.

"No buts. They will stay here, and you will welcome them both. Now apologize to your brother, and show Winter to the reptile section."

The reptile section? Simon glanced at Winter, who pointedly ignored him.

"Once she's settled," continued Malcolm, "you and

Winter may join the others in the pit. Do not let me catch you anywhere else."

Nolan's mouth opened and shut several times, making him look like a fish out of water, and finally he narrowed his eyes. "And if I say no?"

"Then maybe Winter's right after all. Maybe you are just a bully with a crown."

Nolan turned red and, without another word, stormed out of the room. Winter smirked and followed him, but Simon could barely keep his panic at bay. Malcolm might have thought he'd done them a favor, but by humiliating Nolan in front of them, he had guaranteed that the only thing Nolan would ever be was their enemy. Their very powerful, very dangerous enemy who, unlike Bryan Barker, really *could* destroy the rest of Simon's life.

Simon began to follow them, but Malcolm closed the office door before he could leave. "Not just yet," he said. "First you're going to tell me what you're doing here."

So Winter was right. Malcolm may have been the Alpha's son, but if he'd had anything to do with her sending the rats or taking his mother, he would have known exactly why they were there. And Simon was absolutely certain that if that were the case, he would be locked away in a cell somewhere, not meeting his twin brother in a fancy office. That didn't mean he could trust Malcolm though. Winter had been right about that, too. The most Simon could do was play into the lie Malcolm already believed.

"An eagle tried to kidnap me," said Simon. "Darryl and my mother held him off, but we got separated, and a bunch of birds started to chase us. Winter's my friend—she thought we'd be safe here."

"I see." A crease formed between Malcolm's eyebrows, and Simon couldn't decide whether that meant he believed him. "And how often did you see your mother?"

"Almost never." He started to tell Malcolm about how his mother sent him postcards every month, but he bit his tongue before he let it slip. Instead he asked the question he had been dreading. "Does she live here with—with Nolan?"

"Yes," said Malcolm, and he sat on the couch. "She travels most of the time, but while she's in the city, she stays here."

Betrayal snaked through him. All this time, she had been right across the park. She'd been here with his brother, being his mother instead of Simon's.

"I don't get it," he blurted before he could stop himself. A lump formed in his throat. "If she was here the whole time, then she should've come to see me. I don't understand why she didn't."

Malcolm said nothing for several seconds, and Simon knew from the pinched look on his face that he was wondering the exact same thing. "When she shows up, we'll ask," he said at last.

She wouldn't be showing up though, not without Simon's

help. His cheeks burned, and he turned away, focusing on the portrait of the man with sandy hair.

"Did you know that's your father?" said Malcolm suddenly. "Luke. He was older than me, younger than Darryl. The glue that held us together."

Simon stared at the painting. *Luke.* His father's name was Luke. He was smaller than Malcolm and Darryl, with lighter hair and eyes, and he wore a playful smirk that would have seemed unnatural on either of his brothers. But Simon looked like him, and the thought made his heart race. All his life he'd wondered who his father had been, but this . . .

"You didn't know about Nolan, did you?" said Malcolm.

Simon shook his head. And while it was the truth, it hurt even more to admit that his mother and uncle hadn't trusted him with who he really was. "Nolan's going to hate me, isn't he?" he said.

Malcolm glanced at the painting of Darryl. "Brothers don't always get along."

Simon's mouth went dry. His uncle must be frantically searching the city for him by now, but there was nothing Simon could do except find his mother and get out of there as fast as possible.

"Come on," said Malcolm grimly. "I have to speak with the Alpha, and I'm not leaving you on your own. You can drop off your things first."

Malcolm headed back into the living area, and Simon

trudged after him. He saw the atrium with new eyes now—it was the place where his mother had lived. With his brother. And without Simon.

Resentment coiled in the pit of his stomach. Why had she chosen Nolan instead of him? Had Simon done something wrong? He wouldn't have an answer until he found his mother, so despite his hurt and anger, he kept his mouth shut as he followed Malcolm toward the glass spiral staircase. They climbed past the second floor and up to the third, and just as Simon felt too dizzy to take another step, they finally reached the top.

"In here," said Malcolm, pushing open another door to reveal a lavish bedroom larger than Simon and Darryl's entire apartment. A four-poster bed with gold curtains sat in the center, with a fireplace crackling cheerfully in the corner despite the late-summer warmth.

Simon set his backpack down, but Malcolm made no move to leave. "I, uh—I need to use the bathroom," he said.

Malcolm nodded toward another door. "It connects to Nolan's room, so don't walk out the wrong door. And don't be long," he said, finally ducking outside.

As soon as Malcolm was gone, Simon lifted his backpack onto a leather couch. Unzipping it, he dug through his socks until he found Felix.

"Still alive?" he whispered. Felix bobbed his head.

"You really have a brother?"

Simon frowned. "Stay away from him, all right?"

"I spent ages in your apartment with your uncle never spotting me," said Felix. "I can handle that pipsqueak."

For the first time since this whole mess had happened, Simon smiled, but it quickly faded. "I need your help searching for my mother," he said. "Malcolm doesn't know about the rats, and I doubt Nolan does, either. The Alpha must be keeping her somewhere neither of them would go."

"I'll do my best," promised Felix. "You stay safe and keep your ears open for anything that might help us find her or figure out what's going on. The Alpha took her for a reason."

"To get to me," said Simon, but the mouse shook his head.

"Maybe, but she wouldn't have gone to the trouble if she didn't need your mom, too. Isabel lives here, remember?" said Felix. "If we can find out why the Alpha captured her instead of letting her go, we might have a better idea of what we're up against."

"Simon?" said Malcolm through the door. "Who are you talking to?"

Felix scampered behind the couch. "Myself," called Simon, and he opened the door. "Sorry, bad habit."

Malcolm eyed the bedroom over his shoulder, so reminiscent of Darryl that Simon felt a pang of guilt. "Right. Ready?"

Simon nodded, and he followed Malcolm out of the room.

He hated putting Felix in any sort of danger, but with Malcolm breathing down his neck and Winter stuck with the reptiles, he would need all the help he could get if he ever wanted to see his mother again—and find out why she'd kept him secret all his life.

10

PECKING ORDER

Simon followed Malcolm back down the spiral steps and into the atrium. Every so often, his newfound uncle looked back at him, as if he was trying to reassure himself that this was all actually happening. Simon felt exactly the same way.

"My office is on the upper level," said Malcolm. "You can watch the pit while I call the Alpha."

"What is the pit, exactly?" Simon asked.

"It's where students train in their Animalgam forms," he said, weaving between the tree trunks. "If the Alpha decides to keep you here, you'll put in your time soon enough. Have you shifted yet?"

"I—" Simon faltered. "Mom said I would soon."

Malcolm raked his hand through his short hair in another

gesture that reminded Simon all too much of Darryl. "Of course you haven't," he said. "All the other students have, so unless you want a nice scar to help us tell you two apart, don't get in anyone's way. Got it?"

Simon nodded, and Malcolm headed into the corridor that led around the entire school. "Reptiles' section at the end of the hall," he said as Simon jogged to keep up. "Don't go in there unless you have to, and if you do, watch your step. We only have so much antivenom."

"What does it look like?" said Simon, remembering the forest and the aquarium from the other sections.

"A desert. Thirty seconds in there, and you'll spend the next three weeks washing sand out of places you didn't know you had. The insects' section is beyond that, on the other side of the entrance hall. Not even I go in there. They filled the hallway with a maze of thick webs no human can navigate."

Simon shuddered. "Wouldn't that stop other insects from being able to get inside? The ones with wings and lots of legs and stuff."

"There's space above and below the webs for them to enter, though we've had incidents of spiders trying to trap them as a joke," said Malcolm. "Spiders technically aren't insects, though they are both arthropods, along with the other members of their section. They insist on being called the insect kingdom though—I suspect because they dislike being referred to as bugs. Or maybe because the spiders hope we'll forget about them. Spiders are the spies of the animal kingdoms, and they aren't exactly fond of others. I wouldn't be, either, if I were their size. But as secretive and cunning as they are, we accept all promising students from the allied kingdoms."

"Except birds," said Simon.

"Yes, well, they're not interested in being our allies, are they? Unless you think Orion was just trying to invite you over for a nice cup of tea."

Orion had been trying to protect him from the pack, but Simon couldn't say that. Instead he followed Malcolm up another spiral staircase. He could hear faint cheering but couldn't tell where it was coming from. "If spiders are the spies of the animal kingdoms, then what are mammals like?"

"Fierce. Competitive. Brave." Malcolm paused when he reached the balcony, waiting for Simon to catch up. "We're the warriors of the five kingdoms. The sworn defenders of all. We do what we have to do in order to protect those who can't protect themselves."

Which meant they also had the brute force to control the other kingdoms. Simon decided that if Bryan Barker were an Animalgam, he would be one of them. Surely not all mammals could be bad though. Darryl was a wolf, after all. Then again, Simon didn't ever want to be on his uncle's bad side. "What about the fish?" he said.

"You're just full of questions, aren't you?" Scowling, Malcolm led him into the inner ring of the Den. "Strict military society. They place high value on diligence, obedience, and working together, and they patrol the oceans and protect our lands from invaders. They're led by a general instead of an

Alpha. Insects have a queen," he added. "Birds have a lord. Reptiles have a council, though they're mostly nomads."

"Nomads?"

"Means they don't usually live in groups like we do. They tend to wander around by themselves and make their own rules. The laid-back, *creative* types." Malcolm's tone made it obvious what he thought about that. "Don't make great fighters, but most of the ones here are venomous, so they have their uses. This way."

Malcolm led Simon down another stone hallway filled with more portraits of animals that looked like they could have come from the postcards his mother had sent him. They passed several doors bearing plaques, though Simon recognized only one name, at the end of the hallway: Malcolm Thorn.

"Stay in the hall." Malcolm jerked his head toward a nearby window that took up nearly the entire wall. "Pit's right there. You can watch, but don't go in, and stay out of sight."

Malcolm disappeared into his office, and Simon inched toward the glass, feigning interest. To his left, a door opened onto a platform, and another staircase led down into what looked like a giant sandbox. Encircling it were rows and rows of bleachers, crammed with what must have been the whole school packed together to watch. In the center of it all, a viper rose up, threatening a cowering grizzly bear that looked an awful lot like Tomas.

Before Simon could get sucked into the match, Malcolm's

voice floated from underneath his door, loud enough for Simon to make out the words. ". . . know about this?"

"Of course not," said a woman in a clipped voice. *The Alpha.* Simon sneaked closer to the office door, careful not to make a sound. "I'll believe Darryl is alive when I see him myself. But *twins*—and you say the other one knows Isabel?"

"Simon. Yes," said Malcolm. "Orion attacked them, and Isabel hasn't returned. I need you back here."

"I cannot cut this summit short—not if we want to keep the alliance with the Black Widow Queen," said the Alpha. "If you would like her as your enemy, then by all means. But I will return in two days, once we've reached an accord."

Malcolm growled. "The flock is circling the zoo, and their assaults have been growing more and more frequent—"

"I will take the boys out of the city and into mammal territory when I return," she said. "If your supposedly dead brother was able to keep this boy safe all these years, then surely you can manage to keep an eye on him until then. Or has Darryl yet again managed to show you up, even from beyond the grave?"

Malcolm was silent for several seconds. "Two days."

"Don't let him out of your sight."

Heavy footsteps echoed through the office, and Simon rushed back to the window, trying to make it look as though he'd been watching the pit the whole time. *Two days.* He had two days until the Alpha returned, and then she would whisk him and Nolan away from the city, undoubtedly to a place where not even Orion could help him. If he ever wanted to see his mother again, he had to find her before then.

Malcolm joined Simon at the window and stared down into the pit. The bear and the viper were gone now, and instead, two students slowly circled one another in the sand. It didn't look like much of a fight. The first boy was almost twice the size of the second, who wore a hood pulled up over his head, and was so slight that he made Winter look like a giant.

Simon furrowed his brow. "Is that even fair?"

"Probably not," said Malcolm, looking murderous. "Just watch."

Finally the larger student lunged. The other student sidestepped him though, and he landed facedown in the sand. A long magenta braid swung out from underneath the smaller one's hood, and Simon gaped. She was a girl.

The boy slowly stood, baring his teeth and growling so loudly that Simon could hear him through the open door. He then let out a ferocious roar, and all at once his body changed from human to mountain lion.

"He's going to kill her!" said Simon, frantically searching the crowd for someone who could help. He spotted Winter at the very top of the bleachers, sitting apart from the rest of the students while Nolan lounged near the bottom, surrounded by a group of cheering boys. The prince didn't join them though—instead he looked bored, as if watching a giant cat devour a girl half his size was something he saw every day.

Fine. If Nolan wouldn't help, then Simon would. He

darted through the door and out onto the balcony above the pit. Behind him, Malcolm swore, but Simon was halfway down the stairs by the time his uncle caught up and grabbed the back of his shirt.

"What did I say about staying out of sight?" said Malcolm. Some of the students had noticed them, and they were pointing and murmuring to their friends. He groaned. "Terrific. Everyone in the five kingdoms is going to know you exist by morning."

"I don't care," said Simon. "You need to stop him."

"And you need to watch."

Simon struggled against his grip, but Malcolm was too strong. Eventually he had no choice but to give up and observe the match. Nearly everyone in the crowd was now staring at him, but he ignored them and focused on the fight in the pit instead. The mountain lion snapped at the girl, who wore a stony expression and didn't take her eyes off her opponent. Simon's heart pounded.

At last the cat attacked. Again the girl was ready for him, and she sprang aside a second time. With impossible speed and strength, she flipped the beast over in midair and pinned him to the ground, her knee against his throat. The mountain lion fought back, his massive paws striking her again and again until—

The girl disappeared. The cat froze in place, and the crowd quieted. Nolan straightened, his eyes wide and eager, and asked, "Do you yield, Garrett?"

The mountain lion growled, barely audible, and Simon stared. What had just happened?

"No point in staying up here, since everyone's already seen you," said Malcolm, and he led Simon down the rest of the staircase, his heavy footsteps echoing around the stone walls.

When they reached the bottom, they stood at the edge of the pit, and Simon could hear the buzz of whispers as all eyes seemed to turn to him. Nolan was the only person who wasn't staring. Instead he glared resolutely at the mountain lion, who lay only a few feet away from Simon and Malcolm. He hadn't moved.

"What will it be, Garrett?" said Malcolm. "Your pride or your life?"

The cat growled again, but at last he grumbled, "I yield."

A shiny black spider emerged from his ear, and it crawled onto the ground and across the sand. As soon as it reached the center of the pit, it shifted, and the pink-haired girl stood in its place. Now that Simon was closer, he noticed that she wore a black armband with a silver spider printed on it. For a second their eyes met, and she did a double take.

"No *way*," she said, a grin spreading across her face. "You've got to be kidding me."

"Not bad, Ariana," said Malcolm, pointedly ignoring her reaction. "One more match before dinner. Who will it be?"

No one volunteered, though Simon wasn't sure whether it was because no one wanted to fight Ariana or because they were all too busy staring at him, Malcolm seemed to be doing his best to act nonchalant, but he couldn't hide his scowl.

"Who's left?" said Nolan with a smirk. "Everyone's already lost to her at least twice."

Garrett the mountain lion shifted back into a hulking boy and climbed to his feet, his face red. He glanced at Simon, but he didn't look surprised like the others. Nolan must have told him already, Simon figured. "Ariana's not invincible," said Garrett. "One stomp in the right place and—"

"You want another round, Puss in Boots?" Ariana said. "Spider or not, I can take you down any day of the week."

"*Enough*," said Malcolm. "We are not here to show off or to bully and intimidate others. We are here to keep the peace between our kingdoms, and that cannot happen if you choose to take these matches personally instead of learning from them. Do you understand?"

Ariana nodded, and Garrett kicked sand as he joined the others at the bottom of the bleachers. He focused on Simon again and leaned in, whispering to Nolan.

"Good," said Malcolm as he looked around. "Now, who's brave enough for one more fight?"

Several of the students fidgeted uncomfortably. Others who had been staring at Simon suddenly looked at their hands. There had to be a hundred of them, Simon guessed— some as old as sixteen or seventeen, and all with silver silhouettes of predators on their armbands. Wolves, vipers, spiders, bears, wasps, scorpions, panthers, and even a few sharks and stingrays. He wasn't sure how they fought on dry land, but now wasn't the time to ask. Instead he searched for any armbands with dolphins to see if he could spot Jam.

"None of you has the courage to face Ariana again?" said Malcolm. "Have you all given up so easily?"

"What about Simon?" said Nolan. "I want to see what he can do."

Ariana tucked her braid into the back of her shirt and grinned. "Sure, if you want chicken legs for dinner."

Simon didn't care how small she was. If she could take down the best of the mammal kingdom, then she was right. He didn't stand a chance. "She'll kill me," he said.

"You don't have to," said Malcolm, clapping Simon's shoulder. "Probably better if you don't."

"Afraid of spiders?" said Nolan. The boys surrounding him burst out laughing, and Simon's face grew hot. If he agreed to fight, no doubt Ariana would take him down faster than he could blink, and he would be the laughing-stock of the entire school. But at least he would prove he was willing to be one of them. No one could call him a coward.

"It's fine," he said, shrugging off Malcolm's hand. "I'll do it."

"Always happy to provide a few bruises." Ariana took her place on the opposite side of the pit. There was something maniacal about the way she watched Simon, and she flashed him another grin.

He was going to die.

DOG EAT DOG

"Good luck," said Malcolm, patting Simon on the shoulder. "All you have to do is get her to yield. And don't kill her."

"Is she allowed to kill me?" said Simon.

"Only if you let her."

"Please tell me that's not actually possible," said Simon faintly as Malcolm took a spot on the bleachers.

"Of course it is," said Ariana with a smirk. "I'm a black widow. One bite and you're dead."

"That makes me feel tons better, thanks," Simon said. The sand shifted beneath his feet, making it hard to stay steady.

Before he could think too much, someone blew a whistle. It was on. Ariana began to circle him and, not knowing what else to do, Simon tried to mimic her. She moved easily across the sand, but Simon stumbled and constantly had to search for new footing.

"So, what are you?" said Ariana. "A wolf, like Nolan claims to be?"

"Human," said Simon. "Right now, at least."

"And when I attack?"

"Probably still human." Unless his body decided to shift at the absolute worst possible time. Which, considering his luck today, wouldn't have surprised him at all.

Ariana narrowed her eyes and moved closer. Simon tried to circle away, but she was always there, just out of reach. "Come on," she said. "You know what I am."

"You really think I'm about to give up the one thing I have going for me?" said Simon. "You'll win. Don't worry about it."

"I'm not worried," she said, but there was an edge to her tone that hadn't been there before.

"Less talking, more fighting," said Nolan in a regal voice. Ariana must have liked it about as much as Simon did, because she scowled.

"As your royal halfwit wishes," she said, and before Simon could blink, she flew through the air toward him.

Simon tried to sidestep her the way she'd sidestepped Garrett, but she grabbed his sweatshirt and twisted him around, and Simon fell hard on his back. All the air left his lungs, and he gasped.

Ariana didn't give him any kind of break. She tried to pin him, but Simon expected it. Still wheezing, he pushed her off and scrambled back up, once again struggling to find his footing.

"You're worse than I thought," said Ariana. She advanced toward him. "You could just yield now, you know."

And risk all the students treating him the same way Bryan Barker had? The same way Colin had? Not a chance. Simon held his hands up in a protective guard, ready for her. Or as ready as he could be.

"Oh, look, you're actually trying. That's adorable." Ariana effortlessly danced from side to side. "What are you going to do? Stare me to death?"

"Something like that," said Simon, but even as she said it, an idea appeared in his head. This time, when Ariana pounced, Simon let her reach him. But as they fell in a heap on the ground, he turned, pinning her to the sand instead.

He buried his knee in her stomach and pressed his arm across her neck, the same way Bryan had pinned him. Simon may not have been very big, but he was bigger than Ariana, and he held her down as she struggled. There was no way she could get out of it. Unless—

Ariana's human body shrank almost too fast for Simon to follow. But he did, and as she shifted into a black widow, he was ready. Simon scooped the spider up and cupped his hands together, trapping her inside.

"Got you," he said. "You bite me, I squish you. They have antivenom here, so I'll probably survive. But you won't."

He heard a tiny string of curses from the spider in his hands, but she knew he had her. And so did he.

Everyone on the bleachers was silent. Several mouths hung open, and even Nolan stared in disbelief. At last Malcolm headed over, navigating the sand with ease.

"Do you yield, Ariana?" he said. The spider didn't respond.

"I'm not letting you go until you do," said Simon. Her legs tickled his palms as she paced, and his skin crawled with the instinct to drop her, but he kept his hands clamped together. Now that he had her, he wasn't letting go.

Finally the spider grumbled, "I yield."

Simon opened his hands and set her gently on the ground. She shifted back into a human, and the moment she was full-size again, she shoved Simon hard. "Cheater! That was *completely* unfair!"

"Was not," said Simon. "Besides, you're the one who won against everyone else."

"Simon has a point," said Malcolm. "With all the experience you've gained, you should have anticipated this possibility."

"But he didn't even *shift*."

Malcolm shrugged. "Sometimes remaining human is our best strategy." He raised his chin to address everyone on the bleachers as well. "Relying on our Animalgam forms can expose weakness, and we have to remember that we're not only wolves or vipers or spiders— we're also human, and we must learn to utilize our strengths in both forms. Simon has been here for less than an hour, but he bested your greatest opponent by analyzing her weaknesses and using them against her."

Simon bit his lip. Malcolm made him sound like some kind of tactical genius, but he hadn't analyzed anything. He'd gotten lucky, that was all.

Nolan leaned forward. "Seems like you do have a flaw after all, spider girl," he said. "No point in having you here if you can't even defend yourself against someone that pathetic."

The boys surrounding him laughed and jeered. Ariana turned red, and she stormed toward a door that must have led out of the pit. As she passed Simon, she paused, her eyes flashing. "I don't care who you are. If you ever humiliate me again, I *will* bite you. And this time there won't be any antivenom around to save you."

The boys continued to laugh as she disappeared into a hallway, and Simon's heart sank. He hadn't meant to do anything except prove he could be one of them. But wasn't that exactly what Colin had done, trying to impress Bryan Barker? Look how that had turned out.

"Enough," called Malcolm. "Pit practice is over. Dining hall, all of you."

Simon stepped aside just in time to avoid the stampede of students, many of whom elbowed and jostled one another for a better view of him as they passed. He could feel their stares on him, and his cheeks burned. Still a freak, just like at school.

Malcolm ambled up beside him, and one glare from him had the remaining students scattering. "Next time you disobey me, I'll put you up against Garrett. He won't be so easy to beat."

Simon made a face at the thought of the mountain lion's claws. "I thought he was going to hurt her."

"Still. And I'd be careful if I were you. Ariana doesn't take defeat lightly, and I can't be there to protect you all the time. Now come on. Dining hall's this way."

Winter was waiting for them when they exited the pit, and she fell into step beside Simon as Malcolm led the way down a grassy hallway. Simon gave her a questioning look, but she shook her head minutely. If she'd had time to look for his mother, she hadn't found anything.

To Simon's surprise, the dining hall wasn't anything like the bland cafeteria back at Kennedy Middle School. Instead it looked like a restaurant, with an elaborate buffet lining the wall. Students filled their plates with not only chicken and pizza but also cheeseburgers, roast beef, potatoes and gravy, a rainbow of fruits and vegetables, and something on ice that looked suspiciously like sushi.

"Stay here until I come back for you," said Malcolm. "If anyone gives you trouble, I'll take care of it."

Simon wasn't sure that would help, but he nodded

anyway. As soon as Malcolm was gone, he said quietly, "We should look for my mom now, while everyone's eating."

"*That's* your big plan?" said Winter. "We got captured by a pack of hungry wolves so you could check a few empty classrooms?"

"I didn't expect this, okay?" said Simon. "I thought . . . I don't know what I thought. But I couldn't just sit there and wait for Orion to rescue my mother. And in two days, the Alpha's going to come back and take me and Nolan out of the city into mammal territory, and—"

"Two days?"said Winter.

Simon nodded. "I heard her and Malcolm talking about it. If I can't find my mother before then, I'm never going to see her again. I need to do *something*."

Winter sighed and tucked her dark hair behind her ears. "It isn't safe for you to go searching on your own. Everyone in the Den is talking about you, and if you're not where you're supposed to be, they're all going to wonder why."

Simon hesitated. She had a point, as much as he hated to admit it. "I sent Felix to look around," he whispered. "Can you check the reptile section to see if there are any hidden rooms or ways out of here? They wouldn't have built this place with only one exit."

"Of course not," said Winter. "You're just figuring that out now?"

He shrugged. "Why did Malcolm stick you there, anyway?"

Scowling, she crossed her arms. "My mother was from the reptile kingdom," she muttered, as if she were admitting some horrible family secret. "I couldn't give them my real last name, so I thought I'd give them hers. She ran away from home and never told her family she married a member of the bird kingdom, so we should be safe."

"Wait," said Simon. "If your mother was a reptile, that makes you a—a Hybred, too."

Winter stopped suddenly and whirled around to face him. "If you say anything, I'll tell Malcolm about your stupid pet mouse."

Simon's eyes widened. "I won't. I don't care what you are. Besides, I think it would be kind of cool, getting to be part of two kingdoms—"

"Simon?"

A blond boy wearing glasses approached them, and Simon immediately caught sight of the dolphin on the boy's armband. "Jam?" he said uncertainly.

The boy lit up. "You remember me!"

"It's sort of hard to forget," said Simon. "A dolphin's never spoken to me before."

Jam beamed. "I just thought, with how important you are—everyone's talking about you, you know." He nodded to the tables, and as if to prove his point, several conversations ceased as soon as Simon looked. Perfect.

He cleared his throat. "Uh, Jam, this is my friend, Winter. Winter, this is—"

"Benjamin Fluke. Most people call me Jam." He stuck his hand out for Winter to shake. "You're really pretty."

"And you look like an owl," said Winter, clearly not happy about being interrupted. "Jam is a terrible nickname for Benjamin. It doesn't even make sense."

Simon opened his mouth to apologize for her, but Jam shrugged sheepishly and dropped his hand when it became obvious that Winter wouldn't take it. "My sisters like to get me in trouble all the time, so my mom used to joke that I was always in a jam. It just stuck."

Winter looked unimpressed, but to Simon's relief, she didn't make any more comments. "I like it," he said.

"Thanks. Me, too. Do you have someplace to sit? You can sit with me, if you want," added Jam. "Unless you want to sit with the land mammals. But they don't like you very much."

"I don't like them much, either, so that's okay," said Simon. "If there's room, I'll sit with you."

"There's always room." Jam picked up a plate at the start of the buffet and headed straight for the fish. "What do you like? I've heard the fries are good, but nothing beats sushi. You should try it."

Though Simon politely declined the sushi, the rest of the food looked even better than it smelled, and once they'd each filled plates and grabbed something to drink, the three of them headed to the table. Before they could reach it, however, Nolan stepped into their path, flanked by several large boys, including Garrett.

"Oh, look, the losers found each other," said Nolan. "How sweet."

Jam's smile faded, and he gripped his tray hard enough to make his water teeter. "Hi, Nolan. Congratulations on finding out you have a brother. That must be cool."

Instantly Simon could tell Jam had said exactly the wrong thing, as Nolan's face clouded over and he balled his hands into fists the same way Simon did when he got angry. "I don't have a brother," he spat.

Jam frowned and looked at Simon. "But—"

"I *said* I don't have a brother!" Without warning, Nolan shoved Jam's tray into his chest, spilling water all down Jam's front and mashing sushi against his shirt.

The entire dining hall fell silent. Jam stood there, dumbfounded and pale, and all Simon could think about were the times Bryan Barker had done the exact same kind of thing to him in front of everyone.

The knot in his chest felt like a hot coal burning him up from the inside out, and without thinking, he grabbed the glass of chocolate milk from his tray and marched up to Nolan, dumping the entire thing over his head.

"What—" sputtered Nolan as chocolate milk ran down his body, and his expression twisted into an enraged snarl. He lurched forward and tackled Simon to the floor, ripping at his shirt and tearing at his hair.

Every instinct he had screamed at Simon to fight back, but no matter how much Nolan might've deserved a chocolate milk bath, he was still his brother, and Simon couldn't hit him. Distantly he heard Winter shouting at them to stop, but all he could do was shield his face from Nolan's punches and protect his chest with his knees the same way he had against Bryan earlier that afternoon.

"*No-lan, No-lan, No-lan!*" chanted the other mammals, and Simon opened his eyes enough to see that a tight circle had formed around them. Several of the students had shifted into their animal forms, and Simon spotted a mountain lion and a pair of coyotes lurking on the edge of his vision. No doubt they would jump in with their claws and fangs if Simon tried to retaliate, but as long as Simon kept his fists to himself, it was just Nolan. He wasn't even hitting that hard—nothing like the eighth-grade bullies who had had years of practice. Judging by the way Nolan grew winded after only fifteen seconds, Simon guessed this was his first time beating someone up by himself.

"*Enough!*" A vicious roar cut through the cheers, and the students scrambled back to make way for Malcolm and the three hulking wolves that flanked him. Nolan ignored them and raised his fist again, ready to strike.

"Did you not hear me?" said Malcolm, grabbing him by the back of his collar and lifting him into the air. One of the wolves padded up to Simon and sniffed him.

"Still alive, pup?" she said, shifting into a tall brunette.

Simon nodded, pushing himself upright. His nose ached, and when he wiped his mouth, there was a smear of blood on his hand, but otherwise he felt all right.

"He dumped his milk over my head in front of everyone!" cried Nolan. His face was flushed and his eyes were watery, and he squirmed against Malcolm's unyielding grip.

"And does the sushi on Benjamin's shirt have anything to do with why he did it?" said Malcolm. Nolan opened and shut his mouth. "I thought so. The four of you, come with me. The rest of you, finish your dinner and get back to your dorms. And you lot—" He glared at the mammals who had shifted in anticipation of Simon retaliating. "Threaten to attack a member of the Alpha family one more time, and I will personally make sure that you never again see the inside of this or any other Animalgam academy for the rest of your miserable lives."

The three boys shifted back sullenly, while Malcolm dragged Nolan out of the dining hall. The woman with the brown hair touched Simon's shoulder and led him after them, and when he glanced back, he saw that Winter was helping Jam wipe sushi off his shirt as they followed.

"Ow, ow, *ow!*" cried Nolan, but as far as Simon could tell, Malcolm didn't loosen his grip. Instead he dragged him to the atrium inside the Alpha section, where he shoved him onto a sofa against the wall.

"You will never lay a hand on your brother again," he snarled, looming over him. "And if I ever catch you so much as thinking about it, so help me, you'll be more prisoner than prince for the rest of your education. Do you understand?"

Nolan shrank back into the couch cushions, rubbing his neck. "Yes, sir," he muttered, and he shot Simon a look so venomous that Simon could practically feel his insides curdling.

"Here, hold this to your nose," said the woman as she urged Simon down on the other end of the couch. She offered him a handkerchief, and Simon took it.

"Is his nose broken, Vanessa?" said Malcolm, and she shook her head.

"Just bloodied. No loose teeth, either, from what I can see."

"I'm fine," said Simon. "He didn't hit me hard."

Nolan's expression darkened, and Simon realized that once again he had said the wrong thing. But he wasn't sure there was ever going to be a right thing to say, so instead he turned his attention to Jam, who was now trying to soak up soy sauce from the front of his shirt with a wad of napkins.

"Are you okay?" he said.

Jam nodded. "I'm fine, but the captain won't be pleased. Laundry day isn't until Sunday."

Malcolm began to pace in front of the sofa, his jaw working and his biceps flexing. "You two"—he jerked his head toward Simon and Nolan—"can be each other's greatest allies, or you can be each other's greatest rivals. Maybe you think you've already decided, but, so help me, I will do everything in my power to make sure you get along."

"But—" began Nolan.

"No buts. Tomorrow, while we're above ground, you will spend every moment together, is that understood? You will sit next to each other on the bus. You will stick together during the visit to the exhibit, and you won't leave each other's side."

Nolan's mouth dropped open. "The whole day? But—"

"The whole day," cut in Malcolm. "Argue, and I'll make it the week."

"Wait—we're going to be leaving the Den tomorrow?" Simon said. He had only two days before the Alpha returned. He couldn't leave now, before he'd even had the chance to look.

"Don't you know anything?" said Nolan nastily. "It's Unity Day. The day the Beast King was overthrown. The whole school goes to his old Stronghold and celebrates."

That name again. Simon swallowed. Asking would only invite more of Nolan's insults, but he had to know. "Who's the Beast King?"

"Who—" Nolan's eyes widened, and he gave Malcolm an indignant look. "And you want to chain me to him for the whole day?"

"It'll be good for you," said Malcolm, and he shifted uneasily. "The Beast King and his history is a very long story best left to another time. All you need to know is that he was a tyrannical ruler, and hundreds of years ago the five king-doms banded together to overthrow him. Tomorrow is the anniversary of that victory, and we cannot miss the celebration. It's the most important holiday in our world."

"But—I thought the flock would attack us if we left," said Simon.

"I would rather keep you both here, away from the skies, but you'll be safe in the Stronghold. I'll be with you the entire time, and the underwater kingdom has already agreed to augment our forces. If Orion dares to come after you, then he'll pay the price for his stupidity."

Simon glanced at Winter. Their time was already dwindling. Unless they got enormously lucky, losing an entire day would only make finding his mother that much more difficult.

"Vanessa, make sure Mr. Fluke and Miss Rivera return to their dormitories and have dinner delivered to them," said Malcolm, and she nodded. "Nolan, you have homework."

Nolan all but leaped to his feet and ran up the spiral staircase, and the slam of his bedroom door echoed throughout the atrium.

"And Simon," added Malcolm after silence fell once more, "you've had a rough day. Tomorrow can't be better if you don't get any rest."

Taking the hint, Simon stood, too. "I'll see you tomorrow," he said to Winter. She shot him an amused look, though what she found so funny, he didn't know.

"Right. Tomorrow." She headed out of the room without waiting for Vanessa, making a sharp right toward the reptiles' section. Simon watched her go, feeling more and more hopeless with every step she took.

"I'll be there tomorrow, too," said Jam, who smelled like the seafood restaurant around the corner from Simon's apartment. "I'm sorry about your nose."

Simon shrugged. "Sorry about your shirt."

"Never liked it much, anyway." And despite everything that had happened in the dining hall, Jam grinned. "See you, Simon."

Once Vanessa led Jam out of the atrium, Simon shuffled over to the spiral staircase, weariness hitting him like an eight-hundred-pound gorilla. Before he could start the climb, however, Malcolm put a hand on his shoulder.

"I'll send a sandwich up for you," he said, and then hesitated. "You're sure you're okay?"

Simon wasn't sure he would ever be okay again, but he didn't know how he was supposed to tell that to Malcolm. "You're a lot like him, you know," he said. "Darryl, I mean."

Malcolm's grip on his shoulder tightened. "He's really alive?"

Simon nodded, and something flashed across Malcolm's face—something Simon recognized all too well. He wasn't the only one who had been blindsided by a brother today. "I'm sorry he lied to you."

"I'm sorry he lied to both of us," said Malcolm, and he

cleared his throat. "Right, then. Upstairs with you. If Nolan gives you any problems, I'm two doors down the hall."

"Do you think there's a way you can let Darryl know I'm here?" said Simon, worry knotting in the pit of his stomach. It had been there all day, lurking in the background, but he could no longer avoid it. He might have discovered a whole family he'd never known about, but his uncle was still the one who had been there for him his entire life.

"I've already sent out a messenger," said Malcolm. "Now that we know Darryl's alive, we'll find him."

If the last twelve years had proven anything, it was that his uncle had an uncanny ability to hide right under someone's nose. But Simon was too tired to do anything but accept that Malcolm knew what he was doing.

When he reached his bedroom, Simon briefly considered collapsing into the huge four-poster bed without changing into his pajamas, but then he saw the origami swan sitting on his pillow.

Exhaustion momentarily forgotten, he picked it up and examined it. On one wing, someone had written OPEN ME, SEAWEED BRAIN in neat, blocky handwriting.

Winter. He unfolded the swan, careful not to tear the edges. On the back of what looked like plain paper was a note.

Stop panicking—you're going to give us away. If she's here, I'll find her. Just trust me.

Simon glanced around the room, searching for any sign of her. But somehow, in the short time he'd spoken with Malcolm, Winter had managed to get into his room from the reptile section, write him a note, turn it into folded art, and disappear completely.

He smiled. It seemed he wasn't the only one with secrets in this place, but at least someone was on his side.

THE BEAST KING

True to his word, the next morning Malcolm paired Simon and Nolan together, forcing them to sit at the front of one of the two buses that would take the whole school to the Beast King's Stronghold. Simon had tried everything to get out of going, including feigning illness, but Malcolm had none of it—instead, all he'd succeeded in doing was making sure his new uncle watched him even closer.

Felix hadn't made an appearance that morning, and every time Simon tried to ask Winter if she'd had a chance to search for his mother, Nolan or Malcolm hovered nearby, and he'd had to quickly change the subject. To make matters worse, Nolan barely said two words to him, instead staring out the window with his hands clenched. Any hopes

Simon had had of his brother helping him find their mother were gone.

After only fifteen minutes, the bus stopped at a private dock on the East River. "We're going by boat?" Simon said as he pulled on his backpack, and Nolan scoffed, the first sound he'd made since boarding.

"It's an *island*. What did you think we'd do, swim?"

In the spirit of making the day as tolerable as possible, Simon chose not to reply.

A burly man with hair the color of steel was waiting for them in front of a ferry big enough to hold the entire school. As they passed, Jam squared his shoulders and raised his chin.

"Captain," he said, pausing long enough to salute.

"Fluke," said the man. "At ease, soldier."

Simon followed Jam up the walkway. "He doesn't look too scary on land," he said. "Fewer teeth, for sure."

"That's the shark we saw yesterday?" Winter said nervously.

"He's harmless out of the water," said Jam in what he must have meant as a reassuring voice, but Winter only paled.

Nolan protested when they chose a seat in the back of the lower level, as far away from the older mammals as they could get, but the last thing Simon wanted was to give Garrett and the others a chance to throw him overboard. Eventually, once Malcolm joined them on the other side of the aisle, Nolan ceased his griping, though he continued sulking for the rest of the ride there.

"So what's this place like?" said Simon as the ferry rocked in the wind.

"This is my first year at the Academy, so I've never been," said Jam. "But I know it's where the L.A.I.R. used to be, before the Bird Lord started the war and destroyed part of it. Now we only come here to celebrate Unity Day."

"When the kingdoms defeated the Beast King," said Simon. Jam nodded. "Who was the Beast King, anyway?"

"I still can't believe you've never heard of the Beast King. That's like not knowing who the president of the United States is," said Jam, baffled.

"He's an idiot," said Nolan, and he scooted even farther away from them. Ignoring him, Simon shrugged.

"Malcolm told me he ruled hundreds of years ago."

"Right—he killed countless Animalgams who refused to bow down to him. Eventually the rulers of the five kingdoms united to overthrow him, but we nearly went extinct in the process," said Jam.

"What made him so powerful in the first place?" said Simon. It was hard to imagine any single Animalgam being able to overcome a whole wolf pack. Or a bird flock.

"Because he could shift into any animal he wanted," said Winter from Simon's other side. "You try defeating an enemy who can suddenly grow venomous fangs or dive underwater or fly away. Not to mention he had thousands of followers willing to fight for him."

"The kingdoms won eventually though," said Jam. "And afterward, they transformed his Stronghold into the original Academy. It's supposed to be really cool. My sister said the section that's still standing has all kinds of artifacts from the war, and—"

"It's boring," interjected Nolan, his arms crossed. "Just lots of old stuff no one cares about anymore."

"It sounds cool to me," said Simon, and Jam gave him a grateful smile.

Suddenly there was a flurry of motion near the middle of the ferry, and a magenta-haired girl darted out the side door—Ariana, the black widow Simon had fought the day before. Even with the loud drone of the engine, he could hear the sounds of her being sick.

"Is she going to be okay?" he said as Vanessa also disappeared out the side door, presumably to join her.

"She'll be fine," said Malcolm from across the aisle. "Stay in your seat."

Eventually Ariana returned, green-faced and looking as if she was seconds away from being sick again. Vanessa sat her down near the door with a paper bag, and she spent the rest of the journey with her head between her knees. Simon watched her while Nolan, Winter, and Jam argued over which kingdom must've been the one to finally kill the Beast King, but after Simon had beaten Ariana in the pit, he was sure he was the last person she wanted to see.

At last the ferry docked. Several students let out loud whoops as they rushed to shore, and Simon trailed after them, one of the last off the boat. Nolan rejoined his friends, and rather than endure an entire day dealing with their taunts and whispers, Simon chose to remain in the back with Winter and Jam. It wouldn't work forever, but maybe he could get away with avoiding Nolan long enough for him to cool down and—

"Simon," barked Malcolm as he stood beside a sign that said PRIVATE PROPERTY. He gestured for Simon to join his brother and the other mammals. Simon sighed.

"You two stay here," Simon said to Winter and Jam. "I don't want you getting caught in the cross fire."

Jam protested, but Simon insisted, and soon enough he joined Nolan up front. Several of the bigger boys snickered, and if looks could kill, the one Garrett gave him would have had him six feet under in half a second flat.

Simon shoved his hands into his pockets and ignored their jeers as Malcolm led the way up a well-worn stone path. When the trees gave way to a large meadow, Simon stopped. The Beast King's Stronghold wasn't just a mansion—it was an actual castle, built of black stone and iron. It rose several stories and expanded across the entire meadow, but though the main section stood tall, the wings tapered off into mountains of rubble. No wonder the school had been abandoned. But what really caught Simon's attention was the huge iron door that stood at the entrance, bearing a crest that looked strangely familiar.

Before Simon had time to think about it, someone ran into him from behind. "Watch it," said a girl as she brushed past him. Ariana, he realized a second too late. By the time he began to ask how she was, she had disappeared into the crowd, and he had to trot to catch up to Nolan.

The iron door opened into an entrance hall that rivaled those of castles Simon had seen in movies, with high ceilings, dark corners, and flickering lights that led the way deeper into the Stronghold. There was no sign of destruction here, even though Simon had the uneasy feeling that the ceiling might cave in at any moment. Malcolm called for the stragglers to keep up, his voice echoing.

They stopped in the middle of what had once been the Beast King's throne room. Scattered throughout the room were paintings of both humans and animals, along with glass cases full of artifacts. Peace treaties written on ancient parchment, swords with handles carved into animal silhouettes— even a collection of tiaras and crowns that had once belonged to the rulers of the five kingdoms. If he had the entire day to explore on his own, Simon would still never have been able to study it all.

Thankfully Malcolm didn't seem to be paying too much attention to Simon now that they were safely inside, and he slipped away while Nolan and his friends were laughing at a painting of a bear crushing a hawk under its paw. Winter stood in front of a glass case that held a silver scepter, her brow furrowed as she examined it.

"The . . . Predator," said Simon, reading the label on the case. It didn't look like anything terribly interesting.

"This is how the Beast King conquered the entire

Animalgam kingdom," said Winter. "That single weapon is responsible for the deaths of countless people."

Simon blinked. Suddenly it didn't seem so boring. "But it's just a scepter—there isn't even a sharp edge."

"That's because this isn't the whole thing." Winter set her hand on the glass. "When all the pieces are in place, the Predator can absorb the power of everyone it kills and transfer it to the person who holds the scepter."

"That's what made the Beast King so dangerous," said Jam. He'd made his way through the crowd, closer to where Simon stood. "He killed so many different Animalgams that eventually he could shift into anything he wanted. Lion, whale, ladybug, python, woodpecker—you name it. But I don't think this is the real thing." Jam pointed to the end of the scepter and squinted. "It's a very convincing replica, but I'm pretty sure the grooves on the end are supposed to be deeper. That's where the pieces go."

"Where are they?" said Simon, while Winter stood on her tiptoes to examine the scepter.

"No one knows," said Jam. "When the rulers of the five kingdoms killed the Beast King, they tried to destroy the Predator, and the end shattered into five pieces. They each took one and hid it in their kingdoms. Without all five, the scepter is as harmless as a stick."

"There are tons of legends about people trying to hunt down all five pieces," said Winter, dropping back down on her heels. "No one's found any of them yet though."

"Because it's impossible," said Jam. "My father's the

general of our kingdom, and he said ours is moved every generation so that no one can track it down. That's how it should be. If anyone put the Predator together, they could gain the power of the Beast King, and we'd be at war all over again."

And they would be able to wipe out their enemies completely. The knot in Simon's chest tightened. Suddenly he was glad the scepter was just a replica. "I don't see why no one smashed their piece so it couldn't be used at all," he said.

"You can only destroy the Predator when it's completely assembled," said Winter. "And no one wants to risk putting it together to try."

A loud whistle pierced the air. "Simon, up here," called Malcolm from the front of the room. Simon winced, and he offered his friends an apologetic look before trudging back to Nolan and the other mammals. His brother didn't seem to notice his return, but Malcolm gave Simon a stern warning to stay nearby.

Shortly after, the adults ushered the students into an empty room, though at first Simon didn't understand—there was nothing to see here. But when the lights in the center of the room dimmed and the walls illuminated, his eyes widened.

An elaborate mural decorated the walls, wrapping around the entire room. Even though he didn't know much about the Animalgam world, he instantly recognized what it illustrated: the Beast King's defeat. Mammals fought mammals. Birds fought birds. Spiders trapped their own kind in webs, snakes squeezed their brothers to death, and, on another wall, sharks leaped out of the sea, catching dolphins in their massive jaws.

In the center of it all, surrounded by loyal Animalgams fighting to the death, was a wolf. No—Simon took a step to the side, and the figure shimmered into an eagle. Another step, and the eagle was replaced by a spider. Again and again, as Simon moved through the room, the figure shifted into a seemingly endless number of animals. None of the others changed forms—just the Beast King.

Vanessa, the pack member who had checked Simon's nose the night before, stood on a platform in the center of the room. "Today, on Unity Day, we remember not only those who died so that we might have a future but also the power we have when our five kingdoms come together as one," she said. Nolan and his friends snickered, but Malcolm appeared out of nowhere and dragged Nolan closer to Simon. "Had the five great leaders not put aside their differences and animosities, we would never have achieved victory over the Beast King, and today we honor their triumph by working together once more."

From her pocket she pulled what looked to Simon like a glass Christmas ornament in the shape of a five-pointed star. It meant nothing to him, but the other students began to whisper excitedly.

"The Heart of the Predator," she announced. "You will split up into teams of four and search for it throughout the island. But be careful who you choose—without a member of each of the represented kingdoms to help you, I guarantee you will lose."

Immediately chaos broke out as everyone scattered to find their friends and create teams. Simon started toward Jam and Winter, but Malcolm set his hand firmly on the back of his neck. When Simon glanced up, he noticed Malcolm was holding Nolan in place, too.

"You said I could do the hunt," said his brother, trying to jerk out of Malcolm's grip.

"That was before I knew the danger you're both in. Today, you stay in the Stronghold with me."

Nolan's mouth dropped open. "But—"

"No buts. I am your Beta, and you will listen to me. Is that understood?"

Glaring at Simon, Nolan muttered, "This wouldn't have happened if *you* hadn't shown up."

Simon stayed silent. There was no use trying to tell Nolan how he would have given anything to go back to yesterday morning and never come here in the first place.

While the rest of the students formed teams and filtered outside to eat before the start of the hunt, Malcolm led Simon and Nolan down a hallway and into a small library stuffed floor to ceiling with books. "Stay here," he said. "I'm going to grab lunch for us."

Simon didn't argue. The books in the room must have held the entire history of the Animalgam world, and he eagerly explored the shelves. Nolan, on the other hand, paced the length of the library for several minutes before finally huffing and heading for the door.

"Where are you going?" said Simon as he climbed a ladder, hoping to explore the higher shelves.

"You can stay here like some caged animal, but I'm joining the hunt," said Nolan, and he stormed out of the library, leaving Simon on his own.

Simon started after him but stopped before he reached the door. Following him would be pointless. Malcolm was keeping them inside because he was afraid of Orion's flock, but Simon knew there was no real danger, not when Orion was only trying to protect him. And Nolan wouldn't listen to him, anyway.

Simon returned to the shelves, trying to distract himself with a volume entitled *The Spy in Spider: Secrets Untangled*, when a voice boomed from the doorway.

"Where's Nolan?"

He jumped, nearly dropping the book. Malcolm stood by the door, holding a tray with three sandwiches and drinks. "He, uh—he said he was joining the hunt."

Malcolm swore and set the tray on the nearest table. "Don't move," he ordered, and headed back into the hall, snarling under his breath.

Simon turned back to his book, sure Nolan would somehow find a way to blame him for this, when a sharp *psst* filled the air. "Simon!"

He whirled around again. This time Jam stood in the doorway. "What are you doing here?" said Simon. "Aren't you supposed to be hunting?"

Jam shrugged. "I'd rather spend the day with you. Besides, Winter—"

She appeared beside Jam and walked deliberately through the small library. Stopping in front of a bookcase located behind an old desk, she stood on her tiptoes, as though trying to read titles too high for her to see.

"What are you looking for?" said Simon. "There's a really cool book on how to tell whether a snake is venomous or—"

She reached for a large unmarked book Simon hadn't touched, and instead of pulling it off the shelf, she tilted it like a lever. Something clicked, and suddenly the bookcase creaked and swung open.

Simon's jaw dropped. "Is that—"

"A secret passage? Yes," said Winter, and she gave them an annoyed look. "Are you coming or what?"

"But—how did you know—"

"Do you really want me to answer that now?" she whispered, glancing at Jam, who was crossing the library toward them. Orion must have told her, Simon realized.

"Have you been here before?" said Jam as he came over to inspect the entrance to the tunnel. An empty metal cylinder that looked like it was meant to hold a torch was mounted to the stone wall.

"My grandfather told me about it," said Winter, and she

stepped inside. Simon hesitated. If he left, no doubt Malcolm would panic the way he had when Nolan disappeared. But technically he wasn't leaving the Stronghold. Or the library. And Winter was going whether Simon went with her or not. It was his fault they were stuck in this situation in the first place—the least he could do was make sure nothing happened to her.

"What's down here?" he said as he followed her through a narrow passageway that seemed to wind in on itself.

"I don't know," said Winter, though the edge to her voice made it clear to Simon that she knew exactly where they were going. He didn't press her though—not in front of Jam. As much as Simon trusted him, there must have been a reason Winter wasn't willing to explain where Jam could hear her.

Somehow she had acquired a flashlight, and as the tunnel darkened, she turned it on. Eventually the passageway descended into a spiral staircase that must have gone below ground, because the temperature dipped the farther they went. When Simon was sure they couldn't go any deeper without his ears popping, Winter finally stopped. In front of her stood a dirt wall with a thick wooden door in the center. A rusty iron ring hung from it in place of a modern knob, and Simon got the distinct feeling that they were the first people to see this place since the L.A.I.R. had moved beneath the Central Park Zoo.

"This must be below the part of the Stronghold that the

flock destroyed," said Jam, and he looked back up the spiral staircase. "It could crumble in on us at any moment."

"Stop being such a chicken. If it hasn't caved in yet, we'll be fine," said Winter, and she pulled on the rusty ring. Something squeaked, but the door remained steadfastly shut. Growling, she tried again. Nothing. "Are you really just going to stand there, Simon? It's not like I haven't done anything lately to help *you*."

Simon wanted to ask her what was on the other side, but with Jam lingering so close, he couldn't risk it. She'd told Simon to trust her, so he would. "Fine—we'll try together," he said. Winter handed her flashlight to Jam, and she and Simon grabbed the iron ring. "One . . . two . . . *three!*"

Together they pulled, and Simon braced his foot against the wall, trying to use it as leverage. The door squeaked, and he pulled even harder.

"Come on . . . ," he muttered, throwing his whole body into it. At last, with a squeal, the door burst open.

"Yes!" cried Winter, but something above them rumbled, cutting her victory celebration short.

"Uh, guys?" said Jam, eyeing the ceiling. "I'm not so sure this is a good ide—"

Suddenly the walls trembled, and a shower of pebbles and dust rained over them. Immediately Simon pushed Winter through the doorway and grabbed Jam's sleeve, dragging him inside.

It was a good thing, too, because the instant they passed

over the threshold, chunks of rock began to fall, some as big as Simon's head. Grunting, he shoved the heavy wooden door shut, and the three of them stood huddled together in the darkness while the walls quaked.

"There goes our way out," said Jam.

"My grandfather said there's another tunnel," said Winter, though she didn't sound entirely sure of herself. "We'll find it."

"We have to," said Simon. "Unless you want to spend the rest of our lives trapped beneath the—"

"Open this backpack at once!" an enraged voice squeaked from behind Simon.

"Felix?" he said, and he quickly set down the bag and opened the pocket. The little mouse emerged, his whiskers bent and his fur sticking straight up.

"You have a pet?" said Jam, pushing his glasses up his nose. "That's so cool. I've always wanted one."

"He's my friend, not a—" Simon stopped and sighed. "Sometimes they're more trouble than they're worth. What are you doing here, Felix?"

"What am I doing here? What are you doing *here*?" he said, looking into the darkness and shuddering. "You could've been killed. What is this place?"

"I—" started Simon, but he faltered. "Uh, Winter, where are we?"

"We're exactly where we're supposed to be," she said, taking the flashlight from Jam and shining it against the wall to reveal a switch. She flipped it, and the buzz of electricity filled the air. Light flooded the darkness.

They stood in the front of a hall as big as the throne room upstairs, with a ceiling made of rock. In it were dozens of huge bookcases rising several stories high and displaying hundreds of years' worth of texts, all of them far older than any Simon had ever seen before.

"Whoa," said Jam as he stepped forward to touch one of the spines. "This looks handwritten."

"We need to find that second passageway immediately," said Felix, and he scrambled out of Simon's backpack onto the stone floor. "Since no one else is bothering to look, I will."

"I'm right behind you," said Simon, skimming the titles. He paused at *Hybred: The Bridge between Two Kingdoms*. "Winter, you have to see this."

No response. He turned around, but she wasn't there.

"Winter?" he called. He heard the shuffle of footsteps, and he snatched his backpack and darted after her, leaving Jam to explore the books. "Winter, slow down."

In the distance he spotted her dark hair between the shelves, and he darted down a particularly musty aisle, barely suppressing a sneeze from all the dust.

"Winter—"

He skidded to a stop in front of an alcove that, at first glance, looked to be full of junk. Someone had thrown together broken furniture, a stack of empty portrait frames, and even several gutted book covers, and hidden them behind an ancient tapestry. Winter knelt beside a wooden crate, digging through it.

"I take it we're not down here to read books," said Simon. "You need to tell me what's going on, Winter."

She ignored him and continued her search, tossing aside bound scrolls of parchment and something that looked like the hilt of a sword. In the time it had taken Simon to find her, she had somehow managed to get through two crates. Hissing with frustration, she pushed the current one aside and started into another.

Within seconds, she crowed triumphantly and pulled a metal rod out of the crate. No, not a rod, Simon realized.

The scepter. She was holding the scepter.

13

HEART OF THE
PREDATOR

"That's the Beast King's scepter," said Simon in disbelief, inching closer to Winter as they stood in the dusty library alcove. Beaming, Winter finally turned to him, hugging the scepter to her chest.

"The Alpha doesn't have it. I thought for sure she did when I saw it in the case, but of *course* that wasn't the real thing." She must have seen the confusion on his face, because she added, "Before the Alpha ran Orion out of the Stronghold, he hid it from her so she wouldn't be able to find it. He must have made a copy, too."

Simon inspected it. Like the replica in the throne room, the real thing was still just a scepter. "I don't see what Orion's afraid of, unless he thinks the Alpha will throw it at him."

"Why do you think she's been taking over the kingdoms one by one?" said Winter. "It isn't just to control them. She wants their pieces of the Predator, too."

Simon blinked. "But—the only reason she would want the pieces is if she were trying to reassemble it."

"Exactly," said Winter. "She already has four. Orion's piece is the only one she's missing. That's what he's really trying to do—stop her from gaining the power to kill every last one of her enemies. Including us."

A horrible sinking feeling came over Simon. It made sense. If the Beast King had been as powerful as everyone said thanks to the Predator, then reassembling it would mean the Alpha would gain instant control over the entire Animalgam world. "There's no way the rulers would hand their pieces over."

"I don't think they did," she said. "Orion said the Alpha sent a representative to negotiate an alliance and steal the pieces from right under their noses. They probably don't even know they're missing."

As unsettled as Simon was by the idea of anyone hunting down the pieces of the Predator, an even more troubling thought dawned on him, and he stared at Winter. "This is why you agreed to help me find my mom. So you could come here and steal the scepter."

Winter hesitated. "No. Of course not. I just thought that while we're here . . ."

A bitter taste filled Simon's mouth. "Put it back."

"*Excuse* me?"

"You heard me. Put it back."

"Don't you get it?" she said. "If the Alpha finds all five pieces *and* the scepter—"

"But she won't," he said. "Orion isn't going to hand his over."

"He will if it means saving your life," said Winter hotly. Simon faltered. The idea of his grandfather risking all five Animalgam kingdoms in order to protect him wasn't something he'd been prepared for, and it hit him right over the knot in his chest. He knew Darryl and his mother loved him enough to do crazy things to keep him safe, but Orion . . .

"It won't matter," said Simon. "Not if she doesn't know where the real scepter is. Put it back. Hide it. Make sure she can't find it, and even if Orion hands over his piece or someone steals it, the Alpha will never be able to assemble the Predator."

Winter glowered. "But—"

"Simon? Winter?" called Jam from several shelves away. Simon lowered his voice.

"She won't look for it down here, and the door's blocked now, anyway. Even if she did find the passageway, she'd never be able to get through."

"But the second tunnel—"

"We'll worry about that when we find it. Put it back, Winter."

She clenched her jaw, but at last she relented and returned

the scepter to the pile of junk, burying it deep within the books and frames. By the time Jam caught up to them, she'd restacked the crates, leaving no sign that they'd been disturbed.

"What are you two doing?" said Jam.

Simon shrugged. "Nothing, just—"

"Simon!" Felix appeared at the head of the aisle. "You have *no* idea how lucky you are. I think I found the way out."

Jam's expression fell. Clearly he'd wanted time to explore the books. Simon said quickly, "I'll make sure it's safe. You both stay here."

Winter didn't seem too eager to leave the scepter, anyway, and Simon gave her one more warning look before following Felix down the aisles. The mouse led him to the back corner of the cavern, where another tapestry hung. When Simon pushed it aside, he revealed a second wooden door.

"How do you know it leads out?" said Simon, but Felix darted under the door. Steeling himself for another cave-in, Simon gingerly pushed it open. It was lighter than he expected, and though the hinges creaked, they didn't protest nearly as much as the ones on the first door.

Simon found himself in a much smaller antechamber. It also had modern lights flickering overhead, and the majority of the room was taken up by a wooden table covered in open books, piles of yellowed parchment, and, much to Simon's surprise, several spiral notebooks and pens. Nearly everything was covered with a thin layer of dust.

"There's another door through here," said Felix, but one of the notebooks on the table caught Simon's attention. The handwriting—he had only ever seen it on the postcards taped to his wall, but he would have recognized it anywhere.

It was his mother's.

He picked up the notebook and examined it. On the top page, his mother had drawn a pair of family trees. The first he recognized: Celeste Thorn was at the top, with lines leading down to Darryl, Luke, and the youngest, Malcolm. *Celeste must be the Alpha's real name*, he figured.

But his father's name, Luke, had an arrow pointing to the second family tree. It was longer than the first, outlining multiple generations, but there was only one name at the bottom:

Luke Thorn.

His brow furrowed, Simon turned to the next page. It was a time line that started in 1537. A series of dates roughly twenty to thirty years apart ran down the page, each with a name written beside it—some male, some female. But as Simon followed the list, he realized what he was looking at.

It was the second family tree, expanded into a single, unbroken line. And at the very bottom, once again, was his father's name.

"Felix—did you see this?" said Simon.

"I can't read," said the mouse, climbing up the table leg to join him. "What does it say?"

"I think—I think my father was adopted." It made sense,

he supposed. His father didn't look anything like Malcolm or Darryl. But he didn't understand why no one would have told him, or why his mother would have been investigating it in the first place.

Simon took a harder look at the open books on the table. Some were as thick as dictionaries, with tiny, cramped handwriting that was difficult to read, but they all had one thing in common: they were open to chapters about the Beast King. What did that have to do with his father?

He flipped to another page in his mother's notebook. *Horse. Iguana. Jellyfish. Sparrow. Wasp. Tiger. Crane. Butterfly.* It was a list of every animal Simon could think of, each with a small checkmark beside it.

"She must have been researching what the Beast King could shift into," he said. But it wouldn't matter anymore, not when the Beast King had been dead for centuries.

Unless—

A bead of sweat formed on Simon's forehead, and he searched the open books. Most of them were vague about the Beast King's history, but at last, underneath another massive leather book, he found a thin biography. Holding his breath, he flipped through the brittle pages until he found what he was looking for.

Though no one has learned the Beast King's true identity or from which of the five kingdoms he hailed, scholars have concluded he was born in the year 1537 . . .

Simon turned back to the page in the notebook with the unbroken family line. The very first date listed, the only one without a name, was—

1537.

"Would . . ." Simon's throat went dry. "Would the Beast King's powers have been passed down the way normal Animalgams' are? Parent to kid?"

Felix blinked. "How am I supposed to know? They don't cover that on *Animal Planet*. Besides, there's only ever been one Beast King."

His mind whirling, Simon skimmed every open page, looking for any sign that his hunch was wrong. But he couldn't find any. The conflicting family trees. The time line that began with the Beast King. The animals his mother had listed, and the checkmarks beside them—she hadn't been researching the Beast King's powers at all.

Simon had finally discovered why Darryl had hidden him. Why his mother had risked everything to keep him from the Alpha. Why his entire life up until now had been one giant lie.

His father was the Beast King's heir.

Simon felt as though Bryan Barker had punched him in the gut. Maybe he was wrong. Maybe he was connecting dots that weren't there. But he would have bet every single one of his mother's postcards that he was right.

"Is there a way out through here?" said a voice. *Winter*. Simon jumped and hastily shoved the notebook into his backpack before turning around to face her.

"Felix thinks so," he said lamely. Jam lingered behind Winter, peering at the open books on the table. "We should go before Malcolm tears apart the whole Stronghold trying to find us."

Walking away from that table full of answers—and more questions than Simon could ever have dreamed of—was one of the hardest things he'd ever had to do. But as the hot knot burned in his chest, he did exactly that, following Felix through another wooden door and into a narrow cavern. Jam walked beside him, but it wasn't until Simon looked over his shoulder and saw Winter sulking over her abandoned scepter that another piece of the puzzle clicked into place.

The Alpha must have known. That was why his mother had never been able to leave with Nolan. Because the Alpha knew exactly who Nolan was—and now, who Simon was.

If she assembled the Predator, she wouldn't have to kill countless Animalgams in order to gain their powers.

She would just have to kill whichever one of them was the Beast King's heir.

14

DOGFIGHT

After a long, winding walk through a narrow cavern that seemed never to end, they emerged from the mouth of a cave into the shallow ocean near shore. Jam was delighted about their discovery, talking endlessly about the titles he'd glimpsed and how old and rare the books must have been, and while Simon remained silent, Winter eventually snapped.

"I thought birds and reptiles were supposed to like reading, not fish."

"I'm not a fish. I'm a dolphin," said Jam. "We're mammals, you know—we just live underwater. That's why the general leads us instead of the Alpha."

"Mammals aren't exactly known to be big readers, either," said Winter.

"Why do any of us have to be defined by our kingdoms? *You don't* exactly seem like a typical snake," said Jam, and they spent the rest of the walk back to the Stronghold arguing.

When they were halfway there, Simon heard a faint chirp. Only then did he remember Malcolm's warning about the bird flock, and he quickened his pace, hoping Orion didn't choose that moment to rescue them. Now, more than ever, it was imperative that he find his mother before the Alpha returned. And somehow he had to talk Nolan into going with them. If the Alpha managed to assemble the Predator after all, they had to be as far away from her as possible before she had the chance to kill one of them.

As they made their way up to the entrance with the familiar crest, Malcolm stormed out of the Stronghold, even more furious than he had been when Nolan had left. "Where have you been?" he growled, grabbing Simon by the collar of his shirt.

"We just—the walls were rumbling—we thought the Stronghold was going to collapse," he sputtered. It took several minutes and a chorus of agreements from Jam and Winter, but at last Malcolm ushered Simon back inside to rejoin Nolan.

Simon was impatient to read the rest of his mother's notebook, but after their separate escapes, Malcolm didn't let them out of his sight. They stayed in the library until the ceremony following the hunt, when Malcolm marched them side by side to the throne room. Simon watched, fascinated, as the winning team—led by Garrett—presented the glass star to Vanessa. She broke it into five pieces and offered one to each member, keeping the last for herself. That star must have symbolized the second part of the Predator, Simon realized—the part the Alpha was trying to put together. The part that would get either him or Nolan killed if she succeeded.

They arrived back at the Central Park Zoo late that evening, most of the students still talking wildly about the hunt. As everyone headed into the Arsenal and down the staircase that led to the Den, Simon, who was at the very back of the group, shoved his hands into his pockets. His fingers brushed up against something metal—the pocket watch his mother had given him.

Simon stopped halfway across the front hall of the Arsenal and pulled it out. Flipping it over, he examined the back. There it was—the same crest that he'd seen at the Stronghold. The same five animals, all drawn together.

The symbol of the Beast King.

"Simon," said a gruff voice, and his head shot up. Standing in a corner, mostly hidden by shadow, was Darryl.

He dashed over, and Darryl caught him in a hug. His uncle still wore the same clothes he'd had on the day before, and Simon made a face. "You smell."

"Good to see you, too," said Darryl with a chuckle, his scar crinkling. His humor was short-lived though, and he gripped Simon's arm. "We need to get out of here. It isn't safe."

"I'm not leaving," said Simon, and the joy of seeing his uncle dissolved. "Mom's here somewhere. The Alpha took her, and I'm not leaving until I find her."

"Even if your mother is here, I can't let you stay. It's too dangerous. We'll find some other way—"

"There *is* no other way. The Alpha's coming back in twenty-four hours."

Darryl's expression grew pinched. "Simon, I'm sorry, I really am, but you have to understand—"

Something inside him snapped. "No, *you* have to understand. I'm not going with you. I have a brother, and you never told me. Mom's been in the city my whole life, and you never told me. I'm part of this—this *world* where people can turn into animals, and you *never told me*. You let me go on thinking I was weird or crazy, and all this time—I had a right to know who I am. Now Mom's been kidnapped, my brother hates me, and the Alpha is after a weapon I don't understand, but I know that if she gets it, a lot of people are going to die, and I have to find Mom before that happens. If you're not going to help me, then—then you need to go."

The accusations tumbled out of his mouth before he could stop them, and his face grew hot once he realized what he'd said. Darryl stared at him for several long seconds, and at last he cleared his throat.

"Your mother wouldn't want you to risk your life for her,"

he said quietly. "You or Nolan. And I'm sorry I never told you about all of this, Simon—it's a discussion your mother and I have had countless times, but ultimately we both decided it was safer if you didn't know. Not until you absolutely had to."

"I absolutely had to yesterday," said Simon. "I absolutely had to when the rats started chasing us."

"And we were going to tell you. Your mother had already started to," said Darryl.

"It was too late by then." Simon hesitated. "It doesn't matter. I'm not leaving Mom or Nolan."

The scar running down his uncle's face twitched. "Simon—"

An infuriated roar filled the entrance hall. A hulking wolf stood at the top of the stairwell, his hackles raised and his teeth bared.

"I was wondering when you'd show your face," said Malcolm in a dangerous voice as he advanced on them. "I see you're not nearly as dead as you wanted us to believe."

Darryl's grip on Simon tightened. "We were just leaving."

Simon opened his mouth to protest, but Malcolm cut him off. "You're not going anywhere—either of you."

"And how do you plan on stopping me?" The dangerous rumble in Darryl's voice made Simon shiver. "Twelve years or not, I can still take you."

A chorus of low growls echoed through the entrance hall, and at least a dozen wolves appeared from the shadows, surrounding them. Three gathered at the exit, blocking their only escape route. Simon's heart raced.

"Both of you, into the Den," said Malcolm. "I'll let the Alpha decide what to do with you."

Behind him, Simon could feel his uncle shuddering with the effort not to shift. "You have no idea what's going on, Brother. If you did—"

"Then I guess it's a good thing you'll have plenty of time to tell me, isn't it?" Malcolm jerked his head, and the other wolves moved closer, gnashing their teeth. "Stairwell. Now."

"And if I don't?" said Darryl.

"Then I hope your pup doesn't get in the way while we rip you to shreds for treason."

"Please—listen to him," begged Simon. The last thing he wanted was for the Alpha to sink her claws into Darryl, too, but there was no escaping without a fight his uncle would lose. And maybe, just maybe, Darryl knew where she might have hidden his mother. It was becoming painfully clear that Simon couldn't save her by himself, and they had only one more day before the Alpha returned. He needed all the help he could get.

At last Darryl nodded tersely and headed down the staircase, taking Simon with him. The rest of the students had long since disappeared into the Den, and part of Simon was grateful. An audience wouldn't help his uncle's temper.

"If I find out you've touched a hair on Simon's head—" said Darryl as they passed over the bridge.

"Why would we want to hurt him?" said Malcolm, nipping at their ankles. Simon hurried along, but Darryl kept the same slow, languid pace, as if he were daring them to try to rush him. "Now explain. What's going on?"

"Not here," Darryl growled. "Not in front of everyone."

"Then walk faster, *Brother*. I expect you remember the way."

The corridors were strangely empty, and when Simon smelled food, he remembered it was dinnertime. The brothers said nothing as they entered the Alpha's section, and it wasn't until the door shut firmly behind them that Malcolm shifted back. The members of the pack who had escorted them remained outside, and for one horrible second, as Darryl stared at his brother with clenched fists and shaking shoulders, Simon thought he was going to attack Malcolm.

"Now tell me," said Malcolm, not taking his eyes off Darryl. "Why did you abandon the pack? Why did you fake your death and leave me to—" Malcolm stopped, and the cords in his neck stood out.

While Simon perched anxiously on the sofa, Darryl began to pace through the trees. "Had you been in my position, you would have done the same. Luke was dead. Isabel was pregnant with his potential heirs. With the war brewing between Mother and Orion, there was no safe place for Isabel within the kingdoms."

Malcolm glanced at Simon. "Orion didn't know," he

muttered, ducking his head as if it would somehow stop Simon from overhearing. "He would've had no reason—"

"He knew. He caught Luke shifting. Why do you think he suddenly began to support Luke's relationship with his daughter after years of fighting it?"

Malcolm paled. "He wanted to control—?"

"You can say it, you know," said Simon. Both men stopped and looked at him. "My father was the Beast King's heir."

The brothers gaped at him for several seconds before Darryl rounded on Malcolm. "You told him?"

"Of course not."

"Have you told Nolan?" Darryl said, and Malcolm faltered.

"We had to. If he shifted into a member of another kingdom without any warning—"

"Malcolm didn't tell me," said Simon. "But I know now, so you can stop pretending."

Darryl headed over to the couch, sitting beside Simon and clasping his hands together. "That's exactly why we did this, your mother and I. You mentioned you know about the Alpha seeking the pieces of the Predator—"

"What are you talking about?" said Malcolm. "Mother isn't—"

"Of course she is," said Darryl. "Why do you think she's been manipulating the other kingdoms into following her?"

"For peace," said Malcolm. "Since she's brokered the treaties, there haven't been more than a few skirmishes—"

"Except between the mammals and the birds," said Darryl.

Malcolm scoffed. "The birds refuse to join the pact. Isabel assured Mother that as soon as Orion died and she became their ruler—"

"If she trusted Mother so much, then why did she ask me to hide Simon?"

Silence settled over them, and now it was Malcolm's turn to pace. "I don't know. And if you're going to tell me Mother had something to do with you faking your death, too—"

"Mother has *everything* to do with it. She and Orion," said Darryl. "I had to protect Simon. Their war over the kingdoms, their fight to best each other—Mother's been collecting the pieces of the Predator. She wants to put it back together, and when she does, she's going to kill whichever boy inherited Luke's powers, and then she's going to seize control of all five kingdoms."

Simon found nothing gratifying about having his worst fears confirmed, and hearing his uncle lump Orion in with the Alpha nauseated him. His grandfather was nothing like the Alpha, even if he had known Simon's father was the Beast King's heir. Orion hadn't been the one to send the rats after them, and he hadn't been the one to try to kill his family. He had saved Simon.

Malcolm's face twisted as though he'd smelled something horrible. "I don't believe you."

"Think about it, Brother." Darryl closed the distance

between them, taking Malcolm by the shoulders. "Mother's been holding Nolan hostage, using him against Isabel to make her scour the country searching for the pieces. Why else would Mother send her traveling so often? It wasn't for diplomacy. Isabel spent *years* researching the Beast King and the Predator with Luke. If anyone was capable of finding the pieces, it was her."

The hot knot in Simon's chest returned, and everything turned to static as Darryl's words settled over him. His mother was the one putting the weapon together. That was why she almost never came to see him. That was why he'd never had a real family. If she was doing the Alpha's bidding, then she must have been watched closely, which meant it was a risk every time she'd visited him. But she'd done it anyway. She'd still wanted to be part of his life. And that, he realized, must have been why Darryl stayed in the city the whole time. So Simon could have that relationship with his mother.

Knowing the truth didn't wash away the bitterness or fill the hollow ache inside him, but at least now Simon had an answer. At least now he knew that his mother really did love him.

Malcolm shoved his brother away. "And why should I believe a word you say? You abandoned us. You lied to us— you lied to *me*. For twelve years, you let me think I was alone, and now—" His entire body trembled. "I don't *believe* you."

"Mother knew I was alive," said Darryl. "Maybe for years.

She sent the rat army to our apartment yesterday after Orion found us, and they took Isabel. They would've taken Simon if I hadn't stopped them." He took another step toward Malcolm, using his height advantage to look down at him. "If she doesn't trust you with that much, what else is she keeping from you?"

An inhuman snarl cut through the air, and in a flurry of teeth and fur, Malcolm shifted and leaped at Darryl, knocking him to the grass.

Darryl roared. In an instant, he also shifted into his wolf form, and Simon jumped back as they collapsed in a heap of limbs and claws.

The wolves snarled and ripped at each other's fur, pawed each other's snouts, and rolled over and over again as they each fought to gain control. Simon knew he should have panicked—they could kill each other, and he couldn't lose Darryl, too. But he stared at them, frozen, his mind reeling. There was something off about the fight. After several seconds, he realized what it was.

Neither wolf was drawing blood.

At last the larger wolf—Darryl—pinned the smaller one to the ground, putting all his weight on Malcolm's torso. "You're the only one I can trust now, do you understand? Mother wants the twins for their abilities, and I need your help to stop her, Brother."

Malcolm gasped for air. "Mother—only wants peace. She loves—she loves Nolan. She would never—"

"Are you willing to bet his life on it?" Darryl jumped off him, and both men shifted back into human form. "She already has four of the pieces. All she needs is Orion's."

Wheezing, Malcolm sat up and rubbed the red marks on his neck. "If it's true—*if*—then you know I'd never let anything happen to the boys. But you've given me no proof, no reason to trust you, no plan of action—"

"The rats said they took my mom to the Den," said Simon suddenly. Both men turned to face him. "If she's here, then where would the Alpha hide her?"

"She wouldn't," said Malcolm. "It's a school, not a prison."

Darryl snorted. "Tell that to Isabel."

"I'll have the pack scour the grounds, but I promise you, she isn't here," said Malcolm, climbing to his feet.

"But what if we do find her?" said Simon. "Will you believe us then?"

Malcolm's nostrils flared, and his knuckles went white. "Yes. Then I'll believe you."

Darryl clapped his hand on Simon's shoulder. "*We* will not be looking for her. You will stay safe in the pack's care. Is that understood?"

"But—"

"I've already lost you once," he said, his dark eyes flashing. "I won't lose you again. I know every room, every tunnel, every brick below the zoo. If your mother's here, I swear I will find her."

Simon slumped and nodded reluctantly. He didn't doubt his uncle, but he also didn't trust Malcolm, not completely.

When dinner finally arrived, Simon was too tense to eat much. He was painfully aware of both Darryl and Malcolm watching him as they talked tersely about the past twelve years, so he forced down a few bites, but all he could think about was where the Alpha might have hidden his mother. It wasn't until later, after he'd excused himself and headed to his bedroom to read more of his mother's notebook, that his uncle's words echoed back to him.

I know every room, every tunnel, every brick below the zoo.

Simon's insides tightened. Of course. *Of course.* He was an idiot for not thinking of it sooner. Darryl could search the Den all he wanted, but Simon knew exactly where he would hide an Animalgam right under someone's nose, and it wouldn't be a place where someone could accidentally stumble across her.

No—if he was going to hide a golden eagle, then there was only one place that made sense: the Central Park Zoo.

NIGHT OWL

With his heart pounding, Simon dashed out of his bedroom and onto the balcony, looking down into the atrium. "Darryl?" he called, but his uncle was already gone. Instead, Vanessa sat at the base of the spiral staircase, whittling something.

"They've gone on patrol," she said, craning her neck to see Simon. "Anything I can do for you?"

Simon shook his head. "No, I just—wanted to ask him something. I'll do it in the morning."

He returned to his bedroom and closed the door firmly behind him. If he couldn't tell his uncle where he thought his mother was, that left only one choice.

"Felix?" said Simon. The little mouse crawled out of the corner where he'd made a nest of socks, bleary-eyed and yawning.

"If this doesn't involve food, I'm not interested."

Simon offered him a napkin full of bread and cheese he'd saved from dinner. "When you looked for my mom, did you search the zoo aboveground?"

Felix's whiskers twitched. "I was going to, but the idea of being eaten didn't appeal to me."

A small thrill of hope ran through him. If Felix hadn't looked up there, then it meant there was a chance Simon was right. "I need to get into the zoo without anyone finding out."

"There are tunnels," said Felix, his tiny cheeks stuffed with bread. "All over the school. They're big enough for people, and they lead to the zoo. There's one—" He tore off another bite of bread and chewed. "There's one in your evil twin's room."

Simon glanced toward the door that led into the bathroom they shared. "Is that the only one?"

"It's the closest." Felix shuddered. "Unless you want to go into the reptile section."

Braving a nest of snakes was infinitely more appealing than letting Nolan catch him snooping around. But Simon knew the pack would be watching his every move if he tried to leave his bedroom, let alone the Alpha section, and that meant the tunnel in Nolan's room was his only option.

He sneaked into the bathroom and carefully cracked open the door that led into Nolan's room. His brother sat at his desk, reading through a textbook, and Simon closed the door again. "We'll have to wait until he's asleep," he whispered to Felix. "Can you watch him?"

Felix made a face. "If he sees me and tries anything, I *will* bite him."

"I wouldn't expect anything less."

Returning to his room, Simon stretched out across the bed and read his mother's notebook. It was crammed with information, and though Simon didn't understand a great deal of it, the more he read, the clearer it became: Darryl had been right about his mother's knowledge of the Beast King.

Just as he was reviewing the list of animals his mother had written, Felix scampered back into the bedroom. "He's gone—he went through the tunnel."

"Nolan?" Simon hid the notebook under his pillow and scrambled to his feet. Had Nolan overheard their conversation and gone to look for their mother? No—Malcolm had said Nolan wandered off into the zoo. This must have been how he did it.

Simon followed Felix into his brother's empty bedroom. "It's underneath the desk," said Felix as he bounded over. "There's a door—I saw him open it, the weasel."

Simon ducked underneath the mahogany desk. At first he didn't see anything, but as his eyes adjusted, he spotted a faint outline. He nudged it, and the door popped open with ease. Behind it was a brick tunnel.

"Stay here and make sure Darryl and Malcolm don't come

in," he said, examining the narrow entrance. He would have to crawl. "If they do, let me know, okay? I'll be by the birds."

"Really? You want me to follow you into a building full of creatures who eat my kind for dinner?" said Felix.

"Right. Then just—hide. And don't let anyone find you."

The tunnel was dark and sloped upward, and Simon couldn't tell how long he crawled. Ten minutes, twenty—it felt like he would never find the end, and twice he considered turning back, but if Nolan had gone this way, then it had to let out somewhere.

At last he spotted a dim light in the distance. As he grew closer, he realized it wasn't a light at all: it was the moon. Simon pushed a metal grate aside, wincing as it creaked. The tunnel ended behind a statue of an eagle at the edge of a square in the Central Park Zoo, next to a building that smelled like fish. It was lighter than it had been in the tunnel, but it was still too dark for Simon to spot his brother.

Now all he had to do was figure out where they kept the birds. He searched for any sign of a map, but even though he had to be close to the entrance, he didn't find one. While the zoo was small, it was full of winding paths, and the last thing Simon wanted was to get lost.

Shivering in the cool night air, he started forward. The bird habitat couldn't be far. He would comb through every single building if he had to, and even if it took all night, he would find his mother.

Something rustled nearby. Simon stilled, and as soon as

he was sure no one had spotted him, he dashed toward a set of concrete stairs, climbing upward. He heard the sound again—closer this time—and he turned a corner and ran past a high window. He'd been in the zoo for only a minute, but already he was sure he was lost.

A flash of white beyond the window glass caught his eye. A ghostly figure slept on the rocks, his massive chest rising and falling. A polar bear. What was a polar bear doing out this late?

Another figure moved at the edge of Simon's vision, and he stopped. For a moment he couldn't make out the details, but when the figure turned, he saw the same face he'd seen in the mirror his whole life, and he exhaled. It was his brother.

Except Nolan wasn't taking a nighttime stroll. Somehow he had climbed into the polar bear enclosure and stood atop one of the large rocks overlooking the water, his arms outspread as though he were about to fly. Simon's blood ran cold. What was he doing?

Before he could call out, Nolan did the single stupidest thing Simon had ever seen.

He jumped in.

POLAR BEAR CLUB

Simon watched in horror as Nolan fell into the water. He disappeared beneath the darkness, and Simon broke out into a cold sweat.

"Help!" he yelled. Someone had to be close by. The pack had found him in minutes the night before. *"Help!"*

The polar bear roared, and the hair on the back of Simon's neck stood up. How long before the bear realized Nolan was inside his enclosure and went after him?

Simon watched the water, searching for any sign of his brother. Nothing. Seconds ticked by, and Nolan didn't resurface. If Simon didn't help him, no one else would.

The polar bear roared again. "Intruders!" he cried. "My water. My rocks. My fish."

"No one's going to eat your fish," Simon managed to pull himself up the wall. "If you stay out of the water, I'll bring you a whole bucket, okay?"

The polar bear shook itself. "My fish!"

"Your fish." Simon reached the top of the rock. Nolan still hadn't resurfaced. "I'm going in now. Don't eat me," he said, and taking a deep breath, he jumped.

The cool air rushed around him, and he hit the water hard. Darkness surrounded him. He didn't know which way was up. The icy water attacked every part of his body, turning him to stone. It was cold—so much colder than he ever thought water could be. His feet hit the bottom, and his legs unlocked as they pushed against it. His muscles burned, but he forced himself to kick upward. Air. He needed air.

At last he surfaced. Gasping, he spun around, searching for Nolan. His muscles seized, and his skin was numb. He had to get out of there, or else Malcolm and Darryl would be dragging two bodies from the water instead of one.

Simon started to swim toward a ladder on the other side of the habitat. It wasn't far, but in the cold water, it might as well have been a mile away. He was only a few strokes from the wall when something grabbed the bottom of his jeans, pulling him down into the icy water once more.

Nolan. Simon struggled against his grip. He was going to drown them both. Simon yanked his leg as hard as he could, over and over again, and at last Nolan let go. Simon surfaced once more, water splashing in the quiet night.

Gasping for air, Simon waited several seconds for Nolan to join him. He must have been able to push off the bottom, too. But he didn't. He didn't surface at all.

Panic rushed through him. Nolan had been underneath the water for almost a minute by now. If he didn't get any air soon, he would drown. Simon glanced toward the ladder. If he swam for it now, he could pull himself up out of the water and onto the nearby ledge, and maybe a member of the pack would be close enough to help.

But if they weren't, if Simon and Nolan were all alone out here, his brother would die.

It wasn't a choice. Taking a deep breath, he forced himself down into the freezing water again, groping around in the blackness. At first he felt nothing, and his heart pounded. Nolan had to be conscious—he had to be.

But at last, cold fingers closed around his, and Simon grabbed Nolan's hand. The ladder ran up the side of the wall only a few feet away. Simon just had to drag his brother close enough so that they could both climb up to the ledge.

He started to pull. Nolan didn't resist, and Simon feared he had already blacked out. Digging his heels in, he yanked his brother over, and at last his hand touched the first rung of the ladder.

"Help!" he sputtered as he surfaced. He was completely numb now, and he struggled to drag Nolan above the water. Using the last of his strength, he pushed him onto the ledge. Nolan's legs felt heavy, but Simon hauled them out of the pool before finally climbing up himself. He collapsed, too cold to shiver. His skin didn't feel right. He could barely move, but he somehow managed to clumsily roll Nolan over.

Was he dead? Simon couldn't tell. His eyes were closed, his face white in the moonlight, and he didn't move. He wasn't breathing.

Simon forced himself to his knees. He had never done CPR before, but he had to try something. Sucking in a deep breath, he pushed against Nolan's chest. His sweater squelched, and Simon tried again, harder this time. "Come on," he said roughly. "Come *on*. If you're waiting for me to give you mouth-to-mouth—"

Suddenly an impossible amount of water gushed out of Nolan, and he coughed hard and rolled onto his side. Relieved, Simon fell back against the wall. He was alive. They were both alive.

"Are you okay?" Simon asked.

"Did—did I shift?" Nolan sputtered between coughs.

"Shift?" he said, and realization dawned on him. "Wait— you jumped into a polar bear enclosure in the middle of the night just to make yourself *shift*?"

"Did I shift or not?" demanded Nolan, his voice growing stronger.

"No, but you nearly got both of us eaten. Thanks for that."

Nolan stared at him. His lips were blue. "You jumped in after me?"

"I wasn't going to watch you drown." Although now it

didn't seem like such a bad idea. "Why were you trying to make yourself shift, anyway?"

He drew his knees to his chest. "None of your business."

"I just saved your life," said Simon. "I have a right to know why."

Nolan's teeth began to chatter. His face contorted as though he were having some kind of internal battle, and finally he burst, "It's your fault, anyway."

"My fault? What did I do?" said Simon.

"You're here. You could—you could be the heir instead. You could be—"

"The Beast King," he said quietly, and Nolan's eyes widened.

"You know?"

"Long story," he muttered.

"It's going to be one of us, you know," said Nolan. "Yesterday, Malcolm told me—he told me that since we're twins, one of us is going to be the Beast King, and the other one's going to be an eagle."

He spat out that last word as though it were dirty, and Simon scowled. "There's nothing wrong with that."

"Of course there is," said Nolan. "It's bad enough we're Hybreds. That's when two parents—"

"Are from different kingdoms. Yeah, I know," said Simon. "And you're afraid your family won't love you if you're an eagle instead."

Nolan was silent. He didn't have to answer for Simon to know the truth.

"Birds aren't bad," he said. "They're smart They're loyal. They can fly—"

"If I'm the Beast King, I'll get to fly anyway," he said with a sniff. "The Alpha's mad at me. The mammals have been protecting our line since the Beast King was defeated, and all the ones before me had already transformed by the time they were twelve. She thinks it's my fault that I haven't, but I'm trying." He pulled up his wet pant leg and unstrapped what looked like weights from his shins. "I've *been* trying, but no matter what I do, I can't make myself shift."

"That isn't your fault," said Simon. "I haven't shifted yet, either."

"That was kind of obvious in the pit, you know," said Nolan. "What if we don't shift until we're fifteen or sixteen? We'll be *ancient*."

Simon was beginning to wonder whether that was such a bad thing. At least then they would have time to figure out how to escape before the Alpha killed them. "Nolan, about that—"

"Why did you save me?"

Simon paused. "You would have done the same for me."

"No, I wouldn't have. I'm not even sure I would have called for help."

"You would have," he said firmly. "Because that's what family does."

Nolan hesitated, and after several seconds, he mumbled, "I'm sorry about what I said earlier. You are my brother. I just—I just don't want you to shift first."

"I won't," said Simon. "I didn't even know Animalgams existed until yesterday."

"Really?"

"Really. Yesterday morning, I thought—"

A nearby howl cut him off. A gray wolf appeared through the glass window, and he scrambled up the side of the enclosure as if it were nothing. "What happened? Are you hurt?" said Malcolm.

"Just cold," said Nolan. "Simon saved my life."

Malcolm's blue eyes fixed on Simon. "We'll talk about it later," he said. "We need to warm you up."

"Simon!" Darryl's massive wolf form appeared at Malcolm's side, and he immediately shifted back into a human. "What the—did you two *jump in?*"

"Long story," said Simon as his uncle gathered him up. Darryl was so warm that Simon felt as if he'd stepped straight into a fire.

"You're freezing," said Darryl. "Come on, back to the Den before you turn into a block of ice."

Simon wanted to protest—he hadn't even found the birds yet—but as they climbed out of the enclosure, several other members of the pack joined them. He had no idea whether they were loyal to Malcolm or the Alpha, and with them listening, Simon didn't dare tell his uncle why he was really out here to begin with. Instead he kept quiet, and together Darryl and Malcolm helped them through the dark zoo and into the Arsenal. Exhausted, Simon leaned against his uncle until they hit the warm entrance hall, where the rest of the pack had gathered. Vanessa shifted back to her human form, hurrying to their side.

"What happened? Where were they?"

"They jumped into the polar bear habitat," said Malcolm.

"They did *what?* Is the prince all right?"

"They are *both* cold and need to be warmed up, but they'll probably live," said Darryl. He didn't sound like he was joking. "The reptiles' section?"

"Not unless you want them to get bitten, too," said Malcolm. "Mother's office. She has a fireplace."

Vanessa led the way, her curls bouncing with every step she took. Simon found it almost hypnotic, and he couldn't look away, even when they reached the office. She pushed the door open, but instead of barging in, she stopped suddenly and bowed her head. "Your Majesty."

"What on earth is going on?" said a regal voice. Had Simon not already been too cold to move, he would have shivered.

A pale woman with a sheet of dark hair that hung to her waist stood behind the desk, wearing a white pantsuit and a long silver chain around her neck. Her eyes were steely blue, and within seconds, they fixed on Simon.

He gulped. There was only one person she could be.

The Alpha.

17

THE ALPHA

Simon couldn't take his eyes off the Alpha. He'd expected her to be taller and strong, like her sons. Instead she looked as though a gust of wind could snap her in half if she wasn't careful. As she stepped out from behind the desk, however, there was strength in the way she moved. She might not be able to lift a boulder, but Simon had no doubt she was the Alpha—and that she was someone he would be crazy to cross.

But she wasn't supposed to be back until tomorrow. She'd returned a day early, and panic crashed through him. Would she take them out of the city immediately, or did Simon still have time to find his mother?

"These two geniuses jumped into the polar bear

enclosure," said Malcolm as he helped Nolan to the sofa nearest the fireplace. "They're fine. Just cold."

Darryl followed suit, and once Simon was settled on the couch, the Alpha approached them. Her unforgiving stare flitted back and forth between Simon and Nolan, as if she were trying to find a difference between them. Simon refused to look away.

"So it's true," she said coolly. "There really are two of them. And you . . ." She focused on Darryl. "I see you're still alive."

"No need to pretend, Mother," said Darryl. "You must have known for a while now."

The Alpha made a noncommittal noise, and her lack of denial spoke volumes. Simon glanced at Malcolm, who knelt to tend to the fireplace. A muscle in his jaw twitched, and he poked a log harder than was strictly necessary.

"Dare I ask how you managed to get that hideous scar?" said the Alpha to Darryl as she turned back to Simon and Nolan, regarding them once more. Simon could practically see the wheels turning in her head, and he shifted uncomfortably.

Darryl frowned. "Orion, after Isabel left . . ." He cleared his throat. "Anyway, I got his eye in return."

"You should have ripped out his heart." The Alpha knelt in front of Simon, touching his chin and turning his head from side to side. The news that Darryl and Orion had maimed each other sent a shock wave through Simon.

Now he understood why neither of them was willing to trust the other. "Have you shifted?"

"Not yet, he hasn't," said Darryl, and the Alpha's eyes narrowed.

"I did not ask you."

"I—I haven't," said Simon, his voice sticking in his throat, but his defiant stare didn't waver.

"Hmm." She stood, smoothing nonexistent wrinkles from her suit. Vanessa brought a pair of warmed blankets for the boys, and Simon shuddered as the heat slowly chased away the numbness. She politely excused herself from the office, and the Alpha waited until she was gone before she continued.

"Do you both have a death wish?" she said, folding her hands in front of her.

"N-No," said Nolan, and Simon shook his head as well.

"Then what were you doing in the polar bear enclosure in the middle of the night?" There was no hint of concern in her voice, only irritation. "Did you think it would be fun to drown or to be eaten by a hungry animal?"

Simon didn't want to think about what the polar bear could have done to them if he'd tried. But he did know that if his brother got into trouble for this, it would only be one more thing Nolan held against him, and he couldn't let that happen. Not when they'd finally made progress. "I'm sorry," he said. "I thought—I thought I would go exploring, and I fell in. Nolan rescued me—"

"Don't," said Nolan. The color was starting to return to his cheeks. "I'm the one who went aboveground. He must have followed me. I jumped into the water, and Simon pulled me out. He saved my life."

"Is this true?" said the Alpha, and Simon nodded. "Why would you do such a thing?"

"Why wouldn't I?" he said, baffled.

"I heard about the way Nolan has been treating you." Under her stare, Nolan paled and looked at his hands. "Yet you still risked your life for him."

"He's my brother. He would have done the same for me." Even if Nolan didn't believe it.

The Alpha was quiet for several seconds. Focusing again on Nolan, she said, "Why did you decide to take a midnight swim with a polar bear in the first place?"

He fidgeted silently. She looked back and forth between them, but Simon kept his mouth shut, too.

"Isn't it obvious?" burst Malcolm. "You've been pressuring him to shift since his eleventh birthday. I've had to keep half the pack on him to make sure he doesn't kill himself trying. It's a miracle he hasn't succeeded. And if Simon hadn't been there tonight—" Malcolm stopped suddenly, and he swallowed hard. "If you continue to pressure him, one day we're not going to be so lucky."

She narrowed her eyes, and though Malcolm stood at least a foot taller than his mother, he lowered his head and slumped his shoulders. The Alpha sniffed. "Luke shifted at age eleven. His father before him shifted at eleven." She turned to them. "You are both twelve, and yet neither of you have come into your abilities. For all I know, you never will, and what use will you be then?"

Simon didn't care what she thought about him, but out of the corner of his eye, he could see Nolan turning red as his fists tightened. Suddenly the numbness didn't matter, and the hot knot returned, pulsing until it felt as if it was going to burst out of his chest.

"You only care because one of us is going to be the Beast King, and you want to know which," he said hotly.

"Simon," warned Darryl sharply, and Simon fell silent before he could accuse the Alpha of worse. But she merely leveled her gaze at him once more, and a shiver that had nothing to do with the cold ran down his spine.

"You're exactly right," she said. "If the rest of the kingdoms discover the existence of the Beast King's heir, I want to know which of you will need my protection. I want to know which of you they will want to kill. If there is a crime in that, then so be it."

It was more than that, and she knew it, but Darryl gave Simon a look, and he kept his mouth shut.

"Do you know which boy was born first?" the Alpha asked Darryl.

He shook his head. "If Isabel knows, she never told me."

"It must be Simon, right?" said Malcolm, though he didn't sound sure of himself. "If Isabel wanted you to hide him—"

"Does it matter?" said Darryl. Beside Simon, his brother had turned the color of sour milk. "The ability to shift is in our genes. Nature doesn't care who's born first. All we know is that one will be Luke's heir, and the other will be Isabel's. They aren't the first identical twins born to our kind."

"No, but they are the first born to the Beast King's heirs," said the Alpha. "I suppose we'll just have to wait and see, won't we?"

So Simon would either be heir to the kingdom the Alpha wanted to destroy, or every Animalgam on the planet would want him dead. He wasn't sure which was worse.

"We'll leave for the country manor tomorrow," she added. "Take the boys upstairs and make sure they get some rest. And Nolan, Simon—if either of you risk your lives like that again, I will lock you both up until you're old and gray. Is that understood?"

"Isn't that what you're already doing?" said Simon, but the Alpha pointedly ignored him.

Darryl helped him up, but before they could leave, she said coldly, "A word, Darryl."

"Can't it wait?" he said.

"It's already waited for twelve years. Stay. Malcolm, you take the boys."

Simon started to protest—he had to tell his uncle where he thought his mother was, and he couldn't do that with the Alpha listening. But Darryl shook his head.

"Go with Malcolm, Simon. I'll be right outside later if you

need anything." He hesitated, and then brushed a lock of damp hair out of Simon's eyes. "You know how much you mean to me, right? If I lost you . . ."

"I know," said Simon. "I'm sorry. I won't do it again."

"Yes, you will. You're a Thorn. We spend our lives getting into tight corners and finding our way out of them. Just be smarter about it the next time, all right?"

"I will." He paused, and before he could stop himself, he blurted, "Love you, too, Darryl."

To his surprise, Nolan didn't make a sound, not even a snort of laughter. His uncle nodded briskly, and Simon let Malcolm lead them out of the office and through the atrium in silence.

Malcolm dropped Nolan off at his room first before leading Simon to his. "You need to hold your tongue around the Alpha," he said quietly. "I've spent half my life pushing her, and it doesn't work. Trust me."

"Do you at least believe us now?" said Simon.

"It doesn't matter what I believe," said Malcolm, though his brow furrowed. "What matters is that we have time to figure out what the truth is. As long as you two haven't shifted, you're safe."

"And what about Darryl? What's going to happen to him? The Alpha doesn't need him—not when she has you."

Malcolm let out a noise that sounded halfway between a guffaw and a choking animal. "Never in my life, when faced with a choice between us, has she chosen me. I assure you that hasn't changed."

There was a note of bitterness in his voice as he said it, and also a hint of relief that Simon couldn't help but wonder about. It wasn't hard to imagine how Malcolm must have felt being overshadowed by his older brothers, even if it was strange for Simon to think of Darryl as anyone's brother. "You don't know that for sure," he said. "What if she decides she doesn't need him, or that he can't be controlled?"

Malcolm sobered. "Then that will make this decision a whole lot easier."

Simon didn't ask what he meant, and Malcolm didn't explain. He exited the bedroom and closed the door behind him, leaving Simon alone with the all-too-real possibility that no matter what he did, no matter how much help he had from his uncles and Orion, the Alpha would win one way or the other.

The next morning, Simon awoke with a plan.

It wasn't a very good plan, but Simon couldn't just sit still and wait for his world to right itself again—he had to *do* something. After changing into the only clean clothes he had left, he checked outside to see if Darryl was in the atrium, but there was no sign of his uncle. That was it, then. Simon was on his own.

He returned to his bedroom, but before he could begin putting his plan into action by sneaking into Nolan's, Felix scampered in front of the bathroom doorway to block him.

"You almost died last night," he said, crossing his tiny arms in front of his chest. "I won't let you put yourself in danger again."

"You don't even know what I'm going to do," said Simon.

"Do, too. You're going to look for your mother."

"I *have* to," he said. "The Alpha's back. We're leaving today. I've got to find her, and we need to get out of here."

"But Darryl's here," said the mouse. "He'll be able to look—"

"I didn't have the chance last night to tell him where she is, and there's no time now. I'm her only shot," said Simon.

Felix's whiskers twitched disapprovingly. "And how exactly do you expect to get past your brother?"

"I—" Simon hesitated. "I'll tell him the truth. That Mom's missing, and I think the Alpha is hiding her somewhere in the zoo."

"You trust that bumbling baboon with this?"

"I don't have a choice, do I?"

Simon stepped around Felix and pushed open the bathroom door. To his surprise, Nolan was crouched on the other side, his mouth agape and his eyes wide.

"Mom's missing?" he said. "Why didn't anyone tell me?"

Simon instantly kicked himself for not mentioning it earlier, but when could he have? While they were freezing to death fifteen feet from a polar bear? While he was pouring chocolate milk over Nolan's head? While Nolan was snickering at him with the rest of the mammals and refusing to admit he had a brother at all? "I'm sorry," he said. "Since you knew the Alpha, I thought—"

"Why do you think she took Mom?" said Nolan, and Simon launched into everything that had happened. Well, almost everything—he didn't mention Orion, and he didn't mention the library beneath the Beast King's Stronghold. Simon wanted to trust his brother completely, but he couldn't just yet, not when he didn't know whether Nolan would believe him. But Simon did tell him about the rat army, about their mother and Darryl protecting him, and about the Alpha's plan for them and why she was taking control of the other kingdoms.

Nolan paled and began to pace the length of the bathroom floor. "If the Alpha really wants to put the Predator together and kill one of us—and I'm not saying I believe you, but if you're right—then we have to find Mom and get out of here," he said once Simon had finished. "Are you sure she's in the zoo somewhere?"

"It makes sense, doesn't it?" said Simon. "If Malcolm and the pack don't know where Mom is, then the Alpha couldn't have hidden her in the Den. Unless you can think of someplace else."

Nolan shook his head. "No, you're right." He glanced at his watch. "The zoo opened ten minutes ago. We can blend in with the crowd and look for her."

Simon brightened. "You're really going to help?"

"Of course," said Nolan. "She's my mother, too."

Behind him, Simon could hear Felix sigh, but he ignored him. This was worth the risk.

Nolan led the way into his room and through the tunnel that let out in the middle of the zoo. The sunshine made Simon squint as they crawled from behind the eagle statue, and before he could ask where they were going, Nolan started toward one of the buildings across the square. Simon followed. They blended in easily with the crowd, and no one seemed to look too hard at the twelve-year-old twins walking toward a building labeled TROPICAL RAIN FOREST.

"Golden eagles don't live in the tropics, but if Mom is in the zoo, this is the only place they keep birds," said Nolan as they stepped through the glass doors and into what seemed to be a miniature rain forest. All kinds of trees rose high above them, with a stream running through the middle and a wooden walkway for visitors to follow. A wave of heat and humidity hit Simon hard, and instantly he felt beads of sweat form on his forehead.

"Where would she be?" he said, craning his neck. Dozens of birds flew from branch to branch, chirping to one another in a chorus of words that ran together, each indistinguishable from the rest.

"There are a couple of rooms through there," said Nolan, nodding toward another door. "They have snakes and other animals, but I don't know if there are any birds—"

"Wait!" Simon ducked down, tugging Nolan with him. When his brother began to protest, Simon clapped his hand over Nolan's mouth and pointed. On the other side of the room, crossing the walkway, was a woman with a familiar sheet of dark hair.

The Alpha.

Nolan's eyes nearly popped out of his head, and he fell silent. Together they watched as she disappeared through a door, and as soon as she was gone, Simon pulled his brother along the walkway to follow her. The Alpha turned down a dark hallway full of dimly lit glass display cases, and at the end of the corridor, she pulled a key from a long chain she wore around her neck and unlocked a door that blended in with the surrounding wall.

"What's in there?" whispered Simon as they darted down the hallway, hoping to catch the door before it closed. He reached it with half a second to spare, shoving his shoe into the crack to stop it.

"It's where the zookeepers keep food and stuff for the animals," said Nolan, peeking through the opening. Instantly he pulled away and flattened himself against the wall. "I think I see her."

Simon counted to five, and then chanced a glance inside. At first he couldn't see much of anything through the crack, but he quickly found a better angle.

The Alpha stood in front of a pair of cages, her hands folded and her chin raised regally. She focused on the top cage, in which a golden eagle perched, its wing bandaged and its eyes halfway closed. His mother.

"I do hate to see you like this, Isabel, but you've given

me no choice," said the Alpha as she used the key around her neck to open the cage and drop in several freshly killed rats. "I've been nothing but generous, and you repay me by trying to run away with Simon? Even if you had succeeded, you must have known that I would have tracked you both down eventually."

Simon's palms grew sweaty. So he was right. The Alpha really had captured his mother. How were they supposed to get her out of there when the Alpha had the only key?

Before he could formulate a plan, something moved in the larger cage below his mother's, and Simon squinted. A gray tail slipped through the cracks, and a low, drowsy groan sounded from inside.

"I see you're awake," said the Alpha. "This would all have been so much easier if you hadn't tried to fight me, my darling son."

The face of a gray wolf came into view, a muzzle wrapped around its snout, and Simon's blood turned to ice.

Darryl.

18

SPIDER GAMES

The Alpha was holding his mother and his uncle hostage.

That was all Simon could think about as Nolan dragged him back through the tropics and out into the sunshine. The cooler air washed over him, a relief after the sweltering heat inside, but Simon barely noticed.

"Do you know if there's a copy of that key?" he asked as they strode toward the eagle statue at the edge of the square. The zoo was even more crowded now, and they had to dodge families and a school group full of children wearing matching orange T-shirts.

"There's only one," said Nolan. "It'll open any door in the entire zoo, but she wears it all the time. I've never seen her take it off."

"So we have to get it," said Simon.

"If you have a plan, I'm listening."

But Simon didn't have a plan—not for this. They reached the eagle statue in silence, and as Nolan ducked behind it, Simon stopped suddenly. On the wings sat two pigeons who hadn't been there before. His grandfather had helped him once. Simon could only hope he was willing to do it again.

"Do you know who Orion is?" said Simon. The pigeons glanced at each other.

"Food?"

"What are you doing?" said Nolan, looking around anxiously.

"Trying to rescue Mom." Simon dug into his pockets and found a stale piece of bread he'd been saving for Felix. He held it out in his palm, and the pigeons pecked at it eagerly. "Do you know who Orion is or not?"

"The Bird Lord," said one pigeon through a beak full of bread.

"Do you know where he lives?" he said, and the second pigeon bobbed his head.

"Tower in the sky."

"Sky Tower—right."

"No," said Nolan in a choked voice. "Whatever it is you're doing, *no.*"

"It's our only choice." Simon's heart pounded as the pigeons picked at the last of the stale crumbs. "I need you to fly to Sky Tower and tell Orion that Simon and Isabel are here. I need you to tell him that they're holding her captive in the Tropical Rain Forest, behind a door down the south hallway. Can you do that for me?"

"Simon and Isabel," said the first pigeon, while the second chirped, "South in the hot room."

That was the best he was going to get out of them, and he hoped it would be good enough. "Don't forget, all right? You have to go now. Tell him I promised you food."

"Food?" The first perked up again.

"Lots and lots of food after you tell him," said Simon, hoping his grandfather wouldn't mind.

The pigeons took off, and Simon ducked into the tunnel, where Nolan was waiting for him. "I can't believe you want to trust *Orion*," said his brother.

"Two days ago, he saved me from the rat army, and he's been watching over me ever since. If anyone can help us, it's him."

"He's a *bird*," said Nolan. "They want to kill us."

"No, the Alpha wants to kill us. Orion wants to stop her. Please," said Simon. "If you can't trust him, then trust me."

Nolan grumbled, but at last he relented, and he led the way through the tunnel. Relieved, Simon followed, crossing his fingers that the pigeons made it. Sky Tower wasn't more than a few blocks away—with a little luck, the pigeons would reach Orion before Simon and Nolan returned to the Den. But they wouldn't be able to open the cages, not without the key.

By the time they crawled into Nolan's bedroom, Simon had racked his brain for any inkling of a plan. But short of tearing the key from the Alpha's neck and running as fast as possible, he couldn't think of anything, and despair began to creep through him. There had to be something he was missing—a way to free his mom and Darryl before the Alpha took him and Nolan out of the city.

"What now?" said his brother, pacing back and forth. "I can't just face the Alpha and pretend nothing's wrong."

"We have to, unless you want to end up like Mom and Darryl," said Simon. "Orion's coming. He'll help us, and until then, we keep our heads down, all right? And don't tell anyone."

"Not even Malcolm? Maybe he could help."

Simon hesitated. "Okay—find him and tell him what's going on. Make sure he knows the Alpha has Darryl, too. Are you sure Malcolm doesn't have a second key?"

"Positive," said Nolan.

"Then we'll figure something out. Go to breakfast, tell Malcolm, and we'll meet back here after, okay?"

His brother nodded, and Simon slipped back into his room. He expected Felix to be waiting for him, but it was Winter who perched on the sofa, her arms crossed as she drummed her fingers against her elbow.

"Where have you *been*?" she burst, jumping to her feet. "Your bloodthirsty rat said you sneaked out."

"Felix isn't . . ." Simon sighed and knelt beside his

backpack, digging through it. He had to be ready to leave at a moment's notice, and he couldn't leave the pocket watch behind. "Where is he? You didn't hurt him, did you?"

Winter made a face. "Of course not. I might've threatened him, but I didn't actually touch him. He ran off somewhere. Now tell me—what's going on?"

Simon frowned. "I found my mother. The Alpha's holding her in the zoo with the birds. And—she has Darryl, too."

Winter's mouth fell open, and her expression softened. "Where are they? Orion—"

"I already sent a pair of pigeons to tell him." When she scoffed, he added, "I bribed them with food. They should already be at Sky Tower. But there's a key we need, and the Alpha has it. My mom and Darryl are in cages, and we can't free them unless we somehow get our hands on it."

Winter shook her head. "There's no way the Alpha will hand it over. Orion will figure out a way to break the locks, I promise."

"Even if Orion can break my mom out, Darryl's the one who took his eye," said Simon. "He won't free him, too."

"Yes, he will. Darryl means something to you, and Orion won't let him die," said Winter firmly.

He wanted to believe her, but Winter didn't know, not really. Orion had suspected Darryl was working for the Alpha. Simon was positive his grandfather wouldn't release him.

"Nolan's gone to tell Malcolm," he said. "We need to get out of here."

"What about the Predator?" said Winter, and Simon blinked. "Don't look at me like that. You and Nolan can run away to the other side of the world for all I care. It won't change the fact that the Alpha has almost all the pieces, and I guarantee you she'll find a way to get the last one. If anything goes wrong, if she captures you or Nolan again, Orion or your mother will hand it over. You know they will."

"So what?" said Simon. "We haven't shifted yet. We're useless to the Alpha until then."

"You could shift tomorrow, for all we know," she said. "Once we leave the Den, we're never going to get another chance like this. If you really want to stop the Alpha—if you really want to save your family—then we need to get the pieces of the Predator, too."

"But she can't assemble it, not without the real scepter."

Winter hissed with frustration. "Eventually she's going to realize hers is a fake, and she'll go looking for the real one. When she does, all she'll have to do is follow our scents, and she'll find the real deal that *you* stupidly made me leave right under her nose. We have to steal the pieces, Simon. If we don't, it won't be long before she can assemble the Predator, and—"

Winter stopped suddenly and grew still. At first Simon thought she had had some sort of epiphany, but instead she picked up a water glass from his nightstand.

"I like you, Simon. We're friends, and I don't want you to die," she said. "Once the pieces are out of the Alpha's control, Orion will overthrow her and free the other kingdoms. And once that's over, he can return the pieces to their rulers, and—ah *ha*!"

The glass clinked against the wall. Bewildered, Simon watched as Winter used a piece of paper to cover the mouth and promptly set the glass upside down on the nightstand.

"Who sent you?" she demanded.

"What? Who are you talking to?" said Simon, moving closer to the nightstand.

"See for yourself."

Simon peered inside. A shiny black spider with a red hourglass belly huddled underneath the glass.

"Ariana?" said Simon, stunned. "What are you—"

"She was spying on us," said Winter. "Probably heard everything. How long have you been following Simon?"

Silence. Simon tried to take the glass, but Winter snatched it away. "You have to let her shift back," he insisted.

"And give her a chance to escape? No way."

"What are you going to do, keep her locked up?" said Simon. "If she tries to shift like that, the glass will break, and she might get cut. Or lose a limb or something." He wasn't entirely sure how it worked.

"It would serve her right," muttered Winter, but she let go of the glass and picked up one of Simon's books instead.

"Here's the deal, spider. Simon's going to let you out, and if you try to run, I'll squish you. Got it?"

As far as Simon could tell, Ariana couldn't nod or otherwise show she agreed, but after a few seconds, Winter seemed satisfied. "All right. Pick it up."

Simon slowly lifted the glass. "Don't run," he said. "She really will squish you."

The spider twitched, but at last she began to grow. Simon blinked, and the pink-haired Ariana sat on the nightstand, looking—happy?

"I knew it!" She hopped off and grinned at both of them. "I knew there was a reason you were here."

"I *will* still throw this at you," said Winter, brandishing the book.

"What? Oh—I won't tell anyone," said Ariana. "Are you kidding? My mother is the Black Widow Queen, and she isn't exactly crazy about the Alpha assembling the Predator, either. You think the other kingdoms just submitted to her on a whim?" She shook her head, and a wisp of pink hair fell into her eyes. "No one wants her to get that final piece. But Winter's right. She'll look under every single rock until she finds it, and she'll have the entire mammal kingdom to help her."

"Is—is that why you were listening?" said Simon. "Because you thought we had something to do with the last piece?"

Ariana shrugged. "I thought something was going on

when you showed up and the bird flock went crazy, so I've been following you. You're pretty interesting, Simon Thorn. Especially your family tree."

Simon's cheeks warmed. So she knew everything. "You can't tell anyone. If you do—"

"Relax. The queens of my kingdom have known about the Beast King's heir for generations," said Ariana. "I'm not going to rat you out."

Simon eyed her, not entirely sure he believed her. "Why are you telling us this?"

"Because," said Ariana, her mouth twisting into a smirk, "I know where the Alpha's hiding the pieces of the weapon."

19

TWO BIRDS
AND ONE STONE

"This is crazy," whispered Winter as they followed Ariana down the spiral staircase in the Alpha's section. "She's a spider. Never trust a spider."

"Do you know where the pieces are?" said Simon, and she shook her head. "Then we don't have any other choice."

"You know I can hear you, right?" said Ariana as she sashayed through the empty atrium, looking extremely pleased with herself. Winter scowled at the back of her head.

"It's true, isn't it?" she said. "Spiders are the spies of the Animalgam kingdoms."

"And we are *extremely* good at it," said Ariana. "If I wasn't willing to be caught, I wouldn't have been."

"Easy to say now," said Winter, and Simon nudged her. Whether they could trust Ariana or not, she was trying to help them. That was the important part for now.

"We don't have much time before the Alpha comes looking for me," he said. "Where is she hiding the—"

"*Simon!*"

A strange cry filtered in from the hallway. Simon, gripped by fear, ran over to the door and pulled it open.

A hair-raising screech filled the air, and he gasped. Dozens of birds flew through the hallway. Pigeons, falcons, hawks—every kind of bird Simon had ever seen in the city swooped between the branches, screaming at the top of their lungs with their talons poised to attack. Orion had received his message.

"It's the flock!" he shouted over his shoulder. "They invaded the Den."

"Don't let them in!" called Winter. "If they take us to Sky Tower now, we'll never be able to come back."

As relieved as he was to see them, Simon knew she was right. The key, the pieces of the Predator—they couldn't leave the Den, not yet. He tried to close the door, but a hawk swooped into the atrium, narrowly missing getting its tail feathers caught. Simon slammed the door before any other birds could get inside.

"Simon Thorn," said the hawk. "You must come with me at once."

"Not yet," said Simon, recognizing him as Perrin, the bird

Orion had commanded to watch the pack. "I'll be there soon, but my family—"

"We've sent a team to retrieve your mother," said Perrin. "I will not leave without you."

The hawk shifted in midair, landing on his feet with a thud. He was a tall, thin man with muddy hair, but he moved with undeniable power as he closed in on Simon. Ariana squeaked and disappeared, shifting into her spider form.

"I know a way out of here," said Winter. "I'll bring him back to Sky Tower as soon as we're done."

"I'm afraid that is not an option." Perrin grabbed Simon's arm. "We go now, while our soldiers have the pack distracted."

"I'm—not—*leaving!*" Simon tried to break his grip, but Perrin dragged him toward the door.

"I don't think you heard him," said Winter, stepping between them and the exit. "I'll give you one last warning to let him go."

Perrin shoved her out of the way, hard enough to make her stumble, and Simon cried out in protest. "You can't do that!"

"I have my orders," he said, reaching for the knob. Simon fought, digging his heels into the grass, but it was no use. As soon as Perrin opened the door, dozens of birds would come flying in, and they wouldn't stand a chance of breaking away.

"I said *let—him—go.*"

The air around Winter began to shimmer, and as Simon watched, her body began to shrink. Her dark hair seemed to melt into the rest of her, but her arms didn't grow into wings the way he expected. Instead they disappeared into her sides, and her legs molded together, forming one long body. Her face grew flat and her nose pointed, and before Simon knew it—

She was a snake.

Her green eyes looked brighter than usual against her black scales and pale rings, and she hissed, baring sharp, curled fangs and a white mouth. Perrin paused, shock registering on his face.

"When Orion discovers what you are—" he began, but Winter didn't let him finish. In a flash, she shot toward him, sinking her fangs into Perrin's ankle. Winter must have been venomous, because instantly his grip loosened enough for Simon to shove him away.

Perrin stumbled, his eyes wide. "You—"

But whatever he was going to say never made it past his lips. His eyes rolled back into his head, and his knees buckled as he collapsed to the ground.

Simon stared at the viper coiled in the grass, her forked tongue tasting the air as her head bobbed up and down, as though she wasn't sure what to do with herself now. "Is this the first time you've shifted?" he said, his voice so high that he was fairly sure only dogs could hear it.

"I've been shifting into a cottonmouth for months," said

the snake—Winter—miserably. "But if Orion finds out I'm not a bird, he'll disown me."

"No, he won't," said Simon. "He loves you, and you're his family. You were the one who told me how important family is to—"

Suddenly the door to the Alpha's office opened, and cold fear washed over him. But it was Ariana, not the mammal queen, who stuck her head out. "I hate to break up the love-fest, but we have work to do." She spotted the unconscious Perrin, and her eyebrows shot up into her pink hairline. "Whoa. Impressive."

Winter shifted back into a human. She was paler than usual, and her hands trembled as she examined Perrin. "I've never—I've never bitten anyone before. Will he be okay?"

"Depends. How much did you give him?" said Ariana.

"All of it?" said Winter in a small voice. Ariana cursed and lurched forward, kneeling beside the man and checking his pulse.

"You'll be useless for the next few weeks, while your venom replenishes," she said as she searched her pockets. Finding a tiny syringe, she administered its contents into the side of Perrin's neck and settled back on her heels. "There. That should keep him alive. Someone will find him eventually. Now, if you don't mind, I'd rather not be caught."

Winter continued to watch Perrin as though she couldn't believe what she'd done, and Simon took her by the arm and led her toward the Alpha's office. "You heard Ariana. He'll be fine," he said.

"Probably," said Ariana, and Winter let out a choking sound. "You really need to learn to control your dosage. Come on, the safe's back here."

They stepped through the doorway into the Alpha's office. The portraits on the wall stared down at Simon, and he couldn't shake the feeling that they were silently accusing him. "Where are the pieces?" he said, eager to get them and leave.

"Right in front of you, Simon." Ariana strode behind the Alpha's desk, where the picture of Simon's father hung, and began tugging on the frame. "Just have to find the—there!"

The portrait swung open, revealing a safe. Simon inspected the dial, and the bubble of excitement in his chest deflated. "Don't suppose you have the combination, too?" he said.

"No, but I'm sure we can figure it out," she said. "I'll shift back into a spider, and when the lock clicks, I'll be able to hear it, and—"

"Move over." Winter stepped between Ariana and the safe, and she began to spin the dial.

"What are you doing?" said Simon. "How do you know the combination?"

"The insect kingdom isn't the only one with spies," she said, pausing before she twirled the dial the other way. After one more switch in direction, Winter pulled the latch, and the safe opened effortlessly. "Take a look at this."

Inside was a black box roughly the size of a dictionary. Simon picked it up and set it on the desk. "Do you think it's . . . ?"

"Open it and find out," said Winter.

Simon fumbled with the gold clasp, his stomach doing somersaults. The case was lined with black velvet, and within it lay four triangular crystals. They sparkled in the low light, emitting a soft glow as if each contained an ember. Simon had never seen anything like them in his entire life.

"Are you sure we should give Orion all four pieces?" he said. "Won't it be better if we separate them?"

Winter shook her head. "Orion's going to give them back to the leaders of the other kingdoms, but we can't do that yet—not while they're still under the Alpha's thumb. She'll just steal them again. And if we leave her a piece, that's one more she won't have to track down. Besides," she added, "they're useless without the scepter, remember?"

A loud growl echoed from the atrium, and Simon's skin prickled. Ariana immediately shifted back into a spider, and Winter closed the safe as Simon snapped the box shut.

"How are we supposed to get out of here?" he said.

"This way," said Winter as she scrambled around to the Alpha's portrait. It swung open, revealing another hidden tunnel. It was dark, like the one in Nolan's room, but it was also wider.

"Where does it lead to?" whispered Simon.

"Near Turtle Pond. Come *on*."

Simon shook his head. "That's too far from the exit. We'll never make it before they discover we're gone."

"What other choice do we have?"

Simon hesitated. Another growl ripped through the air, this one from immediately outside the office door. His palms grew sweaty, and the box slipped in his grip. Even if they could make it to the exit on time, he couldn't leave Darryl.

"I'm staying here," he said. "They won't notice you're gone for a while, and you'll have time to get the pieces to Orion."

Winter stared at him. "I'm not leaving without you. The Alpha will eventually discover they're missing, and the moment she figures out it was us, she'll kill you."

"She won't kill me. I might be the Beast King, remember?"

"And if you aren't? If you're Orion's heir instead?"

Simon stooped down to give her a boost. "They'll have to figure it out first. Now *go*, before she finds us and I don't have a chance to get away, too."

"You have to," she said, finally allowing Simon to help her up. "Orion's already going to be angry when he finds out what I am. If he thinks I left you behind, too—"

"I'll be there," Simon promised, and he handed her the box. "Be careful."

"Same to you. Don't get killed, all right?"

"I'll try not to," he said, closing the portrait behind her.

It was just in time, too. The door to the office burst open. "Simon! What are you doing in here?"

The Alpha. Simon straightened, trying his best not to look guilty. "I—a bird got into the atrium, and he tried to attack me. My friend, she's a snake—she fought him off, and I went in here for safety."

The Alpha stepped forward slowly, glancing around. "I suppose that explains the unconscious man. Did he harm you?"

"I'm fine," said Simon quickly. "My friend, she went to get help."

"No need," she said, setting her hand on his shoulder possessively. "The packs are chasing the invaders out now, along with the older students and faculty—"

Before she could finish, Malcolm burst into the room, his shirt ripped to shreds. He had fresh scratches on his face and neck, and he gasped for air.

"Where is he?" said the Alpha coldly.

"I—" Malcolm faltered. "The flock knew exactly what they were doing. Several of the mammals are injured, and—"

"I don't care. Where is Nolan?"

Malcolm's entire body shuddered with rage. "The students saw several birds of prey take Nolan hostage. We've searched the entire school, but—" He swallowed hard. "He's gone."

20

DOGHOUSE

Nolan was gone.

The Alpha's nails dug so deeply into Simon's shoulder that he was sure she would leave marks behind, but he didn't care. Orion had rescued Nolan, which meant his mother and brother were safe now. His relief must have shown on his face, because Malcolm gave him a strange look. Simon quickly furrowed his brow, trying to look concerned instead, but it was too late.

"If Orion has my grandson, then what are you still doing here?" said the Alpha in a dangerous voice. "Track them down before they reach Sky Tower."

Malcolm tilted his head. "I'll take the pack. Where's Darryl? The more noses on the ground, the better chance we'll have."

"You've been doing well without him for twelve years. Do not allow his presence to rob you of your agency."

Malcolm turned to leave, his expression sour, but before he could exit the office, the Alpha spoke again. "And, Malcolm?"

"Yes?"

"If you do not find him, do not bother coming back."

Malcolm clenched his jaw and nodded once more, closing the door behind him. Simon tensed as the Alpha crossed the room and slowly slid the lock into place.

"Now tell me, Simon," she said. "How did the birds get into the Den?"

A hard, cold lump formed inside him. "I don't know."

"Of course you do. You're the one who sent for them," she said, and his heart pounded.

"I—"

She stepped forward, her hands folded in front of her. "I know why you're here, Simon. I know you're only trying to find your mother. And I can make that easy for you, or I can make it very, very difficult. It's entirely your choice."

Simon's mouth went dry. "I—I don't know how they got in," he said. "Maybe the birds know about the tunnels."

"Perhaps," she allowed. "But you are still the reason they came."

"I don't know anything about that," he said, the lie thick on his tongue.

She sighed. "Very well. We'll just have to do this the hard way, won't—"

The Alpha stopped, her eyes narrowing. Simon followed her gaze, and suddenly the room seemed to tilt.

His father's portrait, the one that hid the safe, was cracked open.

"What were you doing in here before I arrived?" she said, touching the gilded frame. The portrait clicked shut.

"I—nothing," he said. Winter must not have closed it all the way.

"Are you sure about that?" she said, pulling the portrait open once more. Her fingers touched the dial. "I will give you one more chance to tell me the truth, Simon."

The knot burned in his chest, and he tried to formulate an excuse—any excuse—but the words didn't come. "I—I—"

She twirled the dial expertly, popping open the safe. Silence hung in the air, and slowly the Alpha turned toward him, her face twisted with shock and fury. When she spoke, her voice trembled, as if she were barely able to hold herself together. "Where did you put the pieces, Simon?"

"I don't have them," he said.

"Then you know where they are, and you *will* tell me, or I will make sure you regret it for the rest of your very short—"

The Alpha stopped suddenly, and a strange look passed over her face. She tried to step toward Simon but stumbled. She peered down at her arm, where a black widow clung to the inside of her wrist.

"You—" She tried to bat the spider away. It jumped onto Simon's shirt instead, and she stumbled toward the sofa. "What . . . ?"

The Alpha collapsed onto the rug in front of the fireplace, and her eyes fell shut. Simon blinked. What had just happened?

The spider leaped off his shirt, and a second later, Ariana stood in front of him wearing a smug smile. "Winter had the right idea earlier," she said. "I gave the Alpha a dose of special venom I created last year. It won't kill her, but it'll knock her out long enough for us to get out of here. Now come on—she hit the panic button."

"The what?" said Simon. Ariana pointed to the underside of the desk, where a red button was embedded in the wood.

"Security's probably on their way here already," she said. "We have to go."

"We can escape through the portrait," said Simon, but she shook her head.

"They'll be waiting for us on the other side. We have to go out the only way they won't expect—through the Arsenal."

"But—the bridge isn't high enough. The sharks will stop us."

"Then I guess we'll just have to outrun them, won't we?" She opened the office door. "Are you coming or not?"

Simon hesitated, then bent down and removed the key

from around the Alpha's neck. "We have to make a stop in the zoo first."

"Are you crazy?" said Ariana. "We don't have time for that."

"I don't care," said Simon. "Even if Orion rescued my mom, I doubt he bothered with my uncle. You can go if you want. It's probably safer if you don't come."

She snorted. "As if I'd miss this. If we're caught . . ."

"We won't be, not if we hurry." He wasn't going to leave Darryl behind, not even if it meant going tooth to tooth with a shark to save him.

21

SHARK BAIT

Simon and Ariana crept out of the Alpha's residence and into the hallway. It was eerily empty, though Simon had the feeling that would change soon.

"This way," he said, moving toward the curtain of ivy that separated them from the mammal section. Ariana snorted.

"Are you suicidal? That's where the packs will be coming from. We have to go through here." She headed in the opposite direction, toward the door that led into the reptiles' section. Simon followed nervously.

"I don't think this is a good idea."

"This is the fastest way," she said, exasperated.

"Not if one of us steps on a venomous snake."

"Then just watch where—"

"Through here!" shouted a deep voice from behind the ivy. No time to worry about getting bit—Simon grabbed the handle and yanked open the door that led to the reptiles' section, pulling Ariana inside.

Heat like a roaring fire hit Simon hard. Sweat trickled down his back, and he wiped his forehead. Fine white sand shifted beneath his feet, and the walls shimmered blue, as if the sky itself were a mirage. He'd never been in a desert before, but if he had to imagine what it would be like, this was exactly it.

"Clingy much?" said Ariana, prying her hand from his grip. "Watch where you step."

He glanced down at his feet. A white-and-black snake slithered inches in front of him, and he blanched. "I'm not going into the insects' section."

"Why not?" she said, stepping over the snake. Simon followed in her footsteps exactly.

"Because I want to live long enough to see my mother again." A rattlesnake coiled in the middle of the path, shaking its rattle threateningly.

"You stepped in my drawing," he hissed, and Simon glanced down. His shoe was in the middle of an elaborate sand illustration of the Eiffel Tower.

"Oh. I'm sorry," he said, jumping to the side. "I didn't mean to. We're just cutting through."

"Come off it, Geoff," said Ariana. "You were just going to wipe it clean."

The rattlesnake hissed, but he slumped back down into his coil. "It was a good one, too."

"It was," agreed Simon hastily. "I'm sorry. I'll make it up to you later, Geoff."

The snake sighed, and Simon moved delicately past him. Halfway there.

"The spiders won't hurt you if you're with me," said Ariana. "And we don't kill people we like. Most of the time, anyway. Watch the coral snake."

Simon stopped, his foot hovering half an inch above the tail of a snake with a red, yellow, and black striped pattern. "Sorry."

"You're going to die, Simon Thorn," the coral snake hissed. "We can't help you out there."

"You aren't helping him in here, either," said Ariana. "So unless you plan on getting a little snappy and distracting the pack while we escape, stop being a jerk."

The coral snake hissed, and Simon angled himself between them. "She didn't mean it," he said, and Ariana snorted. "Well, okay, she did, but we really could use your help. If anyone tries to come after us, can you stop them? Don't—don't *kill* them," he added. "Just make sure they don't follow us."

The coral snake slithered around them, forming a circle in the sand. "What do I get in return?"

Simon racked his brain. What did reptiles like? "Books," he said. "I have a whole library at home. I'll bring you as many books as I can carry."

The coral snake seemed to consider this, and finally moved aside. "And charcoal," he said.

"S-Sure. I'll see what I can do." Taking Ariana's hand again, Simon gingerly crossed the rest of the expanse of sand until they reached the entrance to the insects' section.

"Trust me," she said. "We'll be fine."

She opened the door and dragged him out of the desert. The shadowy insects' section was even worse than Simon had imagined. He gulped and despite the muggy air, he shivered. A wall of cobwebs stood inches from the tip of his nose, so thick that all he could see was white.

"How am I supposed to get through this?" he said.

"Crawl, of course," said Ariana, and she knelt down. "Follow me."

She disappeared through a small opening underneath the webs. Simon flattened himself against the floor; there was just enough room for him to fit, though he had to drag himself along with his arms, and spiderwebs caught in his hair. He had the unnerving feeling that someone was watching him, but he kept his eyes on Ariana as she crawled through the maze of cobwebs. And it *was* a maze, Simon quickly realized. Each intersection offered two choices, and he didn't want to think about what would happen if someone chose the wrong one.

At last they emerged on the other side. Simon shuddered, while Ariana ran her fingers through her hair. "That wasn't so hard, was it?" she said.

Simon blanched. "Speak for yourself." He wasn't sure he would ever shake the feeling of a million imaginary insects crawling over him.

From there they broke through to the foyer of the Academy. Simon dashed down the hallway toward the entrance, nearly tripping on the thick rug. He pushed open the double doors that led to the bridge, and—

Nothing. The bridge was gone. In the distance, he could see the doorway to the Arsenal, but unless they wanted to go for a swim, there was no way to cross the moat.

Ariana skidded to a stop beside him. "Well. That's a problem."

Simon's mind raced. They couldn't chance the tunnels—Ariana was right. The pack would anticipate that and be waiting for them. But there had to be some other way across. "I think I might know someone who can help."

Simon headed back toward the school, but instead of returning to the insects' section, he turned right, toward the Aquarium.

"No way," said Ariana. "The reptiles like the mammals about as much as we do, but the fish are completely under the Alpha's thumb."

"Not all of them. Come on." He led her into the underwater tunnel. A shark floated above them, but if he noticed them, he didn't stop.

Ariana shrank down. "You know they can see us, right?" she said, and Simon was surprised to hear her voice shake.

"I know. Through here." He stopped in the middle of the hallway and crouched down. The trapdoor Malcolm had pointed out to him opened easily, and Simon slid through, climbing down the ladder.

"I don't like water," said Ariana as she followed him down into a concrete corridor.

"We don't have much of a choice, unless you want to sneak out through the tunnels on your own."

"Please," she said. "Like I'm letting you do this without me."

He led the way through the damp hallway. The yellow lights flickered, giving off an eerie glow, and finally they reached the barracks. Simon peeked around the corner. It was a long room full of metal bunk beds, and the only decoration was the glass ceiling that showed the Aquarium above them. The members of the underwater kingdom sat at tiny desks, with their heads down as they worked on their homework. All except for one.

Jam stretched out across his bed, book in hand as he happily ignored the furtive looks from the others. His bunk was only a few down from the door, and Simon tried to wave and catch his attention.

Nothing.

"Let me do it," whispered Ariana, and she shifted once more and crawled across the concrete floor. Simon lost sight of her when she reached the bunk bed, but a moment later, Jam jerked and dropped his book.

"What—" he started, but he blinked and then finally looked at the doorway.

Simon waved. Nearby, others glanced at him as well, and Jam pushed his glasses up his nose and stood.

"What are you doing down here?" said Jam as he hurried toward Simon. They stepped into the hallway, and Jam closed the door to the barracks. "If the captain catches you, you're chum."

"We need your help," said Simon. "The Academy's on lockdown."

"I know. The captain wanted me to do extra training, since the general's unhappy with my . . ." Jam stopped, shuffling his feet. "But I said I had homework."

"I didn't know the Lord of the Rings was on the syllabus," said Ariana, suddenly appearing in human form beside Jam. He turned nearly as pink as her hair.

"It doesn't matter," said Simon. "Jam—do you think you can get us to the other side of the moat without being seen?"

"You want to sneak out?" he said, and Simon nodded. "Why?"

"I'll explain everything if you help us. If you don't—"

"If you don't, the Alpha is probably going to kill Simon," said Ariana casually. "We stole the pieces of the Predator."

"You did *what?*" said Jam.

"*And* he and Nolan are the Beast King's heirs. Surprise."

Jam stared at him, agog, and it took a couple of hasty

minutes for Simon to explain the whole story. "And Ariana's right," he added. "When we shift and figure out which of us is the Beast King's heir, the Alpha's going to use the Predator to kill whoever it is and absorb their power. I can't let that happen."

Jam opened and shut his mouth several times. "I—of course I'll help, but—how?"

"We need to get to the other side of the moat," said Simon.

Jam blinked owlishly and pushed his glasses up his nose. "Can you swim?"

Simon nodded, but Ariana made a face. "No way am I getting in the water," she said. "I'll meet you both on the other side of the bridge."

"You're sure you can sneak past the pack?" said Simon.

"You do remember who you're talking to, don't you?" she said. "I'll see you in ten minutes. Don't be late."

She disappeared down the hallway, and Simon turned back to Jam. "Listen, I know it's dangerous. You really don't have to do this."

"I want to. You're the first friend I've had in this place. I'm not going to let the Alpha hurt you," said Jam, and despite everything, Simon decided that if this was what having real friends felt like, he almost didn't want to leave. Almost.

Jam led him to a small chamber at the end of the hall-way. The glass ceiling exposed the moat, and a school of piranhas swam right over their heads. Simon tried not to think too hard about what else was in there.

"How are we supposed to do this?" said Simon. "I can't shift yet."

"They won't hurt you if you're with me. Probably, anyway. Here, put these on." Jam offered him a face mask and a swim cap from a hook on the wall. "This way, they won't recognize you."

Simon had his doubts, especially since they might already have seen him in the tunnel, but he pulled on the equipment. Once he finished, Jam stepped back to inspect him.

"Excellent. Up here." He climbed a ladder and pointed to a hatch. It led to a compartment at the very bottom of the moat. "It's full of air right now. Once we're inside, it'll fill with water, and the other side will open so we can swim out. Come on."

He crawled into the glass chamber and Simon followed, squeezing in beside him. The same school of piranhas swam by again, and Simon's hands grew clammy.

"Take a deep breath," said Jam. "Hope you can hold it for a while."

Simon inhaled as much air as he could, and Jam hit a button on the side. A buzzer went off, and another panel in the hatch opened up into the moat. Jam shifted into his dolphin form, and cold water rushed in around them until they were completely submerged.

"Grab on," he said, his squeaky voice muffled by the water. Grasping the slippery gray fin, Simon held on for dear life as the dolphin began to swim.

Seaweed brushed up against his legs, and the other fish all gave him curious looks, but it seemed that Jam was right; none of them questioned what Simon was doing in the water. It was almost peaceful down here, and for a moment, Simon wished he really was the Beast King, if only so he could stay down there longer.

But he was still human, and it didn't take long before his lungs started to burn from the lack of oxygen. He squeezed Jam's fin. "Almost there," the dolphin promised. "Just a few more meters and—"

"Soldier!" A roar ripped through the water, and a great white shark swam up to them: the captain. "What are you doing with that civilian?"

"Training exercise, sir," said Jam without missing a beat. "Civilian rescue, sir. Malcolm authorized it this morning, sir."

The captain considered them as he showed off rows and rows of razor-sharp teeth. "Did you fill out the paperwork?"

"On my desk, sir. I made copies for you, Malcolm, and my personal records, sir."

Simon grew dizzy. He wouldn't be able to hold his breath much longer. His chest ached, and he considered swimming up to the surface himself. He might be seen, but it would be better than drowning in the moat. He squeezed Jam's fin again.

"The civilian needs air, sir. He isn't used to holding his breath, sir."

"Go ahead, soldier," said the captain. "If I don't see the paperwork before dinnertime, you'll be doing laps for weeks."

"Noted, sir." Jam launched himself through the water, and just when Simon thought he might gulp in a lungful of water, they broke the surface. "There," he said proudly. "Told you we'd make it."

Simon took a great gasping breath and coughed. "Thanks. Remind me never to do that again."

"You did great," said Jam. "Do you think he bought it?"

"I think so. We'll see if any piranhas try to eat me."

"We keep them well fed." Jam swam them over to the entrance to the Arsenal. Simon tried to pull himself up, but his palms slipped, and he couldn't get a grip.

"Gotcha." A hand shot out and wrapped around his wrist. Ariana. "Took you long enough."

"Jam decided to have a chat with the captain," said Simon.

With Ariana's help, he climbed onto the ledge and yanked off the cap and mask. His clothes were sopping wet, but there wasn't anything he could do about it. However, when Jam rolled himself up onto the platform and shifted back, his clothes were perfectly dry.

"How do you do that?" said Simon, and Jam shrugged.

"It's part of whatever makes us able to shift in the first place, I guess."

A muffled howl cut through the air, and Ariana made a

face. "We need to get out of here before the pack finds us. Think you can make it?"

"I'm all right," said Simon, and he stood. "You shouldn't come with me."

"I already told you, you're not getting rid of me that easily," she said.

"Or me," said Jam, readjusting his glasses. "Someone has to watch your back. The more of us there are, the better our chances."

"He has a point," said Ariana. "You won't be able to get to Sky Tower without us."

Simon hesitated. "If the Alpha finds out—"

"She already knows I bit her," she said. "Can't get much worse than that. We'll be fine."

Together the three of them headed into the Arsenal and up the narrow staircase. Simon expected a wolf to burst through the door at any moment, but they made it to the foyer without any problems. A few tourists taking pictures gave them strange looks, but Simon dashed past them and out the front door, with Ariana and Jam following close behind.

"Sky Tower's only a few blocks away," said Jam. "That's where we're going, right?"

"Not yet," said Simon, and instead of heading out into the city, he turned back toward the zoo entrance. "The Alpha has my uncle, and I have to set him free first."

"It isn't safe in the zoo anymore," said Ariana. "Not for you, anyway. If you let me do it—"

"It won't take long, and I don't want you to get caught," said Simon, slowing when they reached the gate. A zoo worker stood taking tickets, and Simon glanced around. Nearby, a large group of tourists ambled toward the entrance, and he gestured for Ariana and Jam to follow him.

"This is a really stupid idea," muttered Ariana as they joined the tourists, who were too distracted by snapping pictures to notice the three of them. "The pack is going to be stationed at every tunnel exit."

"Then we'll just have to avoid them." Keeping to the middle of the crowd, Simon held his breath as the zoo worker tore the tickets and gestured for the group to go through, and then—

They were on the other side of the gate. "Come on," he said, breaking off from the tourists. Jam and Ariana followed, and within minutes, they were inside the sweltering rain forest building, running toward the unguarded door. Simon fumbled with the Alpha's key, relieved when it opened the lock. "Make sure no one comes in," he said before slipping inside.

The first thing he saw was his mother's empty cage. Orion had managed to rescue her after all. Part of Simon hoped he had done the same for his uncle, but when he looked into the second cage, all the air left his lungs.

The hulking wolf lay inside, his sides heaving and his gray fur matted with blood. Scratch marks lined his belly, and the feathers that clung to him made it obvious what had happened. Whoever had rescued Simon's mother had tried to kill his uncle.

"Is he . . . ?" said Jam, his eyes wide.

"He's breathing." Simon quickly unlocked the cage and opened it. "Darryl—are you awake? Can you hear me?"

The wolf opened an eye. "Simon? What are you doing here?"

"We're getting you out of here," he said, and he moved aside so Darryl could climb out of the cage. He did so slowly, wincing with every move he made, and Simon felt like he was going to be sick. He knew the war between the birds and the mammals was bad, but Darryl had been imprisoned—he couldn't have done anything to them even if he'd wanted to.

As soon as Darryl was free, he shifted back into a human and staggered against the wall. Simon helped him to the concrete ground, panicked. His uncle couldn't possibly walk out of the zoo like this, not without attracting too much attention.

"I don't know what to do," said Simon, his voice hitching. "Nolan and Mom are safe with Orion, but—but the birds attacked you, and—"

"We have to leave, before the pack finds us," said Darryl, his breathing labored. His face was scratched up, and the scar that ran down his cheek was a ghostly white. "You're not safe at Sky Tower."

"I'm safer there than I am here," said Simon. But his uncle wasn't. "We can't just leave Mom and Nolan behind."

"We have to," said Darryl. "You don't understand—"

"Simon!" cried Ariana. A snarl echoed from behind them, and with a start, Simon twisted around. Another gray wolf stood in the doorway, blocking their only exit.

Malcolm.

22

SMUG BUG

The wolf growled, and Simon instinctively stepped in front of his uncle. Malcolm was supposed to be their ally, but the fury in his eyes and the rage in his snarl made Simon question whether he'd ever been on their side.

"Don't eat us," begged Jam, holding his hands in front of his face. "I'm all stringy and probably taste like fish. Unless you like fish. Then I probably taste like—like mercury. And seaweed. Definitely seaweed."

"Don't be an idiot, Fluke. I'm not going to eat you." Much to Simon's relief, Malcolm shifted back into a human, and he immediately crossed the room and knelt beside them. "What did Mother do to you?" he said, his hands hovering over Darryl's chest.

"Wasn't Mother this time, shockingly," said Darryl with a rough laugh. "Orion holds a grudge, it seems."

Malcolm grunted. "We can't stay here. Do you think you can move?"

Simon helped Malcolm hoist Darryl to his feet, and his uncle leaned heavily on Malcolm as they trudged back into the hallway. "Where are we supposed to go?" said Simon.

"Anywhere but here," said Darryl. "Or Sky Tower."

"There's a safe house upstate," said Malcolm. "Mother won't think to look for you there, and I'll convince her you're with Orion instead."

"You won't come with us?" said Darryl.

Malcolm grimaced.

"Not while Orion still has Nolan."

They reached the exit and burst out into the daylight, where the breeze immediately cooled Simon off. "We can't leave them," he said. "Mom and Nolan—even if they're safe with Orion, we can't just abandon them like that."

Darryl let out a humorless laugh. He was walking on his own now, though he limped heavily and favored his right side. "The only place any of you are safe is as far from the city as you can get. Nolan and your mother—"

"Malcolm."

Vanessa stepped out from the crowd and blocked his way. Behind her, another half-dozen human members of the pack appeared, forming a semicircle around them. Tourists and families stepped around them easily, not seeming to notice the intrusion, but Simon stopped cold.

"Vanessa," said Malcolm, and Simon could feel his towering presence directly behind him. "I have this handled."

"I'm under direct orders from the Alpha to bring the boy in," she said. Simon gulped. So the Alpha must be awake. "She also added that, unfortunate as it may be, your judgment could be compromised."

Malcolm growled, and the other members of the pack began to flex their muscles. Simon's pulse raced, and he glanced at Darryl. No doubt his uncles could take Vanessa and the others when they were both whole and healthy, but Darryl was too injured to get into a skirmish and win.

"I am telling you, I will escort him back to the Den," said Malcolm, a warning in his voice.

"You are not my Alpha," said Vanessa, reaching for Simon. "I have to obey—"

A thunderous cry ripped through the square, and Darryl pounced, tackling Vanessa. The other members of the pack jumped into the fight, and several people around them screamed.

"Go!" yelled Malcolm, shoving Simon away from the brawl. "We've got this."

"But—" Simon began. His uncle could barely stand on his own.

"We'll find you," promised Malcolm. "Just go."

Ariana grabbed Simon's hand and took off, and he had no choice but to follow. With Jam close behind, they darted down the stone pathway and through the exit.

Only after they had crossed Fifth Avenue did they finally slow to catch their breath.

"Where's Sky Tower?" said Jam, craning his neck.

"Stop that. You look like a tourist," said Ariana.

"It's the tall building there with the glass dome at the top," said Simon.

"Oh." Jam paled. "That's really high."

"Don't tell me you're afraid of heights," said Ariana, grinning.

"You're the one who refused to get into the water," countered Simon. Her smile faded, and they walked half a block in silence.

"Are you sure you want to go there?" she said at last. "You saw what Orion's birds did to your uncle."

Simon raked his hair from his face, keeping his eyes open as they approached the entrance to Sky Tower. He couldn't pretend to forgive the flock's attack against Darryl, but logic overrode his unease. The birds and the mammals had been at war for as long as Simon had been alive, and his uncle *had* taken Orion's eye.

"The Alpha's the one who wants to kill us, not Orion," he said firmly. "He thinks Darryl was helping her. Once I tell him what really happened, he'll understand."

"Even if he does, Orion won't let you leave, you know," she said.

"Where would I go? Out here, the Alpha's after us. In there, my family can be together." And more than anything, that was all Simon wanted. "If you're scared, you don't have to do this, you know."

"I'm not scared," said Ariana, sounding offended by the very idea.

"And I'm not leaving, either," said Jam, though his voice trembled ever so slightly.

Simon tried to flash them a grateful smile, but it felt more like a grimace. "Then when we get inside, let me do the talking."

He pushed open the glass door. The lobby was eerily dark and cold. "Hello?" he called. Something wasn't right. Orion would never let security lapse like this.

A figure stooped behind the desk. Simon moved closer. A security guard was slumped in his chair, and dark liquid dripped from his neck.

Simon recoiled and whirled around. "The guard, he's—"

He froze. Near the doorway, two members of the pack had seized Jam and Ariana, hands clamped over their mouths.

"Dead?" supplied a man with a wicked grin. Ariana's eyes were wide with panic, and Jam's glasses dangled precariously from one ear.

Fear pulsed through Simon, turning his insides to ice. "Let them go."

"I'm afraid we can't do that," said a low female voice. Out of the shadows stepped a wolf, her teeth bared, and Simon knew instantly who she was.

The Alpha.

23

ENEMY TERRITORY

The Alpha approached slowly, her claws clicking on the marble floor. Simon's chest tightened. One slash of her paw, and it would all be over.

"Where are the pieces?" rumbled the wolf. She was smaller and her fur was darker than the others', but she radiated ferocity and danger.

"I don't have them," said Simon. "Let my friends go."

She snarled and leaped into the air, landing hard on Simon's shoulders and sending him crashing to the floor. "Give them to me, or I swear I'll—"

A roar echoed through the lobby, and a pair of enormous wolves tackled the Alpha, heaving her off Simon. They tangled in a blur of fur and teeth, and Simon pulled himself to his feet. Darryl and Malcolm.

"Run!" shouted Ariana. She elbowed her assailant in the abdomen and twisted out of his grip.

Simon hesitated. Jam wrestled with the other man, and though he was several inches shorter, somehow Jam was holding his own. No, more than holding his own—Jam had his attacker's arm wrenched to an unnatural angle. "I'm sorry, if you'd just let me go, I wouldn't have to—" Jam caught Simon's eye. "What are you waiting for? Get out of here!"

Simon dashed across the lobby and hit the elevator button. The doors opened. The elevator guard was gone, but a bloody keycard lay on the floor.

"Wait for me!" squeaked Felix, darting across the lobby of Sky Tower, zigzagging between the wolves, and diving into the elevator at the last second.

"Felix! What are you *doing* here?" said Simon, scooping him up.

"You're the one who left the Den without me," he accused. "What else was I supposed to do?"

"I'm sorry," said Simon, guilt pooling in the pit of his stomach. How had he forgotten Felix?

The little mouse sniffed. "Let me watch television again, and I'll consider forgiving you."

"Yeah, all right," said Simon. "Now that Darryl knows about you, there's no reason to hide."

Satisfied, Felix sat back on his haunches. "Good. Now, what's the plan?"

"The plan is for *you* to stay safe," said Simon. "Besides, I thought you didn't like birds."

Felix shivered. "I don't, but that doesn't mean I'm going to let you waltz up there on your own, either. Orion won't let you leave again."

"It doesn't matter," he said. "All of us—Orion, Mom, Nolan, Darryl, Malcolm, me—now we can go someplace safe where the Alpha will never find us."

"You're forgetting that Orion and Darryl hate each other," said Felix, and Simon hesitated.

"I know." But they both wanted to protect him and Nolan. Surely that counted for something.

At last the elevator opened, and Simon stepped out into the forest that was Orion's penthouse as Felix scampered off to hide. Above him, birds chirped in human voices, their murmurs discontent, and Simon spotted Orion's silhouette in the tree house far above him.

"Simon!" His mother's voice echoed throughout the atrium, and he tensed.

"Mom? Mom!" He sprinted toward the spiral staircase. "Where are you?"

"You need to run!" she called, but he didn't understand. Run from what?

"Ah, Simon. There you are." His grandfather peered through the leaves. "Come join us."

Simon quickly ascended the staircase that led to the upper level. Orion leaned against the railing, an oddly triumphant smile on his face, while Winter sat in an armchair nearby, staring resolutely out the window.

His mother was nowhere to be seen.

"Please, Simon—go," she begged, and he looked down. On a thick branch hidden halfway between the tree house and the lower level of the atrium hung a cage, and inside was a golden eagle. His mother.

Cold horror crashed through him, and he looked back and forth between the cage and Orion. "She shouldn't be locked up. She hasn't done anything wrong," he said, slowly taking a step back toward the staircase. A pair of falcons fluttered down and shifted back into humans, blocking his way.

"Unfortunately, we seem to have a difference of opinion on that," said Orion. "Search him for anything the Alpha may have planted on him."

The guards' rough hands patted Simon down and dug through his pockets. He fought against their grip, but they were too strong. The first guard fished the pocket watch out of Simon's sweatshirt, and when he handed it to Orion, Simon felt a keen wrench in his gut.

"That's mine," he said hotly.

"Is it?" said Orion as he examined the back. "The symbol of the Beast King. How curious that something this valuable fell into your possession. Where did you get it?"

"I found it in the Den," he lied, certain that telling Orion the truth—that his mother had given it to him—would only make it more valuable.

"I see." Orion clipped the chain of the watch to his lapel as the guards backed off, satisfied that Simon wasn't armed.

"How did you escape on your own? I was about to send the flock back to the Den to rescue you."

Simon looked at the caged golden eagle. He wasn't so sure he wanted Orion's help, not anymore. "I ran. The Alpha's downstairs, along with half the pack," he said, fuming. "If we don't leave now—"

"I'm aware," said Orion, "and I very much hope she makes it up here. Because when she does, I will have a surprise waiting for her."

Something on the desk glinted, and Simon's mouth fell open. The pieces of the Predator. He'd put them together, forming the shape of a five-pointed star. "You—you're going to kill her?" he said.

"It's the only way to ensure peace," said Orion, following Simon's gaze and picking it up. "Absorbing the ability to shift into the Alpha wolf will allow me to seize control of the mammal kingdom and right her wrongs."

"But—the pieces are useless on their own," said Simon.

"Indeed," he said. "Which is why I asked my dear Winter to retrieve the scepter from the library and leave it in the cave, where my lieutenants were able to fetch it."

At first Simon wasn't sure he'd heard Orion right. But Winter refused to meet his eyes, and when his grandfather revealed the familiar silver staff on the desk behind him, he knew there had been no mistake.

"This—this was all a setup?" said Simon, and he turned to Winter. Betrayal unlike any he'd ever felt wrapped around his insides, and for a second, he couldn't breathe. "Going to the L.A.I.R. never had anything to do with finding my mother, did it? All you wanted was the stupid Predator."

"You are the one who decided to rescue your mother," said Orion gently. "I tried to keep you safe, knowing the Alpha was after you, but you made that quite difficult, venturing into the Den as you did. Once you were inside, there was little my kingdom could do to help you. I have feared for your safety every hour, every minute, every second since you ran away from Sky Tower. However, with Unity Day approaching and the Alpha so close to assembling the weapon, we could not waste such a golden opportunity to stop her. Winter was able to communicate with the flock and update us on your status, and in return, I gave her the information she needed to retrieve the stolen pieces of the Predator and ensure our future." He smiled kindly, his good eye crinkling. "Don't you see, Simon? You two have saved us. The Alpha will never be able to use the Predator against you or our family now."

Simon knew he should have been relieved, but fear and anger boiled inside him, and the knot in his chest burned unbearably. "You swore no one would have the whole weapon," he said through gritted teeth, glaring at Winter. "You lied to me."

"I'm sorry," she said, her voice breaking. "I had to. Stealing the Predator is the only chance we have at stopping the Alpha. The pack killed my father, and if we don't fight back, if we don't find a way to win, they're going to kill us, too. They'll kill every Animalgam in the bird kingdom until there's no one left to fight them."

"Then what are you so worried about?" he blurted. "Seeing as how you're a snake."

Everything went silent. Even the birds in the trees stopped their murmuring, and the blood drained from Winter's face.

"That's—he's lying," she said, and she looked at Orion desperately. "I haven't shifted. You *know* I haven't."

"She turned into a cottonmouth and bit Perrin when he tried to rescue me," said Simon, fury clawing at him from the inside out. "She's been able to shift for months."

"Is that true?" said Orion quietly. Winter's eyes shone with unshed tears, and she gulped.

"Please—"

"*Is it true?*"

At last, wiping her cheeks, she whispered, "I'm sorry."

Orion took a deep breath, releasing it slowly. "I will deal with you later," he said. "For now, you are dismissed."

Winter stood and stumbled toward the staircase, her eyes red and her lower lip trembling. She shot Simon a venomous look, and even if she'd deserved this for betraying him, he couldn't help but feel guilty.

"There," said Orion once she was gone. "None of the other kingdoms can be trusted, not in this delicate time. Once the Alpha is dead and I control the mammals, perhaps then we can re-form the bonds of trust we all once shared, but until then—"

"Enough with the lies," said Simon's mother, her voice tight with anger. "Killing the Alpha for *peace* may be the first step in your plan, but you're really no better than her. You want to become the Beast King. You want to kill my sons."

Orion frowned, the lines in his face deepening, and he toyed with the star in his hands. "I have no desire to become the Beast King if there are other ways to ensure peace, my dear. And I'm certainly not fond of the idea of killing my own kin. I will not allow any harm to come to whichever boy is my heir. But I am bound to protect the Animalgam kingdoms whatever way I can. Ending the Beast King's line before it can rise up again is, of course, the best option, and I would have succeeded last time if you hadn't given Luke heirs."

"Last time?" His mother said nothing for a long moment, and suddenly she gasped. "It was *you?*"

Simon blinked, confused, and Orion grimaced. "As long as the line continued, our world would always be in danger. I did what had to be done."

In the cage, his mother was breathing rapidly, and even from a distance, Simon could see her tremble. "I knew it was someone from our kingdom, but—he trusted you. He confided in you. He was trying to help you negotiate peace for our world, and you turned around and *murdered* him?"

Nausea washed over Simon, and as the pieces clicked into

place, he was sure he had misunderstood. "Wait. You—you killed my father?"

"A necessity I deeply regret," said Orion. "He was a good man, but as I said, I am bound to protect those who are unable to protect themselves. He had the power to destroy us all—"

"Luke never would've hurt anyone," said his mother, and Simon opened his mouth to agree, but nothing came out. All this time, he'd trusted his grandfather, too. He'd put his life—and his mother's life—in the hands of the man who had killed his father.

"He was under the Alpha's thumb, and you know as well as I do that she was already beginning to gather the pieces," said Orion. "It is not the Predator we must fear, but the one who wields it. If there was a chance the Alpha could use it against us . . . my hands were tied."

"We were trying to find the pieces before she could," said his mother. "If you had only helped us, we could have assembled it and destroyed it completely before she could—"

"My lord!" cried a hawk, landing on a branch nearby. "The pack has taken the bait. They should be arriving in the stairwell momentarily."

"Finally." Orion straightened, and his hands trembled as he slipped the Heart of the Predator onto the scepter, pushing it into place with a sharp *click*. "Let her come."

Simon backed away until he hit the railing, his pulse pounding in his ears. He had to get the weapon before Orion could use it to absorb the Alpha's powers and seize control of the kingdoms. Simon knew that without a doubt, no matter how many alternatives there were, one day Orion would kill either him or Nolan—whichever twin was the Beast King's heir. For his own power, or to stop the Beast King's line from rising again—it didn't matter. One of them would still be dead.

"Take him downstairs to join his brother," said Orion to the guards behind Simon. "Protect them at all costs."

They reached for him, but Simon darted out of the way and kicked the nearest guard in the shin. Startled, the guard stumbled backward down the spiral steps, plowing into his partner and sending them both tumbling down head over heel.

"Simon!" shouted a small voice, and he looked around. Felix crouched beside Orion, and before his grandfather realized he was there, Felix bit him on the ankle.

Orion cried out, doubling over as his grip on the weapon slipped. Simon dashed forward and snatched the scepter, prying it from his grandfather's gnarled fingers and dancing back out of his reach. Now that it was assembled, he could destroy it, and there was only one way he could think of to make sure it wound up in so many pieces that Orion would never have the chance to use it.

Simon spotted the opening at the top of the atrium. If he could only get up there—

A hair-raising screech echoed through the trees. Orion

had shifted, and he flew after Simon, catching up in seconds. His talons scratched Simon's neck and shoulders, and he shoved the bird away, using all his might to tear a handful of feathers from Orion's wing. The eagle screamed and disappeared into the tree.

Dozens of birds exploded from the branches and began to descend on Simon, but Orion called out, "Do not harm him! He is trapped—there is nowhere for him to go. I will handle this."

As they flew back into the trees, Simon looked around, searching desperately for a way to get up to the roof. But there was no ladder. There was no staircase. The only way up was—

He gritted his teeth. Climbing onto the railing, he balanced precariously on the edge and tucked the Predator into his belt. Here went nothing.

"Simon—no!" cried his mother, but it was too late. He leaped across the open air, barely managing to grab on to one of the few branches thick enough to hold his weight. Pain shot through his arms, and he struggled as he pulled himself up. At last he made it, and he scurried toward the trunk and began the shaky climb to the highest branches, where he would be able to reach the opening in the roof.

"Simon—come back down," called Orion. "If you fall . . ."

Simon continued climbing. Twice he nearly lost his grip and plummeted, but he held on, his entire body straining.

At last he reached the edge of the atrium. The branches

at this height were too thin to hold his weight much longer, and he looked around. The wind whistled through the open panel only a few feet away, and Simon took a deep breath. Now or never.

He pushed off from the tree and leaped toward the opening. The weak branch snapped below his feet and tumbled to the ground, and for one horrible moment Simon was sure he would fall, too. In the atrium below, he heard a chorus of shouts, but there was nothing anyone could do. He was on his own. He slammed into the wall, only just catching the edge of the window. The glass cut his palms, but using all his strength, he pulled himself into the open air.

Every muscle in Simon's body trembled as he slid across the glass. The roof was flat except for the dome that surrounded the highest branches, but as he moved closer to the edge, he noticed there was no railing. Only the wind stood between him and a forty-story fall.

The skyline spun around him, and he walked unsteadily toward the edge. All he had to do was drop the Predator. There was no way it would survive intact, and no one would be able to use it ever again.

"I wouldn't do that if I were you, my boy."

Orion appeared on the roof, once again in human form. His sleeve was ragged and his arm bled from where Simon had ripped out his feathers, but he didn't seem to care. With his hand outstretched, he inched toward Simon, his good eye turned toward him.

"Think about what you're doing. If you destroy it, I will have no way of protecting you against the Alpha and the other kingdoms. As soon as they discover that the Beast King's line still exists, they *will* kill you. Or your brother."

"And so will you," said Simon, his voice shaking.

Orion shuffled closer. "If that's what you're afraid of, then I promise the only person who must die is the Alpha. I will keep you and your brother safe. I swear on all I am that we will figure it out together. As a family."

Simon inched toward the edge. He had nowhere to go but down. "Family doesn't threaten to kill each other. Even if I trusted you, no one should have this kind of power. Not you, not the Alpha, no—"

A howl rang through the atrium, and he glanced at the open window. The pack was here. Simon was running out of time.

He was about to let go of the scepter when Orion charged forward. Simon tried to sidestep him, and it took every muscle in his body to stop before he stumbled over the edge. Orion shifted into an eagle before he could fall, and he snatched the weapon from Simon's hand.

"Hey!" said Simon. Running against the icy wind, he darted into Orion's blind spot and threw all of his weight against the golden eagle, tackling him to the roof. They skidded across the glass together, and Simon made a wild grab for the scepter.

"No!" cried Orion. His talons dug into Simon's skin, but

it was too late. Simon's fingers closed around the scepter, and he wrenched his arm from Orion's grasp.

Scrambling to his feet, Simon raced for the edge. Behind him, Orion screamed, but Simon was deaf to his shouts. Just a few more steps, and—

Something slammed into Simon, knocking him down. He kept his hold on the Predator, but his body went sliding across the glass, skidding closer and closer to that forty-story drop. Simon clawed at the roof, but nothing he did slowed him down. He was going to fall.

Just as the roof disappeared out from under him, someone grabbed his arm. For a split second, Simon dared to hope it was one of the wolves. Darryl, Malcolm, even Vanessa— he didn't care, as long as he wasn't alone.

Instead, Orion knelt on the edge of the roof, his nails digging into Simon's wrist.

"The Predator," he gasped. "Give it to me."

Simon dangled off the edge, his sneakers squeaking against the glass panes as he struggled to find purchase. But there were no ledges that would hold him. If Orion let go, Simon would fall.

He couldn't think. He couldn't feel anything but the biting wind, Orion clutching his arm, and the five-pointed star cutting into his palm. He made the mistake of looking down, and his head spun.

"Give it to me!" yelled Orion. "If you don't, we will all die."

Simon's mind went blank, and he couldn't move. He was dangling off the edge of a building, and he couldn't even open his mouth to speak.

"Orion!" a voice boomed over the howling wind. *Darryl.* "Let him go."

"I'm afraid you don't want me to do that right now," he wheezed.

"He could be your heir," said Darryl. "If you kill him, you could kill the end of your line."

"He is not," said Orion with startling certainty. "Isabel knows he isn't—she knows he is the firstborn. That is why she hid him. That is why she told no one of his existence. That is why she gave him the Beast King's pocket watch. She knows, and now so do I."

"And if you're wrong?" said Darryl.

Orion coughed, and his hand began to slip. "There is no use pretending any longer. You have protected him all this time because you know he is the Beast King's heir. As soon as he shifted, you were going to turn him over to the Alpha so she could gain his powers."

Darryl limped into Simon's view, and for a split second, Simon wondered why he wasn't a wolf. But on the glass roof, his claws would only make him more vulnerable. It didn't matter how well his uncle could fight. This far above the ground, he would lose.

"I've protected him because he's my family," said Darryl. "I don't care what he shifts into. He's the most important person in the world to me. And if you drop him off this roof, I will spend the rest of my life making sure yours is as painful as possible."

"I don't want to—kill him." Orion clenched his teeth. His arm trembled, and Simon could feel his grip weakening. "That achieves nothing. All he has to do—is give me the scepter."

Simon's eyes locked onto Darryl's. "I can't," he managed. "He's going to kill me anyway, and if he's wrong, he'll kill Nolan, and he'll kill Mom, and he'll kill you. He'll kill everyone."

"I won't let that happen," said Darryl. "You've done everything you can, but sometimes you have to lose the battle in order to win the war. Whatever happens—you and I will fight it together, and everything will be all right. But if you drop the weapon and he lets go . . ." His voice hitched. "Please, Simon. Nothing is worth losing you."

The knot in his chest ached, and Simon could barely breathe. At last, without taking his eyes off his uncle, he slid the scepter onto the glass roof.

"Thank you, my boy," said Orion. "You've made the right decision, and now I must once again do what is best for my kingdom. I do hope you know it isn't personal."

And with that, he let Simon go.

MURDER OF CROWS

Simon opened his mouth to scream, but nothing came out.

He was falling. The cold wind rushed around him, and the world blurred.

He couldn't breathe. He couldn't think.

It wouldn't matter soon enough, but Simon didn't want it to end like this. Not without saying good-bye to his mother. Not without telling Darryl how sorry he was and how much his uncle meant to him.

The hot knot in his chest burst, and an aching cry escaped from deep within him. He could already feel his limbs twisting, shattering the way they would on impact. His insides clenched, his voice caught in his throat, and he spread his arms—

He was flying.

The wind seemed to rise beneath him, lifting him into the air. He wasn't falling anymore. Instead he glided through the sky above Manhattan.

How? He gave his arms an experimental flap. They weren't arms anymore though. They were wings. And his screams—they were the screeches of an eagle.

He whooped and flapped his wings again. He'd done it. He'd really shifted. He was a living, breathing eagle now, soaring through the air at an impossible speed.

But Simon's exhilaration was quickly dashed by blind panic. He didn't know how to fly, and now he was careening out of control through New York. He might have saved himself from becoming nothing more than goo on concrete, but now there was nothing stopping him from running headlong into a building.

"Flap!" called a voice. "Flap!"

"What?" yelled Simon. A pigeon appeared beside him.

"Flap!" insisted the pigeon again, demonstrating with its own wings. Simon tried to mimic it, and he rose even farther into the air. "Flap!"

"I'm flapping!" he said. "How do I turn?"

"Flap!" The pigeon demonstrated, and with Simon's keen eagle eyesight, he immediately spotted the shift in the pigeon's feathers before it disappeared down another street. Instinctively he followed.

Soon enough Simon could navigate nearly as well as the

pigeon, provided he didn't think about it too hard. That was when he got disoriented and his human mind tried to take over. For now, he let the eagle part of his brain figure it out.

"Thanks!" he called to his new friend. "I owe you one." At the pigeon's confused look, he added, "Food."

"Food?" said the pigeon immediately, and Simon laughed.

"Later," he promised, and he soared through the air, back to Sky Tower.

Even at a distance, he could see two figures fighting on the roof in the sunlight. A wolf snarled, and an eagle hovered out of reach. Relief flooded Simon. Darryl was holding his own.

As he grew closer, however, he spotted a strange cloud swarming the building. Birds, Simon realized. Hundreds of them. And they all went straight for his uncle.

"Darryl!" he yelled, hurtling toward the roof. The wolf snapped at the birds, fighting to break free, but there were too many of them. They pecked and scratched at his face, his throat, his paws, every part of him they could reach. Darryl stumbled, and Orion shifted back into a man, clutching the scepter.

"I was planning to test the Predator on your dear mother, but I suppose this will do," said Orion. "Give Luke and Simon my best."

Time seemed to slow. Seconds turned into minutes. And as Simon watched in horror, Orion lunged toward the wolf, sinking the razor-sharp points of the Heart of the Predator into Darryl's chest.

Simon screamed and dived straight toward them. In the moments before he reached the roof, the wolf curled in on himself, and Orion stared at the scepter, confused.

"Why isn't it working?" he said. "What have you and Isabel done?"

Darryl managed a wolfish grin despite the blood that began to mat his fur. "Can't always win, can you?"

Blinded by rage, Simon collided with Orion in a clash of feathers and talons, ripping at the old man with everything he had. In a split second, Orion shifted into an eagle, and they flew through the air, tangled together five hundred feet above the city.

"You survived," said Orion exultantly, his talons cutting into Simon's chest. "My heir. My prince."

"Let Darryl go," demanded Simon. "He never did anything to you."

The eagle laughed. "He took you, he took my daughter, and before that, he took my eye. He was never getting out of Sky Tower alive. Besides, it's too late. He's practically dead already."

Dizzy with fear, Simon tore himself away from Orion and turned back toward the roof. Nearly all the other birds were gone now. Darryl had shifted back into a human, and a pool of blood expanded beside his motionless body.

Everything went still. All Simon could see was his uncle, the man who had protected him for his entire life, who had given up his family, his pack, everything he'd loved to stay with Simon. Now he was dying, and it was all Simon's fault.

The knot in Simon's chest was gone now, replaced by unshakable fury. He screeched and dived back toward the golden eagle. A primal instinct seized him, the same one that had overcome him the day Bryan Barker had attacked him in the cafeteria, and only vengeance remained. Simon lashed out with his talons, slicing across Orion's face and grazing his one good eye.

Orion screamed. Clutching Simon's feathers, he shifted back to human form. "My eye!" he moaned. "What have you done?"

"Stop it!" cried Simon, struggling to get away. He wasn't sure how he did it, but one moment he was an eagle, and the next his limbs twisted back into a human's.

Orion clutched Simon's wrist. "You fool—you have no idea—" He suddenly gasped, panicked. "The scepter—where is the scepter?"

Simon scanned the roof, but he didn't see anything—only Darryl lying in a pool of his own blood, his chest expanding with his shallow breaths. "It isn't here."

Orion roared. "It must be! You have it—I know you have it, boy! Give it to me!" He tore at Simon, grabbing his shirt and stumbling closer and closer to the edge of the roof. "You don't understand—I must be the one to control it!"

They were inches from the drop now. Simon struggled to pull them backward, but his grandfather was too heavy. "I don't have it! I swear—"

"You'll kill us all!" cried Orion. "Every last one of us will die because of you."

A strong gust of wind hit them both, and Orion teetered. If he fell, he would take Simon with him. Simon might be able to fly, but if Orion kept holding on to him, blind as he was, he really would kill them both.

"Let go." Simon tried to spin them back toward the safety of the roof, but Orion held on. As the old man lost his balance, Simon twisted against his grip, pushing with all of his might.

Orion cried out, and at last he let go. Clawing at the air, he stumbled backward off the roof and fell into the empty sky.

"Orion!" Simon lunged to the edge, reaching for him, but it was too late. Orion plummeted toward the street below.

Horrified, Simon watched as his grandfather fell. Halfway down, Orion shifted into his battered eagle form and spread his massive wings. Simon didn't have time to be relieved though. Unable to see where he was going, Orion dived straight toward a brick building.

"Watch out!" yelled Simon, and a split second before he hit the wall, Orion pulled up and circled back to Sky Tower. Simon's heart hammered as the eagle flew at him, his talons outstretched.

No time to get away. He threw his arms protectively in front of his face and ducked. At the last second, Orion soared past him, close enough for Simon to see that his injured eye was open once more.

With a scream, Orion arched downward, and Simon thought he was going to crash into the roof. Instead, his talons caught something that glinted in the sunlight. *The scepter*. He had found the scepter.

"No!" shouted Simon, but the eagle disappeared into the bright blue sky. He squinted into the sun, but it was too late. Orion was gone.

A wet cough caught his attention. Simon crawled toward his uncle, his chest tight. "Darryl?" he said, hovering over him.

"Simon." His uncle's voice was little more than a whisper, and Simon had to lean in. "You're alive."

"We need to get you to a hospital," he said. "They can help you—"

"Too late for that." Darryl managed a small smile. "I have something for you."

He uncurled his hand. The pocket watch was nestled in his palm, slick with Darryl's blood. Simon took it with shaking fingers, his eyes watering.

"Simon, I need you to listen to me," said his uncle hoarsely. "Whatever happens, you can't go after Orion."

"But—he has the Predator," said Simon, pocketing the watch and pressing his hands against his uncle's chest to stop the bleeding. Even through his blurred vision, he could see that Darryl was right. It was too late. No one could lose this much blood and survive.

"Your mother—she didn't steal the pieces. She and the

rulers of the other kingdoms created copies. No one was sup
posed to know—not until you and Nolan were safe—but the
Alpha never had the real ones."

Darryl said this with a note of triumph, but to Simon, it
only meant that his uncle was dying for nothing. A wave
of guilt and grief crashed into him, and for a moment,
Simon couldn't breathe. "I'm sorry," he said, his voice breaking. "I should have stayed with you. I should've met you at
the ferry. I should never have gone to the zoo. I should've
waited—"

"You have nothing to be sorry for." Darryl touched
Simon's cheek with his cold hand. "You did it to save your
mother. I would have done the exact same thing if it meant
saving you." He coughed again, and blood splattered the
glass roof. "Promise me that whatever happens, you'll get
as far away from Orion and the Alpha as you can. Your
mother—your mother and Malcolm will protect you. That's
all I want, kid. To know you'll be okay."

A sob bubbled up in Simon's throat, and he struggled
to speak around it. "Only—only if you swear you won't
leave me."

Darryl smiled weakly. "It's okay, Simon. I'm ready. Just
promise me you'll stay safe."

Simon pressed harder against the blood pouring from his
uncle's chest. "I—I promise. But—please, you can't—you
can't die. I need you."

"This is how it's supposed to be." Darryl's hand settled

over Simon's. "I couldn't save your father. Let me die protecting you."

"Please," choked Simon. "You're my family."

"And I always will be. I had my time with you, and they were the best years of my life. It's your mother's turn now."

Behind him, Simon heard the click of claws against glass, and a wolf appeared at his side. Malcolm.

"Brother?" said the wolf in disbelief. He set his paw against Darryl's chest as well, but nothing either of them did could stop the flow of blood.

"I'm sorry for leaving you," said Darryl. His gruff voice was fading. "You—deserved better."

"Impossible. No better brother exists."

Darryl touched his paw. "Take care of him, Malcolm. He's your charge now. Heir or not—he's our family."

"Of course." Malcolm lowered his head, and with effort, Darryl refocused on Simon.

"You are strong, Simon. Stronger than you know. Never—never forget it."

Finally his grip on Simon's hand faded, and the light in Darryl's eyes disappeared. A choking sob escaped Simon, and he clutched his uncle's cold fingers. Behind him, the other wolves gathered on the rooftop one by one, but it was too late.

Darryl was gone.

25

PIGEON POOP

Simon didn't know how long he knelt on the rooftop beside
his uncle's body. Long enough for his face to grow numb
in the wind, and long enough for the entire pack to chase
away the remaining birds and join them, their heads bowed.

He didn't let go of his uncle's hand. Over and over again,
he pictured Darryl's eyes opening, and Simon silently begged
for this to be nothing more than a nightmare. But it wasn't
a nightmare. This was his life, and Simon didn't know how
to face it without his uncle.

If only the rats hadn't attacked them. If only Simon
had met Darryl at the ferry. If only Simon hadn't been so
stupid and trusted Winter. None of this would have happened, and they would have found a way to save his mother
together. Darryl would still be alive, and by now they would

have left the city, all three of them. And they would all be safe.

No, Simon realized. They wouldn't all be safe. Nolan would still be at the Den, and his mother would never have left New York without him. Orion and the Alpha would have hunted them down, and one way or another, Darryl would have risked his life to protect him.

But maybe by then, Simon would have found a way to keep them all alive.

Malcolm clapped his hand on Simon's shoulder and cleared his throat. His eyes were red and swollen. "Come on," he said gruffly. "The pack will take care of him. We need to get you someplace safe."

"What—what about my mom?" said Simon.

Malcolm frowned, not quite looking at him. "Orion's lieutenants escaped, and they took her with them."

The world began to tilt once more, and the edges of Simon's vision went black. His mother was still missing. Darryl was dead. And all of it had been for nothing. "I'm sorry," he said softly to his uncle's body. Squeezing Darryl's hand one last time, Simon finally let go and stood, his gaze lingering on his uncle's motionless form. Only when Darryl's face was burned into his memory did he allow Malcolm to lead him back into the atrium.

The climb down the tree was a blur. He couldn't think about his uncle, not yet, not without falling apart, so he focused on his mother. Orion wouldn't kill her, not when he could still use her to find the real pieces of the Predator. But how long would that last? How long would it be before Simon lost her, too?

"About time!" Felix scampered halfway up the spiral staircase, stopping at his feet. "Come quickly—it's your brother."

Any relief Simon felt at knowing Felix was all right evaporated, and he ran down the stairs after him. "What happened? Where is he?"

"Less talking, more running!" called Felix, darting down to the lower level and hurrying through the branch-filled hallway. Simon followed, with Malcolm hot on his heels. As they passed an open sitting room, he spotted Ariana and Jam huddled on the sofa. He would thank them later. Right now, he had to find his brother.

Felix stopped in front of a door at the end of a long corridor. An odd scratching noise came from inside the room, and Simon yanked the door open and stopped cold.

His brother wasn't on the other side. Instead, a young gray wolf paced across the carpet, making a pitiful whining sound.

"Nolan?" said Simon. The wolf sat back on his haunches, and in the blink of an eye, it shifted into a rattlesnake. And then a frog. And then a squirrel, and a robin, and a wasp.

"I'm the Beast King's heir," said Nolan as he shifted back into a wolf, shaking his head in disbelief. "I thought when you showed up that you would be instead, but it's me."

Simon stared at him, stunned, though he quickly

recovered. Of course Nolan was the Beast King's heir, now that Simon knew he was an eagle. His resolve turned to steel. He wouldn't let Orion kill his brother. No matter what it took, no matter what Simon had to do, he would protect him. Orion had already stolen his mother and uncle. Simon wasn't going to let him steal his brother, too.

"Turns out I sprout feathers," he said wearily, and his grief must have shown on his face, because Nolan trotted up to him, his wolf's brow furrowed with concern.

"I'm not going to boss you around, if that's what you're worried about. As long as you do what I want, I mean."

Simon shook his head. "It's not that," he began, but before he could explain, a shadow appeared over Simon's shoulder.

"It's Darryl," said Malcolm as he stepped into the room. "He's dead."

Nolan's face fell, and his tail drooped. "He—he is?"

"And Orion took Mom with him," said Simon.

His brother bared his teeth. "We'll get her back," he growled. "I'm the Beast King now. No one takes my mother and gets away with it."

More than anything, Simon wanted to agree with him. He wanted to scour every corner of New York City—every corner of the country, if he had to—until he found Orion and his mother. But dread coiled inside him at the thought of what Orion would do to his brother if he captured him. Simon couldn't let that happen.

"You."

The Alpha's voice rang out, and she stormed into the room, all pretense of royalty gone. At first Simon thought she was hurrying toward Nolan, but instead she cornered him, shoving him against the wall and putting her nose an inch from his.

"You took the pieces," she said, her face contorted with fury. "You handed Orion the Predator. Now he has control, and because of you, my kingdom will fall." She grabbed his throat, cutting off his air supply. "You will *suffer* for what you've done, if it's the last thing I—"

A furious snarl filled the room. An enormous wolf slammed into the Alpha, and she tumbled to the ground, shifting as she hit the carpet.

But it was too late. Malcolm pinned her smaller form, and he snapped his jaw just above her throat.

"I do not care what Simon did," he growled. "You have only yourself to blame, Mother. You were our Alpha. He's a twelve-year-old boy, and I will not let you hurt him. Not now, not ever."

"How *dare* you." The Alpha tried to claw Malcolm's muzzle, but he was too quick for her. In an instant, he shifted his weight, immobilizing her completely.

"You have let down our kingdom, and you have let down our family," he said. Near the doorway, Simon noticed the rest of the pack gathering in wolf form. "You have no right to call yourself our Alpha any longer. Relinquish your crown before you cause any more harm to our kingdom, or I will kill you."

Silence reverberated throughout the room, and Simon barely dared to breathe. The Alpha stared at her son, her eyes full of hatred. "I am your *mother*."

"And that is why I am offering you your life," said Malcolm. "I will give you one chance. Step down, and you live. Refuse, and you die here."

She bared her teeth. "Take him into custody," she ordered the pack. But none of them moved to help the Alpha. Instead they all rumbled their dissent, and one wolf stepped forward.

"You heard him," said Vanessa. "We follow Malcolm now, not you."

The Alpha clenched her jaw, and several tense seconds passed. "Traitors, all of you," she said, and at last she shifted back into her human form. "Very well. I step down as your Alpha and pass on my title to you, Malcolm." She glanced coldly at Simon and Nolan. "My only living heir."

Malcolm rumbled, and he didn't let her go. "You will leave the city and all our lands, and you will never return. If I ever see you again, I will rip you limb from limb, as slowly and excruciatingly as possible. By the time I'm finished, you will be begging me to let you die."

Finally he climbed off her and positioned himself in front of Simon and Nolan. She rose, and with her head held high, she walked out of the room, the pack parting to give her space.

"Follow her. Make sure she leaves," he said.

"Yes, Your Majesty," said Vanessa, trotting down the hall with another pair of wolves at her heels.

"It's only a matter of time before Orion sends every bird in the city after us," said Malcolm. "We need to return to the Den. You three, gather the other students. Nolan, Simon, you will remain with me and the rest of the pack."

"But—" Simon's mouth went dry. "I'm Orion's heir. Birds aren't allowed at the L.A.I.R."

"You're my nephew," he said firmly. "I will not allow anyone to cast you aside no matter what Animalgam form you take. You are the person you choose to be, not the person others think you are."

Simon was silent. He might not have wanted anything to do with Orion, but that didn't change the fact that he would one day be in charge of the kingdom the mammals hated. Maybe they only hated Orion—maybe now everything would change. But something in his gut twisted, and he had a feeling it wouldn't be that easy. Nothing ever was.

However, if there was one thing he knew for sure, it was that he would be the best heir to the bird kingdom he could possibly be. Malcolm was right about that—he got to choose who he would be. And he wasn't going to be anything like his grandfather.

"You need to shift back, Nolan," said Malcolm. "Can't walk the streets of New York like this, can you?"

Nolan pawed uncomfortably at the carpet. "I don't know how."

"You don't—" Malcolm sighed. "Fine, I'll show you in the atrium. Let's go."

Malcolm guided Simon and the wolf that was his brother out of the room. He hovered closer than usual, and it took Simon a moment to remember that Malcolm had also made Darryl a promise—to protect Simon, even though he wasn't the Beast King's heir. Was this what his life was going to be like now? Trapped in the Den under Malcolm's watchful eye, unable to leave unless he wanted to risk Orion capturing him again?

As they passed an open bedroom door, Simon heard shuffling, and he stuck his head inside. Winter stood in a room decorated all in white, with several large bookcases lining the walls. Classical music spilled from a pair of speakers, and she sniffled as she sat in the center of the bed, staring at something in her hands.

"What are you doing?" he said. Winter jumped, and her expression quickly hardened.

"Orion left me," she mumbled, her gaze drifting back to the thing she was holding—a picture frame. "I tried to go with the flock, but they wouldn't let me."

"Maybe if you'd told the truth, things would've been different," he said.

"No. They would have left me no matter what I did," she said, refusing to look at him. "I'm sorry, Simon. I thought—I thought I was doing the right thing."

Deep down he knew that, but she was still the reason

Darryl was dead. And he wasn't sure he could forgive that so easily. More pictures lined the bookshelf nearest the door, and Simon stepped inside to get a closer look. Most of them were of a man and a woman he didn't recognize, but some of them were of Orion and Winter. At least he was still alive. But he had abandoned Winter without a second thought, and Simon wasn't sure which was worse.

"Are you coming back with us?" he said, picking up one of the photographs. "It's safe now. Malcolm banished the Alpha."

"He won't let me back in after what I did," she said. And while there was a chance she was right, he shrugged.

"If Malcolm's letting me back in, he has to let you in, too."

She scoffed, her voice choked. "Don't pretend you like me. Not after what I did."

"I don't. And I'm not sure it'll ever be okay. But—" He cleared his throat. "You lied to me to protect your family. I get that."

Her face flushed. "I really am sorry," she whispered.

"I know." He pretended to inspect the pictures as Winter hastily wiped her cheek. "Darryl's dead."

"What?" Her eyes widened. Setting the frame aside, she stood and took several steps toward him. "Simon . . ."

"They took my mother, too," he said hollowly. "I don't think I'm ever going to see her again."

Winter bit her lip. "You will. I know Orion better than anyone. He told me all kinds of things, and if anyone can track him down, it's me. I'll do anything to help you find her, Simon. I swear."

He shook his head. "I promised Darryl—I promised him I would stay safe."

"Our world won't ever be safe, not if Orion gets the weapon. I thought he would do the right thing, but . . ." Winter trailed off and glanced at a photograph of the man and woman on her shelves. "I never got to know my mother. But you—you have a chance to know yours. You can't give that up, Simon. You just can't."

He averted his eyes, and a lump formed in his throat. No, he couldn't. "I don't know what to do."

"We'll figure it out," said Winter. "You don't have to do this alone."

A long moment passed, and finally he said, "Everything that happened . . . it's not really your fault, you know."

She hesitated. "It is. I knew exactly what I was doing. But I never thought this is how it would end."

"It's not over yet," said Simon. She was right—no matter what he did, if Orion got his hands on the real Predator, there would be no safe place left in the world for him and his brother. And in the end, that meant the only way to keep his promise to Darryl was to make sure that never happened. "I'm sorry I told Orion you're a snake."

"Don't be. Perrin would have told him, anyway. Besides, I deserved it." She sniffed and took another tentative step toward him. "No matter what happens, Simon—I'm on your side. And I won't let anyone hurt you or Nolan, even if he is a toad. I know you'll probably never forgive me, but maybe—maybe we can be friends eventually. Once this is over."

Simon shook his head. He would never forget this, and he wasn't sure his uncle's death would ever stop hurting, but he'd already lost enough that day. "Winter . . . we're already friends."

Her lower lip trembled, and wordlessly she caught him in a hug. It took everything Simon had left, but at last, he hugged back.

Darryl was buried beneath a stone plaza at the edge of the zoo, beside a statue of a wolf bowing his head. It was his father's grave, Malcolm had explained to Simon in a hushed voice, and a second statue would be erected in Darryl's honor. Neither grave was marked with their names, and Simon hated the thought of tourists passing them every day, taking pictures and rubbing the wolves' muzzles without ever knowing what they really represented.

When the funeral ended and everyone began to trickle back toward the Arsenal for dinner, Simon stopped and gazed across the park in the direction of his old apartment. It was too far to see the building, but he ached to visit one last time. Shoving his hands into his pockets, he approached Malcolm, who stared blankly at the outline of Darryl's grave.

"We should head back to the Den," said Malcolm at last, clearing his throat. "It's getting late."

"I was hoping I could go back to my apartment," said Simon. "I know it's dangerous, but I'll be fast. I just want to get my stuff." He had the important things, like his mother's postcards and notebook and the pocket watch Darryl had returned to him. But he needed proof that his whole life up until this moment hadn't been a dream. And he *had* promised the reptiles as many books as he could carry.

"I want to go, too," said Nolan, popping up behind them. "I've never seen the rest of the city before."

"If he's going, then so are we," said Ariana and Jam, who had come to the funeral as moral support. Malcolm sighed and closed his eyes, long enough for Simon to see a flicker of grief flash across his face.

"All right," he said quietly. "Just this once."

He gathered half the pack, and together they all headed toward Fifth Avenue and piled into three taxis. Nolan and Simon were squished together in the backseat with Malcolm, and as the taxis sped up the street, Nolan glanced nervously out the window.

"You've really never been to other parts of the city?" said Simon. His brother shook his head.

"The Alpha—Grandmother—she said it was too dangerous. She didn't even let me go into the rest of Central Park."

"Darryl didn't let me go alone, either," said Simon, his uncle's name heavy on his tongue. "But I went anyway, before and after school sometimes. There's a path I took that I think you'll like. It's short."

"No," said Malcolm wearily. "No detours."

"It's not far from the apartment," said Simon. "I just want to see it one more time."

To Simon's surprise, his uncle gave in far more easily than he'd expected, and twenty minutes later, they all pulled up to the familiar corner of Central Park. Simon's chest tightened as he glanced down the street toward his old apartment building. Two members of the pack headed over to start boxing everything up, and Simon almost asked to go with them instead. But the excitement on Nolan's face stopped him, and he led them up the sidewalk and into the trees.

It was a warm evening, and the city seemed to melt away. The pack kept a wide perimeter, eyeing each pigeon as it passed, and Simon led Nolan, Ariana, and Jam down the footpath he'd taken to and from school. "This is my favorite place," he said, watching a pair of squirrels argue over an acorn. "It's quiet here, and the chipmunks and birds like to talk. Mostly they just want food though—"

"Look who it is!" called a familiar voice. "Psycho Simon."

Simon felt as though he'd jumped into the icy polar bear water all over again. Up ahead, Bryan Barker and his gang spread out across the path, laughing and throwing sticks at the squirrels. Behind them, once again struggling under the weight of five backpacks, stumbled Colin.

"Who's that?" said Nolan, stepping behind the others

and ducking his head. Simon didn't blame him for trying to stay out of sight.

"No one," said Simon as they drew closer. "Just some jerk who thinks he's important."

Bryan's grin turned into a scowl. Malcolm and the others closed in around them, but Simon shook his head. He had to take care of this without their help.

"I'm more important than you'll ever be, fart face," said Bryan. "*I* actually have friends."

"What do you think we are?" said Ariana.

He eyed her pink hair. "Freaks, that's what. Just like Simon."

Bryan took a threatening step toward him, and Malcolm closed in. He may not have been as big as Darryl, but he was just as intimidating.

Bryan narrowed his eyes. "Where's your uncle, Psycho? Did he finally see what a pathetic loser you are and leave you like your mom did?"

The mention of Darryl was a knife to Simon's gut. He tried not to react—after all he'd faced lately, Bryan Barker was nothing—but Colin piped up.

"Leave him alone, Bryan," he said. "He's not bothering us, and I want to get home."

"Stop being such a baby," said Bryan. "Unless you want to be next."

A pigeon cooed overhead, and Simon glanced up. An entire flock nestled in the branches, watching the action unfold. One brave bird flew down, landing on Simon's shoulder, and an idea formed in his mind. He whispered a few words to the pigeon, which bobbed its head and flew back into the tree.

"Stop talking to the birds, Psycho," said Bryan. "Or are they the only ones who talk back?"

"Sorry, what did you say? I don't speak cockroach," said Simon.

Bryan's face turned bright red. "Who are you calling a cockroach?" He took another menacing step toward them, but before he could reach him, Simon cried out. "*Now!*"

A hundred pigeons exploded from the trees. The first pigeon dived toward Bryan, but just before it reached him, it pulled up and—

Splat.

Splat. Splat, splat. Splat.

Pigeon droppings rained from the sky, landing squarely on Bryan. On his clothes, in his hair, on his face—everywhere. He screamed and danced around, trying to avoid them, but they kept coming. His gang burst into laughter, and Simon crossed his arms.

"I might be a psycho, but you're the one eating pigeon poop," he said. "If you ever call me or Colin or anyone a freak again, I'll send every pigeon in the city after you. Got it?"

Bryan shrieked and ran down the path, looking like a giant moving pile of pigeon droppings. Still laughing, his gang took off after him, leaving Colin behind with the backpacks.

"You should leave them here," said Simon. "They deserve it."

Colin shrugged and shifted one onto his shoulder. "Maybe next time. Thanks, by the way."

"You're welcome. Just don't let Bryan tell you what to do anymore, all right? He's not worth it."

Colin smiled sadly. "We're not all as brave as you are, Simon. See you around."

Simon watched him trudge down the path. Maybe he would see Colin, maybe he wouldn't. Simon's life was changing too rapidly for him to predict anything anymore, and all he could do was try to keep up. One thing he did know for sure though: a week ago, he hadn't been this brave, either.

HOWL AT THE MOON

One evening in the middle of September, after Nolan had left for the dining hall, Simon settled on the sofa with his favorite book. Ever since his uncle's death, he'd been eating his meals in the Alpha's section, too numb to join the others. It had worked out so far, but this time, Malcolm appeared. "My brother wouldn't have wanted you to mourn him forever."

Ten days wasn't forever, but even if it had been ten years, Simon couldn't imagine pretending everything was all right. "I'm not hungry."

"I remember what it was like to be your age, and I was always hungry." Malcolm eased down onto the couch beside him. "It might not seem like it now, but you'll wake up one day and remember what it felt like to be happy. Until then, all you can do—all any of us can do—is go through the motions." He clapped his hand on Simon's shoulder. "You're not alone, Simon. I hope you know that. Now go join your brother for dinner."

Simon dragged himself down to the dining hall, fully prepared to eat as quickly as possible. When he arrived, he spotted Nolan in the buffet line. Before he could join him, however, Garrett and a handful of other mammals surrounded Simon.

"Oh, look, it's pigeon boy," said Garrett with a snicker. Nolan must have told him about the incident in the park. "I've been meaning to ask—why did they call you Psycho Simon? Is it because you have bird-turd brains?"

Simon sighed. So the taunts wouldn't end whether he was at Kennedy Middle School or the Leading Animalgam Institute for the Remarkable. At least they were familiar. "You want to know why they call me Psycho Simon? Find me in the pit, and I'll show you."

A chorus of *oohs* erupted from the mammals, and Nolan walked up beside Simon, holding a tray full of burgers and fries. "What's going on?"

"Nothing," said Garrett with a grin.

Simon shrugged. "Your goons think I'm crazy because I'm Orion's heir."

Nolan scowled. A few boys seemed to shrink beneath his glare, but Garrett stood his ground.

"You will apologize to my brother, and you will treat him with the respect he deserves," said Nolan with surprising authority. Though the fact that he was the Beast King's heir was still a closely guarded secret, finally shifting had done him a world of good. Simon only wished the same had been true for him.

Garrett's mouth puckered as if he had swallowed a lemon. "But—"

"No buts." Nolan raised his chin, and even though Garrett was almost a full foot taller, he took a nervous step back. "If you want to stay in the Den, you'll apologize to my brother right now, and you will bow to him. And call him Your Highness."

Garrett paled, and Simon shook his head. "It's fine," he said, not wanting to cause more trouble for himself. "I'm used to it."

"You're a prince, and my brother," said Nolan. "No one's ever going to insult you again, and if they try, there *will* be consequences. What'll it be, Garrett?"

With a clenched jaw, Garrett bowed stiffly. "Your Highness," he muttered, sounding vaguely like he was trying not to choke. "I'm sorry if I offended you."

"You didn't," said Simon. He clutched his book and looked at his brother. "I'm going to get some food. I'll see you around."

"You're not sitting with us?" said Nolan, and Simon was surprised by the hint of hurt in his voice. He glanced at

Garrett, whose face was turning the color of ketchup. If Simon sat with them tonight, he'd be dead before dessert.

"Maybe for breakfast," he said. "Or you could sit with me."

One look at Nolan's expression told Simon what he thought about that idea. "Breakfast, then," said Nolan. He wandered off toward his friends, and Garrett followed closely behind.

Once Simon filled his plate, he sat down at an empty table and opened his book. He could feel others sneaking furtive glances at him, and he slouched in his seat. By now, thanks to Nolan's big mouth, the whole school knew about what had happened in Sky Tower, but Simon didn't care. They could look all they wanted as long as no one tried to tell him he didn't belong because he had sprouted feathers instead of fur.

He was halfway through a chapter when Jam pulled up a chair across from him. "Is this seat free?" he said.

"Only if you'll eat my fries for me," said Simon.

Ariana dropped her tray onto the table and plopped down beside Simon. "I guess I'll sit with you, too, as long as you promise not to get any of your bird nerdiness on me."

"What, you mean like this?" said Jam, and he reached across the table and rubbed his book on her shoulder.

"Or like this?" said Simon, doing the same. Ariana squirmed.

"Gross! What is *wrong* with you two?"

It might have been his relief at not sitting alone; it might have been the look on Ariana's face as she tried in vain to push them away. But the dam inside him burst, and for the first time since the day Darryl had died, Simon laughed. It felt good, and across the room, he caught Nolan's eye. His brother was sandwiched between Garrett and another boy, and he flashed Simon a grin. Simon returned it.

"Maybe tomorrow, we can get Nolan to sit with us," he said. Ariana and Jam exchanged a look.

"He's the prince," said Jam. "He always sits with the mammals."

"I'm a prince, too," said Simon. "So are you. And you're a princess, Ariana."

She twirled her knife between her fingers. "Call me that again, I dare you."

He pulled his hands away from her. "He'll sit with us tomorrow," he said firmly. "We're all going to be the leaders of our kingdoms someday, and it's about time we all started to get along."

"Hear, hear," said Jam.

"To crazy ideas that are never going to work," said Ariana. "Don't say I didn't warn you."

Simon knew it would take some adjustment for all of them, but as he watched his brother talk animatedly to Garrett and the other mammals, he was sure that one way or another, they would both be the princes the Animalgam world needed them to be, and the five kingdoms would be better for it.

Simon spent the rest of the evening taping his mother's post-cards to his bedroom wall, working well into the night to get the order right. Seeing the colorful pictures of the places she'd been gave him hope he would see her again, and right now, he needed that.

"Where's that one from?" said Felix as he nibbled on an apple slice. After Malcolm had discovered Felix sleeping on Simon's pillow, Malcolm had eventually agreed to let Felix stay, with the caveat that he remain in Simon's room at all times. Felix wasn't happy about missing the television Simon had promised him, but there wasn't much either of them could do about it.

Simon peered at the postcard of a venomous viper. "It's from Phoenix, Arizona. Lots of sand."

"Lots of snakes," said Felix, shuddering.

"Bet Winter would hate it even more than you do," said Simon, and he hopped off his desk. All he had left to put away was his pocket watch. He picked it up off his bed and exam-ined the silver face. Now, instead of being the only connec-tion he had to his father, it was also a constant reminder of what had happened on the roof of Sky Tower, and Simon couldn't stand it. He placed the watch in his dresser drawer, nestling it between two of his thickest pairs of socks. "Have you seen her tonight?"

"She's in her room," said Felix. "Threatened to feed me to the sharks."

"At least she didn't actually try," said Simon. "She's okay though?"

"She's stopped blubbering so much," said the mouse, and Simon supposed that was all he could hope for.

A wolf's mournful howl echoed from somewhere aboveground, where the pack was patrolling the zoo, and Simon tensed. "I'm going out. If Malcolm comes in, tell him I went to the pit to practice. I'll be back before midnight," he said before slipping out of his room and into his brother's. It was empty, and Simon was grateful for it. There were some things he needed to do alone.

He pushed aside the panel that hid the secret tunnel, and soon enough, he emerged into the night air. A cool wind blew, and he closed his eyes and concentrated. Malcolm had talked to him about the finer points of controlling his transformations, and while he'd done it only a couple of times since the day Darryl had died, he thought he had the hang of it. A few heartbeats later, his body began to shift, and soon he had morphed into an eagle.

Simon spread his wings and took flight, soaring over the dark zoo. With his eagle vision, the full moon was more than enough for him to see the smallest details, including where each member of the pack roamed. He circled the area until Vanessa, in her wolf form, moved her patrol to a different spot. Finally, with little more than a soft scrape, he landed on the stone path beside his uncle's grave.

In the days since the funeral, someone had erected the second statue—a giant wolf that was an exact replica of his uncle. He even had a scar running down his furry cheek. The wolf's muzzle was raised as he howled silently at the moon, and a shiver ran through Simon. Shifting back into his human form, he stood beside his uncle's grave.

"Hi, Darryl," he said, searching for the right thing to say. How was he supposed to tell him how sorry he was? How much he missed him? The words didn't exist. But they struggled to escape him anyway, and the knot in his chest throbbed with unbearable pain.

"You're the best family I've ever had," he whispered, and he touched the stone wolf's muzzle. "I'm sorry I didn't listen. I'm sorry I left you, and I'm sorry I never told you how much—" His throat swelled up until he could barely speak. "Most of all, I'm sorry for what I have to do now. I have to find the pieces of the Predator before Orion does. It's the only way Nolan will ever be safe. If I can destroy the weapon, then maybe he'll have a chance. Maybe we both will. And maybe—maybe we'll be able to save Mom. You would do the same thing, I know you would. And—and you're not here anymore, so it's up to me now. I'll protect them, no matter what it takes. I promise."

He took a shaky breath as a mountain of emotions built up inside him. Guilt, anger, regret—each one more excruciating than the last, until finally he couldn't take it anymore. The fire in his chest exploded, and the familiar sensation of his limbs twisting overtook him.

But this time it was different. Instead of feathers, fur sprouted from his skin. His hands and feet shifted into paws, and his face contorted into a muzzle. A tail grew from the base of his spine, and at last, when it was done, Simon sat trembling beside his uncle's grave.

Somehow, impossibly, he was a wolf.

The moonlight caught his eye, and Simon threw his head back and howled.

The adventure continues in
Simon Thorn and the Viper's Pit.

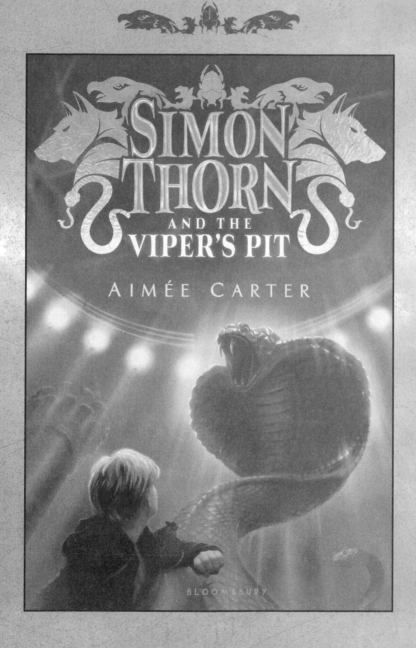

"Simon, *duck!*"

Simon Thorn took one look at the gigantic moose swinging its antlers at his head, and he hit the sand beneath him hard. Scrambling toward the edge of the pit, he stared wide-eyed as the moose threw its head back and laughed.

"What are your options, Simon?" said his uncle Malcolm from the bleachers surrounding the sand pit. Simon's heart pounded as he huddled against the stone barrier, but his hulking dark-haired uncle didn't look concerned. He never did during these early-morning training sessions no matter what kind of animal Simon encountered, and Simon was beginning to resent him for it.

"Yeah, Simon," taunted the moose, prancing across the sand toward him. "How are you going to get out of this one?"

Simon climbed shakily to his feet, never taking his eyes off the moose. It towered over him, and Simon was sure that if his uncle were in the pit, it would tower over him, too. Simon might have been small for his age, but Malcolm was tall and broad. There weren't many humans or animals who would willingly tangle with him. "Run," said Simon plainly.

"You can't run now. Try again," said Malcolm. He was right, of course. Even if Simon hadn't been trapped inside the pit, he was still stuck inside the L.A.I.R.—the Leading Animalgam Institute for the Remarkable far beneath Central Park Zoo, where Animalgam students trained. It was a place that, up until recently, Simon would've never guessed existed, let alone that he might one day attend.

For most of his life, Simon had grown up in New York City thinking he was perfectly ordinary. However, over a year ago, he'd suddenly developed the ability to talk to animals, which had been weird enough. He hadn't told anyone, not even his mom or Darryl, the uncle who had raised him. For a whole year, he let the kids at school think he was crazy, and at first he thought they were right.

But Simon wasn't crazy. Unbeknownst to him, he was really an Animalgam—a human who could not only talk to animals, but developed the ability to turn into one, too. He hadn't believed it at first, of course, like most rational seventh graders. But when he had seen Darryl shift into a huge gray wolf right in front of him, everything in his world had changed.

Now, two months later, instead of studying math or geography like most normal twelve-year-olds, Simon was facing down a moose. If he couldn't run, then what *could* he do?

"Fight?" he guessed. The edges of his vision were growing fuzzy as he tried not to blink. The instant he showed any sign of weakness, he knew the moose would attack again.

"Against those antlers? I don't think so," said Malcolm. Out of the corner of Simon's eye, he thought he saw his uncle whittling a small piece of wood. Great. He was barely paying attention.

"I'm not shifting," said Simon firmly as he inched around the edge of the pit toward the exit that led into the rest of the school. The doorway was narrow, and there was no way the moose could follow him into the hallway with those antlers.

"You need to get over this sooner or later, Simon," said Malcolm. "You can't ignore your Animalgam form forever."

Watch me, thought Simon, though he didn't dare say it out loud. Instead he muttered, "At least I'm not a moose."

The moose made a strange noise that sounded like a cross between a groan and a whine. "You don't like my antlers? Fine. Let's see how you like this."

Rapidly, almost too fast for Simon to follow, the moose morphed right in front of him. Its antlers disappeared, its body and long legs shrank, and its brown fur turned black with a long white stripe running down the middle. By the time Simon blinked, the moose had vanished, and a skunk stared up at him.

Simon turned and bolted toward the door. Yanking on the handle, he groaned when it didn't budge. He was locked in. "Malcolm!" he protested. His uncle glanced up.

"Can't have anyone walking in," he reasoned, even though it was early enough that Simon was sure none of the other students were awake.

The skunk ambled toward him, raising its bushy tail. "Guess what I can do."

"I know what you can do. You don't need to prove it," said Simon, his voice tight as he looked around for an escape route. His only option was climbing over the wall and into the bleachers, but the skunk had him backed against the door now.

"I had a lot of beans for dinner last night," said the skunk, turning to point its rear end at Simon. "I think I feel a massive fart coming on."

Having no other choice, Simon darted forward and leaped over the skunk right as it released a cloud of stink. Covering his nose, Simon scrambled up the bleachers, climbing as high as he could get. The smell was overpowering, and as he reached the top, he was gagging.

"Nolan!" *That* had gotten Malcolm's attention, and he stood, covering his nose as well. "What do you think you're doing?"

"I'm *trying* to make him fly, like you said," said the skunk, his tail puffing indignantly. "The smell isn't that bad."

"Try shifting back into a human and seeing how you like it," said Simon from the top of the pit.

The skunk huffed. "You're just being a baby," said Nolan, and as if to prove his point, he began to change again. This time, instead of shifting into another animal, the black and white fur on his head turned into brown hair, his four legs elongated into human limbs, and his muzzle and beady eyes morphed until a boy identical to Simon stood where the skunk had only seconds before, wearing the same black student uniform the L.A.I.R. required.

Simon had only met Nolan two months ago, on the night he'd unsuccessfully tried to sneak into the school to search for his missing mother. Before that, Simon had lived his entire life on the Upper West Side just a couple of miles away, while Nolan had lived with their mother beneath Central Park Zoo. Simon had only gotten visits from her on Christmas and his birthday, something that still bothered him whenever he thought too much about it. And never, not once, had she ever mentioned the fact that Simon had a twin brother.

The sounds of gagging interrupted Simon's thoughts, and he refocused on his brother at the bottom of the pit.

Nolan could only pretend the smell didn't bother him for so long, and at last he bolted up the bleachers, toward a spiral staircase. "That's *disgusting!*" he shouted as he disappeared into the upper level of the school, where Malcolm's office stood.

"Simon—" Malcolm began.

"Nolan did it, not me!" he called, darting after his brother and leaving their uncle to grumble on his own.

As soon as Simon exited the pit, he took a deep breath, only to discover the foul stench was clinging to his clothes. Terrific. He was enough of a social pariah as it was. If he went to breakfast smelling like skunk, that would give even his best friends a reason to avoid him.

Simon adjusted his black armband, turning the silhouette of an eagle in toward his arm so it was hidden. He had shifted into a golden eagle for the first time two months ago, and while he could think of few things cooler than being able to fly, he was the only member of the bird kingdom who attended the L.A.I.R. His grandfather, Orion, the leader of the bird kingdom, had been at war with the mammals for longer than Simon had been alive, and since the mammals ran the school, they had banned birds from attending. Simon was only allowed because he was Nolan's twin.

"You should help Malcolm clean the pit," said Simon as he found his brother lingering in the upper hallways. Only faculty was allowed up here, but since Malcolm not only ran the L.A.I.R., but was now also the Alpha of the entire mammal kingdom, no one ever gave Simon and Nolan a hard time about being there.

Nolan made a face. "*You* help him. If you had just shifted, I wouldn't have had to spray you."

"I told you, I don't like flying in the pit," he said. And while technically that was true, there was another reason—a much bigger reason—Simon didn't like shifting in front of other people.

Nearly all Animalgams could only shift into a single animal, and they belonged to one of the five Animalgam kingdoms: mammals, birds, insects, reptiles, or underwater creatures. But Nolan was different. He was the heir to the Beast King, a tyrannical ruler who had gained the power to shift into any animal he wanted, making him almost impossible to defeat. Though the five kingdoms had banded together half a millennium ago to overthrow him, his line had continued in secret, and Simon and Nolan's father had been the Beast King's heir before being murdered. Two months ago, they had discovered Nolan was the twin who had inherited his abilities, and that was why Malcolm had locked the doors of the pit even though it was so early that the sky was still dark. If anyone else found out that the Beast King's line still existed, it would start another war between all five Animalgam kingdoms—and this time they would all be trying to kill Nolan.

Simon couldn't let that happen, but he also couldn't tell

anyone his secret and the real reason he was so reluctant to shift in front of everyone while he still wasn't very good at it. Not even Nolan. *Especially* not Nolan. Despite their tentative cease-fire after what had been, to put it lightly, a rocky start to their relationship, Simon was sure that the moment Nolan found out he wasn't as special as he thought he was, he would hate Simon all over again.

"All you have to do is flap your wings a few times, and Malcolm will be happy," said Nolan, annoyed. "I don't get why you won't do that."

"He'll get there eventually," said a voice behind them— Malcolm. He must have followed them. "Just like you'll stop relying so heavily on your mammal forms and start working with the other kingdoms, too."

"I shift into animals from other kingdoms all the time," said Nolan, shoving his hands in his pockets as the three of them stood outside the doorway to Malcolm's office. "I shifted into a hawk yesterday, and an alligator the day before that."

"Mammals make up the smallest kingdom," said their uncle, "yet you almost always revert to a mammal form during morning practice. If you have any hope of protecting yourself someday, you're going to need to be proficient and comfortable in forms from all five kingdoms. And," he added, "you're going to have to start cleaning up after yourself. I can't open the pit until that skunk stench is gone."

"Make Simon do it," said Nolan.

"You're the one who made that mess," said Simon. "I'm not cleaning up your skunk juice, no way."

"But you're the one who made me—"

"Enough." Malcolm pinched the bridge of his nose. "Nolan, you're cleaning up your own mess. Simon, go change. I can smell you from here. But if I don't see your wings in the next twenty-four hours, you'll be the one taking care of any future skunk messes in the pit."

And if Simon knew his brother at all, he was positive Nolan would skunk him every chance he got just to make him clean up.

"That's not fair!" cried Nolan. Malcolm set his hand on his shoulder and started to lead him down the hallway.

"It's perfectly fair. Now come on, the kitchens must have a few extra gallons of tomato juice lying around."

As the sound of their argument faded, Simon headed through the hallway and down into the Alpha section. The underground L.A.I.R. was called the Den, and it was shaped like a pentagon, one side for each kingdom. Since the birds weren't invited to attend, the Alpha and his family stayed in their section instead. Once Simon changed into a clean uniform, he would have the whole place to himself, minus a handful of pack members posted as guards.

He wasn't interested in a nap before breakfast, though. He could hardly believe his luck at getting the rest of the early morning off, and he knew exactly what he was going to do with that extra forty-five minutes: practice shifting the way he couldn't in the pit, not in front of Nolan and Malcolm. Because while his uncle only wanted to see him stretch his wings, Simon could do much, much more.

And that was Simon's big secret, the one he kept from everyone, even Nolan. Somehow, someway, his twin wasn't the only one who had inherited the Beast King's abilities. Simon could shift into any animal he wanted, too. He hadn't had nearly as much practice as his brother, however, and every time he shifted in front of others, he was painfully aware he risked thinking of the wrong animal and exposing his secret. That was why he refused to shift in the pit.

But while he didn't have the experience his brother did, he knew all the lectures Malcolm gave Nolan were right. If he wanted any chance of protecting himself and his brother from the people who wanted to destroy the Beast King's line, he had to learn how to fight in the style of all five kingdoms. If he couldn't do that in the pit, then there was only one other place he could safely practice.

After saying hello to the wolves standing guard near the tall trees that filled the Alpha residence, he headed up the winding glass staircase and into his bedroom. Their section, which had been built to house the bird students, was several stories high, and while it would have been easy enough for Simon to fly around, he wouldn't be able to practice shifting into other animals. Not with the pack members watching.

"You're back early," said a sleepy voice from Simon's bed. Curled into a ball on his pillow lay a tiny brown mouse. Felix was, in many ways, his best friend, but Simon knew where he ranked when it came to the little mouse's priorities: right below naps and television.

"Yeah, Nolan tried to skunk me. Malcolm's making him clean up the pit right now," said Simon, heading over to his dresser.

"That explains the smell," muttered the mouse. "You need a shower."

"And you need to sleep another hour if you're going to be this cranky."

Felix grumbled to himself, not disagreeing, and Simon grabbed a fresh change of clothes and ducked into the bathroom. As soon as he closed the door, however, he headed straight through into the adjoining bedroom: Nolan's.

Beneath Nolan's desk in the far corner of the room was one of several tunnels that led to the Central Park Zoo above. While the Den was one of the safest places in New York City for Animalgams, it had its fair share of secrets, and Simon had discovered this one shortly after arriving. Moving the chair out of the way, he bent down and nudged open the secret panel. On the other side was an opening barely big enough for Simon to crawl through, but he didn't need much space. As soon as he closed the small door and was engulfed in darkness, he closed his eyes and focused. Within a heartbeat, he began to shift.

The cold tunnel expanded as he grew smaller. It didn't hurt, but it did tickle, especially as fur sprouted all over his body. His face grew pointed, and his spine elongated into a tail, leaving him unbalanced for a moment. But before it could bother him, his transformation into a mouse was complete. Simon wasn't sure exactly how many animals he could shift into, but between watching his brother in the pit and the experiments he tried when he sneaked out on his own, he had yet to find any exception.

He scurried through the rest of the tunnel, careful not to make a sound. As soon as he reached the grate that let out into the middle of the Central Park Zoo, he shut his eyes and imagined a golden eagle, and his body once again transformed. His front legs twisted and lengthened into wings, feathers replaced his fur, and his nose and whiskers turned into a hard beak. He hopped out of the tunnel, his long talons scratching the paved stones. The sun was only beginning to creep up between the skyscrapers surrounding Central Park, and with his vision sharpened, he could see everything even in the low light of dawn. Twisting his head around, Simon searched for the wolf pack that patrolled the zoo while it was closed. No signs of life. At least not the kind that would get him grounded.

Confident he was alone, Simon spread his wings and took off, soaring into the sky. At first he meant to only fly around the zoo for a little while, but he climbed higher and higher, his feathers adjusting to take advantage of the wind. He soared above the park, dipping down to swoop among the trees, not realizing where he was headed until he could see the building. His old apartment—the one he had lived in almost his whole life with his uncle Darryl.

It had been two months since Darryl had died on the roof of Sky Tower, and they had been the hardest months of Simon's life. While Simon missed his uncle fiercely, most days he went through the motions and pretended everything was okay, and no one knew just how deeply he was grieving. Sometimes Simon even managed to fool himself into thinking he had adjusted, that the biggest loss of his life was in the past instead of only an errant thought away. But as he circled above his old building, that gnawing ache returned full force, hitting him so hard that he almost forgot how to fly.

He couldn't stand seeing their apartment, not when he knew it would be one more reminder that Darryl wasn't there anymore. Instead, with his insides in knots, he landed on a branch in Central Park near the path he'd taken to go to school. Glancing around, he half expected to see the boys who had bullied him, but it was far too early. Instead he ruffled his feathers and tried to pull himself together. If he spent the morning upset, Malcolm might demand an explanation—or worse, ask if he wanted to talk.

A robin settled onto the branch beside him, puffing up nervously. "Gonna eat that worm?" she said, and Simon spotted a particularly fat one poking out of the dewy grass.

"It's all yours," he said, but the robin made no move to take it.

"You're Simon, right?" she said. "Simon Thorn?"

Suspicion crept through him, and he eyed the robin. "How do you know that?"

As he spoke, several more robins settled onto the trees nearby, along with a handful of blue jays and crows. Not the kind of birds who usually shared breakfast. He dug his talons nervously into the branch.

"Orion said if we find you, we'll have all the worms we want," said the robin, hopping closer to him. "And seeds, and bread. Do you like bread? I like bread."

"I, uh—" He may have been an eagle, but he had no idea if he could fly faster than the others. Over a dozen had gathered by now, all watching him with their beady eyes, waiting for him to make a move.

Perfect.

"I'm late for breakfast," he said to the robin, trying to sound as casual as possible. "But you can have that worm. It looks extra juicy."

For a split second, the robin's attention turned toward the grass, and Simon pushed off the branch and flew toward the zoo once more. Behind him, he could hear the flap of wings as the smaller birds followed. The wind whipped his feathers as he sped up, flying faster than he ever had before. He couldn't risk slowing down, not if Orion was after him.

His grandfather wasn't just the leader of the bird kingdom—he was dangerous, too, and though Simon had been foolish enough to believe Orion had been on his side at first, he now knew the truth. Orion had murdered Darryl, and in the chaos that had followed, he'd also kidnapped Simon's mother, leaving Simon with little hope of seeing her again. It was no surprise the birds were following him. Simon had shifted into a golden eagle in front of Orion, and now his grandfather thought he was the heir to the bird kingdom's throne. But Simon would have rather pulled out all his feathers one by one than ever help Orion again.

It took Simon several minutes of weaving through the trees at dangerously high speeds, but at last he lost sight of the other birds. As soon as he was positive they weren't following him anymore, he dived toward the Central Park Zoo and landed in the courtyard, hopping into the tunnel and pulling the grate shut with his beak. Shifting back into a mouse, he darted through the cold passageway as fast as he could, and by the time he reached the secret door into Nolan's bedroom, he was panting. He stopped, listening hard for the sounds of anyone following him. Silence. Taking a deep breath, he concentrated on shifting back into a human. The tunnel shrank around him, and he had to duck his head, but he relaxed as he grew into himself once more. Being able to turn into any animal he wanted was the coolest thing that had ever happened to Simon, but at the same time, there was nothing like being himself.

Simon shook out his tingling hands and pushed the panel open. He hadn't been gone long. He still had time to read a chapter before meeting his friends for breakfast and—

"Enjoy your flight?" said a deep voice, and Simon froze. In the middle of the bedroom stood Malcolm.

AIMÉE CARTER

is the author of the Simon Thorn series as well as the young adult series the Blackcoat Rebellion and the Goddess Test.

aimeecarter.com

@aimee_carter